SWEETLY

JACKSON PEARCE

LITTLE, BROWN AND COMPANY
New York   Boston

Little, Brown and Company

Hachette Book Group
237 Park Avenue, New York, NY 10017
Visit our website at www.lb-teens.com

Little, Brown and Company is a division of Hachette Book Group, Inc.
The Little, Brown name and logo are trademarks of Hachette Book Group, Inc.

The publisher is not responsible for websites (or their content) that are not owned by the publisher.

First Paperback Edition: August 2012
First published in hardcover in August 2011 by Little, Brown and Company

Library of Congress Cataloging-in-Publication Data
Pearce, Jackson.
   Sweetly / by Jackson Pearce. — 1st ed.
      p. cm.
   Companion book to: Sisters red.
   Summary: When the owner of a candy shop molds magical treats that instill confidence, bravery, and passion, eighteen-year-old Gretchen's haunted childhood memories of her twin sister's abduction by a witch-like monster begin to fade until girls start vanishing at the annual chocolate festival.
   ISBN 978-0-316-06865-9 (hc) / ISBN 978-0-316-06866-6 (pb)
   [1. Witches—Fiction.   2. Werewolves—Fiction.   3. Brothers and sisters—Fiction. 4. Supernatural—Fiction.]   I. Title.
   PZ7.P31482Sw 2011
   [Fic] — dc22   2010043182

10 9 8 7 6 5 4 3 2 1

RRD-C

Printed in the United States of America

To Saundra
(FOR ALL THE CANDY)

PROLOGUE

(Twelve Years Ago)

The book said there was a witch in the woods.

That's why they were among the thick trees to begin with—to find her. The three of them trudged along, weaving through the hemlocks and maples, long out of sight of their house, their father's happy smiles, their mother's soft hands.

A sharp ripping sound bounced through the trees. The boy whirled around.

"Sorry," one of the girls said, though she clearly didn't mean it. Her cheeks were still lined with baby fat and her hair was like broken sunlight, identical to the girl's standing beside her. She held up the bag of chocolate candies that she'd just torn open. "You can have all the yellows, Ansel, if you want."

"No one likes the yellows," Ansel said, rolling his eyes.

"Mom does," one of the twins argued, but he'd turned his back and couldn't tell which one. That was how it normally was with them—they blended, so much so that you sometimes couldn't tell if they were two people or the same person twice. The sister with the candy emptied a handful of them into her palm, picking out the yellows and dropping them as they continued to trudge forward.

"When we find the witch," Ansel told his sisters, "if she chases us, we should split up. That way she can only eat one of us."

"What if she catches me, though?" one of the girls asked, alarmed.

"Well, what if she catches me, Gretchen?" Ansel replied.

"You're bigger. She should chase you," the other sister told him, pouting. "That's the way they work." She was the only one who claimed to know the ways of witches—she was the one with the stories, the made-up maps, the pages and pages of books stored away in her head. She reached into her twin's bag of candy and pegged Ansel in the back of the head with a yellow candy. He didn't react, so she prepared to throw another one —

"Wait...do you know where we are?" he asked.

One of the twins raised her eyes to the forest canopy and scanned the closest tree trunks, while her sister turned slowly in the leaves. They knew these woods by heart but had never ventured quite so far before. The shadows from branches felt like strangers, the cracks and pops of nature turned eerie.

The twins simultaneously shook their heads and their brother nodded curtly, trying to hide the fact that being out so far made him uneasy. He hurried forward, eager to keep moving.

"Ansel? Wait!" one asked, and ran a little to close the space between them. "Are we lost?"

"Only a little," he answered, jumping at the sound of a particularly loud falling branch. "Don't be scared."

"I'm not," she lied. She began to wish she'd packed peanut butter and jelly sandwiches for their adventure, instead of two Barbies and a bag of candy, which Gretchen had almost finished off anyway. What if they were stuck out here past dinnertime?

"Besides," Ansel said over his shoulder, "maybe she'll be a good witch, like Glinda, and help us get unlost."

"I thought you said she might want to eat us."

"Well, maybe, but we won't know until we find her. Unless you want to go back," Ansel said. He didn't entirely believe the stories about the witch, but his sisters did and he didn't want to ruin it for them. Another pop in the woods made him jump; he shook off the nerves and sang their favorite song, one from a plastic record player that had been their father's.

"In the Big Rock Candy Mountain, you never change your socks." The twins began to hum along, adding words here or there, until they got to the line all three of them loved and they sang in unison.

"There's a lake of stew and soda, too, in the Big Rock Candy Mountain!" The familiar words calmed them, made

things fun again, as though their combined voices swept the fear away.

Ansel was about to begin another verse when a new noise came from farther in the forest—not a pop, not a crack, but a footstep. A slow, rolling foot on dried leaves, then another, then another. He grabbed his sisters' hands, one of their sticky palms in each of his. The bag of candies fell to the ground and scattered, rainbow colors in the dead leaves.

They waited. There was nothing.

And yet there was something—there was something, something breathing, something dripping, something still and hard in the trees. Ansel's eyes raced across the trunks, looking for whatever it was that he was certain, beyond all doubt, had its eyes locked on them.

"Who's there?" Ansel shouted. His voice shook, and it made the twins quiver. Ansel was never scared. He was their big brother. He protected them from boys with sticks and thunderstorms.

But he was scared now, and they were torn between wonder and horror at the sight.

Nothing answered Ansel's question. It got quieter. Birds stilled, trees silenced, breath stopped, his grip on his sisters' hands tightened. It was still there, whatever it was, but it was motionless, waiting, waiting, waiting...

It finally spoke, a low, whispery voice, something that could be mistaken for wind in the trees, something that made Ansel's throat dry. He couldn't pick out the words—they were torn apart, and they were dark. Low, guttural, threatening.

The words stopped.

And it laughed.

Ansel squeezed his sisters' hands and took off the way they had come. He yanked them along and ran fast as he could, over brush and under limbs. The twins screamed, a single high-pitched note that ripped through the trees and swam around Ansel's head. He couldn't look back, not without slowing.

It was behind them. Right behind them, chasing them.

Gretchen stumbled but held tightly to Ansel, let herself be dragged to her feet just as something grasped at her ankles, missed. They had to move faster; it was coming, crunching leaves, grabbing at the hems of their clothes.

It's going to catch us.

The twins slowed Ansel down—their joined hands slowed everyone down. They'd promised to split up so the witch could eat only one of them, but now...

It's going to catch us.

Ansel lightened his grip, just the smallest bit, and suddenly his hands were free and the three of them were sprinting through the trees. The thing behind them roared, an even darker version of the words they'd heard earlier.

Both twins knew the other couldn't run much longer. Did Ansel know the way out?

Candy.

On the ground, yellow candies. Ansel was following them, slicing around trees while the twins followed along desperately, eyes focused on finding the next piece, the trail

5

back to the part of the forest they knew. The monster leapt for one of the twins, missed her, made a breathy, hissing sound of frustration. She dared to glance back.

Yellow, sick-looking eyes found hers.

She turned forward and sped up, faster than the others, driven by the yellow eyes that overpowered the sharp aches in her chest, her legs begging for rest. There was light ahead, shapes that weren't trees. Their house, their house was close—the candy trail had worked. She couldn't feel her feet anymore, her lungs were bursting, eyes watering, cheeks scratched, but there was the house.

They burst from the woods onto their cool lawn. *Get inside, get inside.* Ansel flung the back door open and they stumbled in, slamming the door shut. Their father and mother ran down the stairs, saw their children sweaty and panting and quivering, and asked in panicky, perfect unison:

"Where's your sister?"

CHAPTER ONE

The truth is, I can't believe it took our stepmother this long to throw us out.

She's never liked us, after all, especially me—she didn't like the way my father loved me, didn't like the fact that I perfectly matched the daughter she'd never met but my father ached for, the way I looked like his dead wife when she'd been a teenager. She said she just couldn't afford to keep us on anymore and, with me having just turned eighteen and Ansel nineteen, was no longer obligated to.

Obligated. We were obligations left behind by a father eaten alive by mourning, remnants of a shattered family.

"Are we in South Carolina yet? I zoned out," Ansel says, his voice a forced calm as he peers over the steering wheel. Ansel likes to have a plan of attack, like he did back on the football field in high school, but right now, we've got nothing more than the clothes in the car and the gasoline in the tank.

He doesn't want me to see him worrying, but the truth is, I'm happy to be gone. I feel freer without a plan in the middle of nowhere than I did back in Washington.

"Yeah, we crossed the border a few hours ago," I answer, kicking my feet up onto the dash. The backs of my knees are sticky and sweat trickles down my chest—it uses too much gas to run the AC and the heat here is heavy. It's a little easier to bear if I imagine we're on an epic road trip, the kind that's a fun adventure, like you see in movies. "We should be there in another three or four hours, I think," I add.

"There" is the direct result of the folded and refolded pastel brochure in my hands: *Folly Beach, South Carolina: The Edge of America*. I picked up the brochure at a Tennessee rest stop, and ever since, we've been moving toward it, at my behest and Ansel's ever-accommodating apathy.

The photo on the front is of a peaceful, quiet beach with a red and white lighthouse by the water's edge. The sand goes on for miles, golden and flat, while the water peaks into elegant waves. It's the place of my dreams—western Washington State, with its dense forests, was full of places for girls to disappear, to vanish into the trees at the hands of a witch.

A witch. The only term I have for whatever it was that took my sister. I visualize the witch as a twisted villain, an evil woman, a monster, a demon, a near-invisible force, every man in our neighborhood, a trick of the light—something with horribly golden eyes that only I saw and Ansel has long insisted never existed in the first place. Whatever the witch is, she lives among dark trees, deep valleys, craggy ocean cliffs. I've spent my whole life longing for soft, endless sand and crashing waves that blur the sounds of the world so I no longer stare at the trees and wonder where the other half of me is among them. I've spent my whole life wanting to escape the memory of my sister, wanting to start over, and hating myself for wanting that. How could I want to run away from a lost little girl?

But still. I open the brochure again and read.

A picturesque town of painted sunsets, elegant dining, and endless beaches, Folly Beach is truly the Edge of America — where the everyday ends and serenity begins.

Each second we drive, we get closer to the water, the sand, the flat shore where it's impossible to vanish, where I have plans: Plans to start over. Plans to be someone new, someone who isn't haunted by a dead sister. We fly past exits that have nothing at them and finally see hints of the beach only a few hours ahead. Signs advertising resorts and speedboat rentals and little shops boasting floats and giant-size beach towels — it's early June, prime beach season, and most of the other cars on the road seem packed to the brim with vacationing families. I inhale the hot scent of cut hay and try to imagine that it's the ocean's salt.

The Jeep kicks. There's a loud crack, a boom, and the smell of smoke suddenly overpowers the air.

Ansel veers off the nearly empty road just as gray smoke billows from the front of the car. He jumps out, slamming the door as he runs around and opens the hood. I can't see him anymore, but his coughs and curses make their way to my ears. I lean out my window, trying to see what's going on, just as Ansel makes his way back around the car.

"The whole damn thing is burned up," Ansel snaps, throwing himself back into the driver's seat. He shakes his head and punches at the steering wheel. "We only have fifty-seven dollars left and the car burns to pieces."

Ansel mutters another string of curse words, flipping through his wallet as if he may find an extra twenty-dollar bill hidden between old receipts. When he doesn't, he shakes his head, grits his teeth, and breathes slowly. He has a fast temper, but he knows it and tries to keep it at bay around me. It was my mother's suggestion, when Ansel started to heal and I still stared at the forest, waiting for my sister to stumble out.

"Make sure Gretchen knows you're there for her. Don't upset her—be her rock, Ansel. You have to help her move on."

It's a shame my mother couldn't listen to her own advice. She couldn't be anyone's rock, curled up in her bedroom until the grief devoured her. We weren't even allowed to say our sister's name in front of her, because it would set her off, either make her sob or yell at us, scream that *we* had lost her. So we were supposed to act as if nothing was wrong. As if there'd always been only two Kassel children, Ansel constantly trying to find whatever it was that would make up for our sister's absence, doing everything he could to be my rock, the person I hold on to when I feel as though I might slide off the world and vanish like she did.

Ansel leans across me and opens the glove compartment, then pulls out a crumbly map, folded in all the wrong ways.

10

He stares at it for a moment. "We're closer to the town we just passed than we are to the next one. We'll have to walk."

"What if we called a tow truck?"

"I don't think we can afford it, but either way my phone is dead. Wait—yours hasn't been used much. Does it have any bars out here?"

Of course it hasn't been used—no one would think to call me. I wanted friends, really, but at the same time, how could I go to the mall and laugh at movies when my sister was out there in the darkness? Ansel, somehow, forced himself over that hurdle—every time he hangs up the phone, he touches the thick class ring on his finger, as if it's his last connection to normal, to his friends, to their world. I feel bad that he's back in mine, despite how much I need him.

I shake my head at Ansel. "My phone died this morning. I forgot to bring a car charger."

"Then we walk," Ansel says with a sigh. I grab my purse and climb out of the car.

And we start to walk.

Everything seemed hot before, when we were sitting in the car. But now things are *truly* hot, stifling in a way I've never known. The air doesn't move—it sits on us like a weight, crushing us into the long grasses we trudge through. The sky is cloudless, imposing, and for what feels like a million years the scenery doesn't change. The pine-saturated forest feels as though it's growing oppressively closer, and I can sense the familiar fear bubbling up in my chest. There could be something in the leaves; there could be something that makes me disappear. Ansel sees it and quietly moves so that he's in between me and the tree line. He thinks that makes it better, but really, who would I rather the witch take this time around—Ansel or me?

Finally, the exit ramp appears ahead, just as the feeling of insects nipping at my ankles is becoming too much to handle. Rivers of sweat carve down my back and Ansel's shirt is drenched, but we huff and jog up the ramp to a crossroad. There are two signs at the top of the ramp surrounded by black-eyed Susans. One is hand-painted with red and blue lettering and reads SEE ROBERT E. LEE'S RIDING BOOTS. The other is wooden with a white background and red lettering that isn't entirely even, as if it was hand-carved. LIVE OAK, SOUTH CAROLINA. HOME OF THE ACORNS—1969 COUNTY CHAMPIONS.

"1969?" Ansel says, surprised. "And they still have the sign up?"

"Maybe it's the only time they've won," I suggest. Ansel frowns—in Washington, his school's football team won the state championship so regularly that they had to shift the oldest "state champs" plaque off the sign every year to make way for the newest one. Ansel was a defensive lineman—I think I see him smirk a little at the sign as we pass it. He loved all sports, but football was his obsession—he memorized plays, other players' stats, training regimens. He told me once that it was because he liked getting hit. That being knocked to the ground reminded him he was here.

"It looks like our options are limited," he says. There's

nothing but farmland to our right. To our left is a large store—floats in the shapes of orcas and alligators rest in bins outside, and beach towels are hanging in the window. Beside that is a gas station attached to a long diner with giant glass windows. Even from here, I can see people watching us as they eat lunch. They look as if they're glaring at us, but I can't really tell for sure.

Ansel walks quickly to get in front of me, and within a few moments we're close enough that people have stopped staring for fear of being caught. There's a faded red cursive sign over the diner: JUDY'S. Painted letters on the windows advertise famous blackberry pie and muscadine grape preserves. All the people inside are hunched over whatever they're eating, as though they worry someone might snatch it away from them.

When Ansel pushes the door open, a wind chime hung on the interior knocks against it. The diner is mostly occupied by sun-spotted old men wearing baseball caps and jeans, though there are a few soft-looking women as well, all completely silent, eyes on us. I was right—they *are* glaring, but I'm not sure why.

"All right, all right, give them some space," a weary-looking waitress calls from the other end of the diner, waving a rag at the patrons. They give her dark looks but abandon the suspicious glares at Ansel and me. The waitress drops off a stack of napkins by an old man, then walks our way. Her yellow dress stands out against the faded aquamarine and black that decks out the diner. "Forgive them. They don't like outsiders. I see enough that I'm over it, I guess. What'll you have? Coca-Cola? Sweet tea? You look roasted."

"Uh, neither, actually. We broke down about a mile ahead on the road. I wanted to see if we can get a tow truck," Ansel says.

"Closest tow company is over in Lake City, ever since the Bakers left town. They can be out here in about an hour, though, if you want their number," the waitress tells us with a pitying frown.

"Can I use your phone to call?" Ansel asks. The waitress reaches down below the register and pulls up an ancient-looking phone, and she and Ansel begin flipping through a series of tattered business cards, looking for the tow company's number. I ease myself onto one of the bar stools and look around the diner.

Along with a few older blue-collar men sitting at the bar is a man—boy?—about Ansel's age, though something about him feels *old*. It's not his skin, not his hands, but something in the way he holds his shoulders, in the way his head droops down, something that makes me think he's handsome and dangerous at once. Our eyes lock for a small moment through his layer of shaggy, almost-black hair. Bright eyes as green as mine are blue, eyes that don't match the tired look of the rest of his body—the gaze shoots through the air and startles me. I glance down, and when I look back up, the boy is hunched over his coffee again.

I'm jarred away from him by the sound of Ansel hanging up the phone harder than necessary.

"Interested in that sweet tea now? How about a Cheerwine?" the waitress asks Ansel.

"Why not? Two teas, I guess," Ansel mutters in response. The waitress nods and jogs toward a silver urn of tea labeled SWEET with a permanent marker. I don't totally get the need for the marker, because the identical one beside it is also labeled SWEET.

Ansel slides onto the stool next to me. "The guy says it'll cost a hundred and fifty dollars. Might as well be a hundred and fifty thousand. I told him never mind. I didn't even ask how much it would be to fix the car." Ansel sighs and rubs his forehead. "I could do it if I had the tools, but I didn't have room to pack them."

The waitress slides two glasses of amber tea packed with ice onto the counter; I sip on mine tentatively. It's tremendously sweet, so much so that I feel the sugar coating the inside of my mouth. Ansel and I sit in silence for a moment, until an old man a few seats down coughs loudly and wipes his mouth with a handkerchief.

"Okay, okay, you got my pity. You good with your hands, by chance?" the old man asks.

"Good enough," Ansel answers carefully, rising. He walks over and shakes the man's hand.

"Ansel Kassel"—Ansel nods toward me—"and my sister, Gretchen."

"Jed Wilkes," the man replies.

Other people stare at Jed, as though he's broken some sort of oath about talking to strangers. He doesn't notice, though—he takes off his NRA ball cap and runs a hand over his mostly bald head. "Well, if you can do some basic repair sort of stuff, I might be able to point you in the right direction to make a little cash."

"I can do basic repairs—more than basic repairs. What do you need done?" Ansel says eagerly.

"Not me—Sophia Kelly. She runs a candy shop way out in the near middle of nowhere. Had some stuff she needed fixed up, last I talked to her."

There's a sharp movement next to me; I turn to see that the green-eyed boy has lifted his head. "Yeah, *she* needs help," he mutters, slamming his coffee mug down so hard that liquid sloshes out the sides. The waitress cusses at him under her breath, lifts the mug, and runs a wet rag over the spill. Everyone else in the diner seems to share the waitress's sentiment— annoyed eye rolls and irritated glances fly his way. No one offers any sort of explanation before Jed continues.

"Anyway, interested?"

"Yes," Ansel answers immediately. "Absolutely. If I buy your meal for you, would you give us a ride back to my car first? I don't want to leave our suitcases out there all day."

"Hell, don't worry about it, kid. I feel bad for you—you remind me of my grandson, before my daughter up and moved to the city with him. I'll give you a ride to your car. Just remember to tell Miss Kelly how gentlemanly I was," Jed

16

says with a loud chuckle. The green-eyed boy responds by dropping a ten-dollar bill onto the counter and jumping from his seat. He moves to leave the diner but suddenly stops in front of me, eyes piercing my own.

"Stay away from her," he tells me, loud enough that the rest of the diner can hear but so seriously, so desperately, that I feel as though he and I are the only ones in the room. "Stay as far away from her as you can."

Ansel makes it from Jed back to me in record time, but the boy is already gone—he storms out of the diner and slides onto an ancient-looking motorcycle, then squeals out of the parking lot. I'm left shaken, not by what he said, but by the way he looked at me, the way he spoke to me, the way he... everything. I try to swallow my reaction. *Being afraid of a crazy kid in a diner is no way to start a new life, Gretchen.*

"I'm fine. Seriously," I tell Ansel. I hate him and love him for being this way, ready to run to my side. It makes me feel safe, but I wish so badly that I didn't need a rock to cling to.

"Ah, so you do speak, Skittles!" Jed says. Ansel takes the green-eyed boy's vacant seat, still warily watching the cloud of exhaust he left.

"Skittles?" I ask.

"Never seen so many colors since lookin' in a bag of Skittles," Jed says, nodding toward the tips of my hair. Pink, blue, purple, faded strands of orange. I thought that maybe if I made myself stand out, I wouldn't feel so scared of slipping off the world and vanishing like my sister—if people noticed me, they could hold me here. Ansel didn't understand, but I still think it makes sense—you forget the number of wrens and sparrows you see every day, but if a macaw flies by, you notice her. You wouldn't stop using her name and try to forget she ever existed.

It didn't work, though, so I'm left with almost-healed piercings and a rainbow of faded dyes in the lower half of my hair.

Jed continues through my silence. "He's got a thing against Miss Kelly. Don't you mind him, don't you mind any of 'em. People think she's either the patron saint of candy or the first sign of Live Oak's end days. She's the saint, I promise you that."

"Right," my brother says, as if that makes complete sense. If he's as taken aback by Jed's description of Sophia Kelly as I am, he's not letting it show.

"Any reason I should bother trying to find out what you two kids are doing out here all alone?" Jed asks.

"Our stepmother asked us to leave," Ansel says shortly. "So we did."

"Right." Jed shoves a forkful of scrambled eggs into his mouth. "We don't get runaways too often," he says with a laugh. "But then, we don't get too many young people, period."

"We're not runaways," I correct Jed quietly. "We were thrown out."

"Yeah, yeah," Jed says. His eyes sparkle. "But if your stepmother is the type to throw you out, you probably woulda run away sooner or later."

Without doubt, I think. I know I couldn't have lived with

her in the shell of our childhood home for too much longer. Ansel shakes his head and takes a drink of his yet-untouched tea; his eyes widen in surprise at how sweet it is.

"Well, let's head out, then," Jed finally says, nodding at the waitress. She takes a ten-dollar bill from his hand. Ansel fumbles with his wallet to pay for our drinks.

"Don't worry about it, hon. On the house," she says with a kind smile. Usually Ansel would be too proud to walk away without paying, but I suppose being this broke has challenged his pride. He gives her an appreciative look as I follow Jed outside; the diner begins buzzing again behind us, as if they'd been holding in their conversations while strangers were around. There's a faded red truck that I already can tell belongs to Jed—it doesn't surprise me at all when he opens the door and waves us over. I let Ansel have the front, since he's huge and the back is crammed with tools and cigarette packages.

With the windows open, hot wind whipping through the air, we cut down the interstate to Ansel's Jeep. He grabs most of our things, tosses them into the back of Jed's truck beside some rusty animal traps, and we're on our way again.

The first stoplight we see is simply flashing yellow, and Jed coasts through it. The town appears ahead—strings of brick buildings connected to one another, though each with a slightly different storefront. On the sides of the buildings are old signs from businesses long closed, painted on the brick in faded colors. It'd be idyllic, if it didn't have a feel of abandonment about it—as though the buildings are stores merely because that's what they've always been. I feel as if the empty windows are watching me.

Finally, there's a break in the buildings: a town square, with a traffic circle around its border. In the center is a statue of a Confederate soldier on a rearing horse. On the far side of the square, set just off the road, is a wooden building with an American flag out front and a bright red acorn logo above it. The windows are boarded up.

"Is that a school?" Ansel asks over the clattering of the truck's engine struggling down the road.

"Was. Ten or so years ago we stopped havin' enough students to fill it. All the kids are bused down to Lake City now—hour ride, but the government paid for a bus to come and get 'em. Though rumor has it that might stop, what with there not bein' too many kids left in Live Oak."

"You won the county championship in sixty-nine, I saw," Ansel adds with a hint of amusement in his voice.

"Bet your sweet ass our boys did—against Lake City High, biggest showdown in the county. I was second-string, didn't get to play in the game, but Sophia's daddy was the big star of it. Touchdown, seventy-three yards. Proudest moment Live Oak's ever had!" Jed exclaims. If that was their proudest moment, I can't help but wonder what's been going on in the decades since, but I keep my mouth shut.

We emerge on the other side of town and delve back onto roads lined with pastures or trees. Jed begins taking strange turns onto roads that I'm certain can't lead anywhere, since they're all overgrown with branches and the paving is barely there at all, but no, eventually we come out on a decently paved street with forests looming on either side. They're just starting to bear down on me when I spot a break in the trees, and when Jed slows down, I realize what it is — a front yard. We're here.

CHAPTER TWO

It's a cottage, tucked away into a nest of mountainous oak trees that are draped with Spanish moss. The exterior is a cinnamon shade of wood, with a stone chimney that's being devoured by ivy. Flower boxes line the white-trimmed windows, filled with what looks like the peppermint plants our mom used to grow. The door is arced and licorice red and sits behind a covered front porch that holds several rocking chairs. A wooden sign with Coca-Cola advertisements on either end hangs from the porch's mottled tin roof; pale violet lettering in its center reads KELLYS' CHOCOLATIER. The entire thing looks imaginary, like a gingerbread house in a quiet corner of a hot paradise.

Jed's truck rumbles off the main road and onto the gravel drive as he breathes deeply. "It's a spell, I'm tellin' ya. A magic spell."

I'm not immediately sure what he's talking about, but

just as I'm about to ask for an explanation, I figure it out: the air is filled with sweet vanilla, a scent that makes me think of our mom's cooking and morning sun and summertime. It overpowers the cigarette smell of Jed's truck and thickens as we grow closer to the cottage, and I suddenly find that I don't want to speak—I simply want to breathe it in, close my eyes, and rest. I look to Ansel; his expression matches the same blissful, blurry way that I feel.

Jed pulls the truck into the tiny gravel lot in front of the cottage. Ansel gives me a hopeful look before opening the passenger side door and swinging his legs out of the car; I climb out after him. Outside, the humidity makes the vanilla scent almost drinkable. I pull my hair into a ponytail and try to ignore the forest on either side, and the trees and leaves and darkness behind the house. I prepare for the fear, the familiar twist in my stomach, but...it doesn't come. I inhale, exhale, waiting for it to strike, but I can think only about the vanilla smell. For the first time in ages, the trees are simply trees, instead of places for witches to lurk. Jed's right—it is like a magic spell. How else could a single scent erase years of fear from my mind?

Jed inhales again, then shoves his hands into his overall pockets. He crunches across the gravel in heavy work boots, toward the porch. Before he can go more than a few steps, the door swings open.

The first thing I see is the dog: a golden-colored shaggy creature whose pink tongue lolls out of his mouth. He barks in greeting.

The second thing I see is the beautiful girl. I'm not sure

how I missed her on first glance. She's young and built like a dancer, with a heart-shaped face and long hair that spills like dark chocolate curls. She's wearing a pink flowered apron and holds a lime-colored bowl on her hip, the way a mother might hold her baby. Everything about her is lovely — classic, the kind of pretty that can't be created with mascara or lip gloss. The girl's dark blue eyes find Jed first, and she grins.

"Jed! You haven't been here in ages!" she scolds him playfully. She turns to set the bowl down inside the cottage, dusts her hands on her apron, then starts across the front porch with the dog following.

"I know, Miss Kelly. We're repavin' the road to the Clarks' place. Takin' way more time than we figured," Jed says apologetically, sweeping the ball cap off his head.

The girl crosses her arms and laughs, a bell-like sound. Her eyes find Ansel and me. My brother inhales and stands up straighter. He's watching her intently, but melancholy edges around his eyes. He's never really dated. Girls have never been able to understand his — our — baggage.

"And you brought company?" the girl asks. At her words, the dog rushes toward us. Ansel steps in front of me protectively, but the dog simply sniffs around our sandaled feet before licking my toes.

"Sorta," Jed explains, motioning toward my brother and me. "They broke down on the highway and are lookin' to make some cash to fix the car. I was thinkin' if you still needed some work done, this guy might be able to help you out."

"Hmm, okay," she says, nodding. The dog sits at my feet;

I lean down to stroke his head. When I look back up, I discover the girl's eyes on mine—and they're no longer sparkly, no longer happy, but rather, *yearning*. Desperate, even, as if she's searching for an answer within me but coming up empty. Her smile fades not into a frown but into a sad sort of expression, the kind you make before you start to cry. She's looking for something, and though I don't know what, I want to help her find it. I want to be her friend. I take a step forward.

She looks away sharply, and her bright smile reappears. Her eyes sparkle again, whatever sadness that had lingered there instantly vanishing.

"Well, if you're interested—what was your name?" she asks my brother.

"Ansel," he says, his voice shaky and nervous. "And my sister, Gretchen."

"Sophia Kelly. I have a few things that'd probably only take the afternoon to knock out. Simple stuff—a few tree limbs that need to come down, a cabinet door that won't stop sticking, that kind of thing. Interested?"

"Yes, yes," Ansel says breathlessly. Jed snickers, but there's a look of understanding on his wrinkled face.

"Great," she says, grinning. She whistles, and the dog trots back toward her. "Are you going to help your brother, Gretchen?"

"I can—" I begin, glancing toward Ansel.

"No. No, I've got it," Ansel answers quickly. I'm not sure if he actually doesn't need my help or if he just wants to appear extra manly.

Sophia nods. "Come on, I'll get you both a Coke before your brother gets to work," she says to me.

Jed reaches into the back of his truck to haul my suitcase to the ground; Ansel hops onto the wheel and grabs his own in a much more grandiose display than is probably necessary. I pull the handle up on mine and roll it over the gravel toward Sophia.

"Let me help," she says when I arrive at the porch steps. She sweeps toward me gracefully and helps me lug the suitcase up the stairs. Even though we're not that close, I can smell vanilla and strawberries rising from her skin. She gives me another kind smile, then waves me to follow her in. I glance back to see Ansel hurrying to catch up to us, as if he's afraid to let Sophia out of his sight. Normally I'm the one he watches carefully. It's a nice change.

Inside the chocolatier I feel as though I'm somewhere magical, somewhere exciting. Gently sloping light pours in the front windows, illuminating shelves that line two walls of the main room. They're filled to the front with crinkly cellophane bags packed with chocolates in every shape and size. Tiny ribbons are tied into perfect bows, their color reflected in the glass cases on the opposite side of the room. Behind the glass are bright, ripe pieces of fruit dipped into chocolate—white chocolate, dark chocolate, milk chocolate, dotted with nuts or dusted with cocoa powder. Other trays boast chocolate truffles, thick, enormous chocolate cakes and cupcakes, baskets full of cocoa beans, and jars of hot chocolate powder. There's a fireplace and mantel with an antique-looking gun over it; the mantel is lined with stacks of chocolate bars in perfect rectangles with gold and silver foil wrappers.

"I'll put your things in the stairwell for now," Sophia says. Before I can stop her, she heaves my suitcase toward a door at the back of the shop, tucking it just behind the door frame. "What'd you pack, bricks?" she teases me.

"Books," I say, and my cheeks flush. I started reading after my sister vanished because it made me feel as if I were her—as though she weren't lost after all. But then it became something else; in someone else's story, I could become a whole character instead of half a girl.

Our mom used to sneak up, watch me read. She'd always start to cry, and I would close the book to make the tears stop. She wasn't really watching me. She was watching my sister.

I search for words, trying to find a less weighted explanation as to why I brought so many books with me, but Sophia is laughing, bright and happy. "A library's worth of books, from the feel of it. Hey, Jed!" she shouts toward the screen door. "Don't leave yet—I need to give you something!"

"Right, Miss Sophia," I hear Jed call back. Sophia scans the shelves quickly, then snags a bag of chocolate candies and dashes out the door, past Ansel. He looks spellbound and holds the door open as he watches her run toward Jed. I glance at the empty spot on the shelf—pecan clusters, assorted. The remaining bags are full of round white, dark, and milk chocolate circles that look so perfect, I wonder how they can be real.

"Anyway," Sophia says, jogging back in; I can hear the crunching of gravel as Jed backs out of the driveway. Sophia walks to the shelf with the pecan clusters and pulls the remaining bags to the front. Everything she does is intentional—beautiful, in a way. She is confident, and I am jealous, but at the same time I want to study her, copy her.

When I start over, I want to be like her—even though I've known her for only minutes.

"So, you run this shop alone?" My brother's voice is soft, gentle, and even.

Sophia spins back to face us and nods. "Eh, it's a big difference from being at the university, but it's not *that* lonely," she lies. I know it's a lie—it's the same lie I tell people when they comment on how I am quiet or never go to the movies or never talk about having friends. I lie because I'm scared. I'm scared for my sister, scared for Ansel, scared of the witch. But what—or whom—does Sophia need to lie for? I give her a reassuring smile. *It's okay. I get it, really.*

"Don't you think it's risky, though? Out here all alone?" Ansel asks.

Sophia shrugs. "It takes a lot to scare me. Besides, what's left of Live Oak isn't especially welcoming—how many dirty looks did you get in town?"

"A few dozen," I admit.

"It wasn't always like that here, I promise. When I was a little girl, I thought I lived in heaven." She gives me a nostalgic look, then brushes her hair from her face and turns to walk through a set of doors just behind the glass cases. They're shutterlike, something I'd expect to see in a Wild West saloon, and painted jade green. I can see over the top as Sophia opens an avocado-colored refrigerator, grabs three cans, then sweeps back through the saloon doors. After an endless sea of fast-food restaurants with surly employees, having someone like Sophia offer you a drink feels like a great kindness.

"I'll be honest—I can't pay you all that much. I mean, I *can* pay you, but—"

"That's fine," Ansel cuts her off. She nods at him, smiling sweetly. I'm not sure if it's her beauty or hospitality that has Ansel so quick to work for cheap, but I suspect it's some of both.

Sophia leads Ansel through the kitchen; there's a loud clanking as he lifts, then drops, the toolbox—Sophia laughs. I hear a screen door squeal open, slam shut, then silence, broken apart only by the occasional muffled noise of Sophia and Ansel's conversations.

The golden dog trots back in through the kitchen, panting; he stops to grab a rope toy before bounding over to me. He drops the toy and looks at me expectantly. A red leather collar is around his neck, with a silver name tag that says LUXE. I reach down and flip the name tag over. It reads THE KELLY FAMILY, followed by a phone number. *Does Sophia constitute the whole Kelly family?* I think just as she comes back inside and grins when she sees Luxe looking between me and the rope toy in anticipation. I toss it for him; he takes off after it gleefully, a clatter of nails on hardwood.

"He's a lover, not a fighter," she tells me, and I laugh. "I was just making some candied orange slices — want to come back here for some company that isn't going to demand you play fetch?"

"I can help, if you want," I offer, and follow Sophia into the kitchen. It's brighter than the main shop area, with a huge window that opens out to the backyard. There's a swing out there, and a shed with a padlocked door, not to mention more trees dripping with curling Spanish moss. I hear Ansel sawing away as Sophia opens the refrigerator and takes out a bowl of oranges, setting them down on an enormous stainless-steel counter. I take a seat on a bar stool on the other side. She grabs an orange and begins to peel it; I follow suit.

"I love making these, even though I end up eating more of them than I sell," Sophia says absently, brushing the rinds into a little pile. "I swear, they've got magic powers or something. I can be having a terrible day, and I eat these and it feels like everything is right in the world."

"You'll have to sell some to Ansel and me later, then," I joke back.

Sophia laughs. "I don't know if my candy is powerful enough to fix a busted car, but it's worth a try. Do you like almonds? You should try these. They're my specialty," Sophia says, pushing a tray of cooling chocolates toward me. They're molded into little gingerbread men. "They've got gingerbread and caramel in them too," Sophia adds.

I lift one of the gingerbread men and bite into it. It's immediately clear why these are her specialty — they taste amazing. I feel light-headed almost, and the room gets warmer. The taste of gingerbread and chocolate spins through me and makes me feel…like before. I feel the excited, eager way we felt when we first set out into the forest, when we were on an adventure instead of running from a witch. When everything was happy and storybook and we were leaving a trail of candy in the leaves.

"So, what brought you two to Live Oak, anyway?" Sophia asks as I continue to feel as though I'm melting in front of her.

"Our stepmother threw us out because she couldn't afford us anymore. Live Oak just happens to be where we ran out of money," I say immediately.

"What'd you do to get thrown out?" she asks, surprised.

I shrug. "We exist? She never liked us. She just liked our dad, but he wasn't really over our mother dying, and then *he* died—" I pause. Why am I telling her all this? I see Sophia's eyes run over my multicolored hair and she shrugs, then starts peeling another orange.

"She sounds like a nut job. You and Ansel must be close, though, to hit the road together. Is it just the two of you?" she asks as I finish the chocolate. The almonds crunch and the warm feeling grows. Sophia picks up a knife and starts cutting an orange against the grain; the tart and lovely smell fills the room.

"It is now. I had a twin sister, but she vanished."

Wait. Did I just say that? To a complete stranger? I blink. Guilt swims over me, though I'm not sure why. She's not secret. She's just…gone.

31

Sophia looks at me, eyebrow raised. "Vanished?"

I speak without meaning to, as if the words are finding their own way past my lips. "In the forest. Something chased us, and when Ansel and I stopped, she was gone."

Where's your sister?

Words still want to spill from me—I slam my jaw shut to keep from letting everything out, all the memories, the search parties, the nothingness they found among the trees. It was as though the little girl who was half of me never existed at all, as if my family had just been seeing double all these years instead of actually having twins.

"That's so sad," Sophia says, and her voice cracks a little. She hurries over to the sink and pours a glass of water, but I can tell it's mostly to busy her hands and hide her eyes. It's not strange for people to cry for my sister, but Sophia barely knows me. "When was that? Recently?" she asks over her shoulder.

"No. We were just kids, but it didn't stop people from blaming us for her disappearing. My sister and I were six, Ansel was seven. Twelve years ago, I guess."

Sophia's hands freeze; her eyes jump up, find mine. "You're eighteen?" She walks back over to me.

I nod. "My birthday was a few weeks ago. That's why our stepmother threw us out—she can finally do it legally. She hated us. Dad married her a year after Mom died. I think he just wanted to start everything over again."

Sophia slides the glass of water toward me quickly, as if it's a lifeline. She looks alarmed, and I feel my cheeks heating up over telling this near stranger my family history in detail. I take a gulp of water and it cools the warmth that was building inside me. I feel as though I'm just waking up, as if the words spilling from me moments ago were just the result of some kind of stupor.

"I'm sorry," I mutter. "I don't know why I told you all that."

"It's okay," Sophia answers hurriedly, smiling—although her smile has a certain sort of nervousness around the edges. "People say I'm easy to open up to."

"Right." I nod, taking another drink of water. I've hardly had a bite of chocolate since my sister—usually all I can think of when I'm around it is little yellow candies on the forest floor. Is this how it's supposed to make you feel? As if you're happy, as if you're safe?

Sophia drops the orange slices into a cooking pot before speaking. "My dad is gone too. That's why I came back here, actually, to run the chocolatier after he...left." Her final word is heavy, but she looks away so fast that I can tell she doesn't want to talk about whatever the truth about her family is—and I understand entirely. I move on.

"Where did you come back from?"

"College. I was studying philosophy," she says, teasing herself a little in the phrase. "Big money in that, you know. I'm the only one in twenty-three years to leave Live Oak and come back." She pauses to pull a glass jar of sugar from a wooden cabinet and proceeds to sprinkle half the jar over the oranges, then looks up at me. Her eyes look the same way they did earlier outside—as though she thinks I can help her, as if she's desperate for me to help her. "It's hard, losing your parents. Right when you think it's getting better, it starts to hurt again," she says softly, her voice wounded.

I smile a little. "I know. I understand."

Sophia's eyes fill with water and gratitude almost instantly. She sniffs and nods at me. "You know what it's like." I don't say anything as Sophia takes a moment and collects herself, staring intently at the stove as she does so. When she looks back up at me, she's grinning, all signs of sadness gone. "But at least I can make some badass candy oranges," she says.

The afternoon passes quickly—Ansel hauling heavy things by the open door, poking his head in to ask Sophia little questions, dropping in compliments here and there. It doesn't exactly bother me, but it is interesting to watch my brother act this way over a girl—I guess I just never thought of him like this. Sophia and I seem to have somehow instantly bonded over our shared lost parents. She tells jokes and funny stories about her father and we laugh as though we're old friends; it makes me feel grounded, as if in this moment, Ansel isn't my only rock, isn't the only thing keeping me from vanishing. Sophia has a plate of sandwiches ready for dinner when Ansel trudges inside, long after the sun has dropped into the horizon.

"I have to admit, I'm impressed," Sophia says with a grin as she pours him water from an amber pitcher. She hands him the glass and rustles through a flour jar before emerging with a ragged hundred-dollar bill.

"That enough?" she says, passing the money to me. I fumble to accept it mid–sandwich bite.

"Sure, of course," Ansel says quickly. "I don't suppose you'd give us a ride out to our car, by the way? It's still on the interstate. I think this is enough to get us towed."

"Um..." Sophia sways a little, lets her dress twirl around her knees. "I was wondering if you guys would mind staying here tonight? I just realized I've got a few other things you could do tomorrow, if you don't mind..."

"Stay here?" I ask, surprised, but the pink tint around Ansel's ears doesn't escape me.

"No, no, we couldn't," Ansel says quickly.

"It's no big deal, I swear," Sophia insists. "Besides, the hotel in Live Oak closed a million years ago. Unless you want to camp out in your car, you'll have to practically make it all the way to the beach before you get to one that's open."

Ansel looks at a loss for words, floundering in the lack of a plan for us.

"Come on. I've got a spare bedroom and a couch," Sophia tempts us. "Please? I never have company. It'll be fun." Her voice seems almost desperate, and I feel a wave of pity for her. I don't have friends, not really—who am I to turn down someone who wants to be mine?

You're starting over, remember?

"I don't—" Ansel begins.

"Come on, Ansel, you're starting to offend me," Sophia says, folding her arms, but I catch the glimmer of a smile on the corners of her mouth.

"Sorry," Ansel says quickly. "Sorry. It's just always been me and Gretchen and I don't..." He stops. I know what he means, and to my surprise, Sophia seems to know as well: Close your circle long enough, and you forget how to open it back up again.

"Okay. For tonight," he says, giving in. He sends Sophia an appreciative look and plucks a peanut butter and jelly sandwich off the plate.

An hour or so later Sophia leads us through the storefront to a thin stairwell that creaks loudly as we make our way up. There are pictures on the walls: the chocolate shop in what looks like the twenties, then the fifties or so, the eighties maybe, and the most recent one. In each picture there's a person standing out front—Sophia is in the final shot, so I presume it's her father and grandmother in the ones preceding. Our family has nothing like this, and I find myself wondering what it's like to be locked into a life, a profession, a place, even. It can't be the worst thing in the world—I mean, how bad could working in a candy store be?

Upstairs has the feel of an attic transformed into a living space—sloped ceilings and oddly placed beams. That said, it's no less charming than the house below. The main room has a couch and a rocking chair with a crocheted afghan thrown over the arm, and there's a tiny bathroom with white and black checked tile.

"So, bathroom is there—there are towels in the little closet behind the bathroom door. And Ansel, I assume you want to let your sister have the bedroom?"

"Of course," Ansel says without a second thought.

Sophia smiles and motions for me to follow her down the hallway. I glance back at Ansel, who looks strangely large and out of place in the tiny room and as if he longs to go after Sophia—but he sits on the couch instead. I catch a hint of jealousy in his eyes as I walk away with her, and I can't help but be pleased—Ansel is never jealous of me.

"So that's my room, if you need anything," Sophia says, pointing to a large bedroom as we pass it—it's darkened, but there's just enough light to make out a pale blue coverlet on the bed and a large white wardrobe lurking in the corner. "And this is the spare room. Sorry the bed isn't bigger," she says, grimacing. "If it sucks too much, you can have mine. Though that mattress is a little older, so it's kind of lumpy . . . God, I'm the worst host ever, aren't I?" she mutters, blushing a little.

"No, no. Trust me, I've been sleeping in motels or the car for the past few nights. This is great," I answer. Actually, this is beautiful. The room is small and cool, with a steeply pitched ceiling and bead-board walls that have been painted pale yellow. There's a twin bed with a pink floral quilt on top of it. The room itself is perfectly symmetrical—two open windows, two small alcoves (for desks, I presume), matching walls—the single bed and lavender-painted dresser are strange interruptions to the room's reflection of itself.

"Good," Sophia says warmly. "I don't really have company. No one ever uses this room."

We stand for a moment, unsure what to say to each other. I'm not sure why *she* looks concerned, but I'm totally unpracticed when it comes to people being this kind to me. I rock back on my heels, wishing I knew a way to thank her enough, wishing I could blatantly ask, "What's your secret?" and figure out the key to being beautiful, confident, and certain, like she is.

"Well...good night!" Sophia says with a grin and a shrug. I open my mouth to echo the sentiment a moment too late—she's closed the door and I hear her moving down the hall, talking to Ansel about finding extra blankets and pillows for the couch.

I turn to see the the white eyelet curtains stir; a sharp, warm breeze cuts through the room. I thought it was cool in here, but really it's only in comparison to the sweltering heat outside. I step toward a window to tug it shut, pausing for a moment.

The woods are thick and deep, and in the darkness they seem to sway like a single beast, back and forth, hiding, waiting.

There it is—the fear, crawling up through me from somewhere deep in my chest. It's darkly comforting and familiar, a friend I despise. I've never known myself without the fear—as much as I want it gone, I'm not even sure who I'd be if I woke up without it.

I stare into the trees. They're different from the forests in

Washington: thinner trees packed tightly together, pine needles that make tinkling sounds as they fall onto the forest floor below. It has the same eeriness, though, the same depth that all forests have. It looks as if it could *swallow* me.

The parade of pastors, policemen, and volunteers who came to the house used that phrase. They said the forest *swallowed* my sister up. They had a million questions, but the only answer I could give was that a yellow-eyed witch had stolen her, and that was never the answer they wanted. Ansel was more useful to them.

"I don't remember," Ansel said, crying, which I'd seen him do only once or twice before. "I had both their hands, but we had to let go to run faster. I let go of whomever was on my left first, and then whomever was on my right, but I don't know who was where or when she was gone..."

One of us made it out of the forest, but even Ansel didn't know who was truly missing for a heartbeat. He just knew one of his sisters was inside and one wasn't.

Half of me was there, and half wasn't.

Which means, how do I know I'm really the one who survived? What if I'm the one who disappeared? We were the same girl, perfectly identical: the same hair, same eyes, same hands. Yet one of us is gone. A stupid name was our only difference—is that why I survived? Because I'm Gretchen, and she's a girl who doesn't even have a name anymore?

My sister and I—we were born together. I thought we'd die together. I didn't expect her to just...not die. And not live. To just not *be*. We were the same—if I could run fast enough to escape the witch, so could she. But she didn't, and now everything about my life is wrong, wrong, wrong, because of her—

I slam the window shut; it creaks against stale paint and old grime, but I feel the familiar fear and fury subsiding. We'll go to the ocean tomorrow. Calm down. I breathe slowly, like Ansel does, until another fear strikes me—one I had forgotten about until I climb into bed and pull the crisp sheets up over my body. *Stay away from her. Stay as far away from her as you can.*

He spoke as if he was afraid of her. He spoke of Sophia the way I used to speak of the witch.

But what about Sophia Kelly would warrant such a dire warning?

CHAPTER THREE

oud, sharp clanks of a hammer on nails wake me up the next morning. When I peer through the curtains, I see Ansel on the roof of the shed out back, forest looming behind him. I'm not surprised he's good at this handyman role—he kept our home from physically falling apart after Dad died, even if he couldn't repair my family's heart.

In my bedroom, the sun cuts through the white curtains so easily that they might as well not exist. I rummage under my suitcase of novels for a sundress—the last of my clean clothes—and quietly open the door. I've got no idea if Sophia is awake yet. Her door is open; I pause for a moment to look inside.

It's still dark, even in the daylight—I can see the silhouette of one of the large oaks swaying just outside a window and reason it must be blocking most of the sun. There's a small bookshelf packed with philosophy books, and another with classics—*Little Women, Moby-Dick*, the Narnia books, all old and worn down, begging me to flip through their pages. On Sophia's tiny wicker nightstand is a small lamp and, beside that, a Nietzsche book.

A bark startles me; I whip my head toward the staircase and see Luxe panting happily at the open doorway, a tennis ball at his feet. I smile and walk toward him; he sits obediently while I rustle the fur on his head and then descend the stairs.

I'm relieved when the scent of the chocolatier strikes me; something about it makes me relax, makes me forget about the thick forest just outside. Sophia is making something with coconut—she must be, because it smells like islands and sunshine in the storefront. Coming down the stairs, my eyes find a piece of wood nailed above the chocolatier's front door.

The wood is polished smooth, and painted in pale blue are the words "There is always some madness in love. But there is also always some reason in madness."

Odd quote for a chocolatier, I think as I walk around the glass display cases and look over the saloon doors, to the kitchen.

I was right—Sophia is standing over a half dozen split coconut shells. She's gazing out the window, at my brother, I realize, with a sad sort of look on her face. I pause, watching her. It's as if she's remembering something, or wishing for something, something she can't have—

I step through the saloon doors; they creak and Sophia whirls around, smile on her face, any semblance of melancholy gone.

42

"You're up! Are you hungry? Because I'm not so good at making breakfast—actually, I'm not good at making much of anything except candies…but I have a toaster that makes awesome toast, and about a hundred different kinds of preserves," Sophia says, pointing to a cabinet behind me. "My mom, she could make anything. Grits, biscuits, pancakes in the shape of hearts, you name it…" The tangerine-colored radio behind her plays music quietly, and she begins pouring milk from the remaining coconut shells into a yellow mixing bowl.

"Do you want help?" I ask on my way to the toaster.

"With this?"

"I mean, since we're waiting on Ansel, if you want…I don't know how to cook, but I can learn." I've always wanted to learn, honestly—our mom was a great cook. My sister and I practically survived off her homemade macaroni and cheese. I drop two slices of bread into the toaster and pick out a jar of grape preserves.

"I'd love help. I'm kind of obsessive about the way the mixing is done, but can you do the filling? I hate filling." Sophia grins and a look similar to relief washes over her, as though she's truly touched by my offer. "Dad used to pay me a nickel per mold I filled, because he hated it as much as I do." After I finish my toast, I walk to the other side of the counter, where Sophia is standing.

"Just a half spoonful should do it. Don't worry too much if it overflows a bit—we can just snap those edges off once it hardens," Sophia says, passing the bowl to me. "And I've got a bunch more of those trays and am not ashamed of convincing someone else to fill them. Live Oak throws a big Fourth of July party in the square, and I'm way behind."

Sophia turns the radio up a little bit—all oldies, but she tells me it's the only station she can get decent reception for. As Ansel's hammering falls into even patterns, I slowly fill the tiny circles while Sophia pops already-cooled candies from the plastic and puts them into cellophane bags. Luxe settles at my feet and snores softly. There's a consistency to it all, a rhythm that makes me forget time is passing. I don't bother to check the clock till it's almost noon, and I'm shocked that so many hours have passed. It's the same feeling I get after finding out how long I've been absorbed in a book.

I'm about to comment on how quickly the morning has gone when Luxe leaps up and barks happily; he runs out the kitchen's screen door, almost bowling Ansel over, just as I hear a quiet tinkling of bells out front. I glance up to see two girls my age, one blond and one brunette, walking in. Luxe follows at their heels, as if he just strolled in with them instead of racing around the entire house to meet them. Ansel makes it into the kitchen and gives Luxe a weary look.

"Hey!" Sophia calls to the customers as she sweeps through the saloon doors.

"What's up?" the blond girl asks brightly. I peer through the doorway at them. They look unpolished standing next to Sophia Kelly, as though they're made of paint and makeup.

"Nothing too serious. Just about to put out some coconut cordials. Interested?" Sophia asks.

"Hmm, maybe," the brunette says. "Anything new?"

"Not lately," Sophia admits, leaning over the glass counter. "I've got some chocolate and peanut butter bark, though, and I haven't had that in a while."

"Ooh, that sounds yummy," the blonde says, nodding emphatically. I watch her breathe deeply—does the scent of this place make everyone feel carefree, or is that just me?

"It's right over there." Sophia points to a shelf near the saloon doors. She catches my eyes. "Oh hey, wait—Gretchen, Ansel, come up front and meet Jessie and Violet!"

My brother and I make eye contact briefly, and he looks surprised when I'm the first to step toward the saloon doors. I smile as he follows behind me—normally it's me following him, wary to lead.

"Hi, I'm Jessie," the blonde says, and her voice is warm enough that I relax a little as I walk toward them. "You're... working here?" She gives Violet a confused glance that screams: *But they're strangers!* Violet, however, seems focused on Ansel and only gives a faint nod.

"They're just helping me out for a little bit. Broke down crossing through," Sophia explains, handing Jessie a crinkly bag filled with peanut butter bark. The explanation doesn't seem to lessen Jessie's surprise.

"That's cool... Where are you from?" Violet asks Ansel after a moment, glossed lips curling into a flirty smile.

"Um..." He looks at Sophia, as if she can explain Violet's heavy gaze. Sophia stifles a laugh and shrugs, so Ansel continues. "Just Washington State."

"You guys drove here all the way from Washington?"

Violet sounds amazed. I nod. "That means you crossed through practically every state!"

"Not quite, but a few. Lots of fields," I say, reminiscing about the Midwest. "And then once we hit Kentucky, things weren't so different from here."

"Ugh. At least they have an Applebee's in Kentucky. Live Oak just has eight churches and a grocery store, basically. But anyways, how old are you?" Violet asks Ansel hungrily.

"Nineteen. Um, Sophia?" Ansel turns to her, ears bright red. "Do you have a smaller Phillips-head screwdriver?"

"Yep. If you look behind the shed door, there's a whole other set sitting on a box to the left," Sophia answers, waving her eyebrows to tease him. He gives Violet and Jessie an obligatory nod and leaves—I wonder if he'd have been embarrassed if Sophia weren't right here?

"Will *he* be at the festival?" Violet asks Sophia before Ansel is out of earshot. I see my brother cringe and I suppress a laugh.

"You two are still coming?"

"Of course we are!" Jessie says, and looks offended that Sophia would even question it. "You don't think we'd listen to a bunch of old people's opinions? They're all idiots. They just want someone to blame."

Sophia sighs and shrugs. "Seems like more and more people *are* listening to them."

"If by 'more and more' you mean, like...seven people, total," Violet says pointedly.

"In a town like Live Oak, that's a lot!" Jessie and Violet almost simultaneously roll their eyes.

"They're not going to ruin you. The festival is gonna be packed."

"I hope so." Sophia looks down as Jessie turns to me, oblivious to some sort of pain crossing Sophia's face.

"*You* should really stay for it, at least. It's so much fun," Jessie says. "But then make sure you run for the hills as soon as it's done. This place, it sucks you under and drowns you, swear to god. I'm running and never looking back the second I get the chance. I can't believe you came back, Sophia, after you managed to escape."

"Eh, well, someone had to run this place. Besides, the chocolatier gave me something to come back *for*. I can't say I blame people destined for cashier jobs at the Piggly Wiggly for not calling or writing once they break free."

"That's true. I'm not dating anyone who's stocking shelves at twenty," Violet says.

"Oh, shut up, you sound like a Lake City snob," Jessie tells her, then turns to me. "My boyfriend works there. And speaking of, I'm supposed to pick him up in twenty minutes, and there's no way we can speed on Jot-Em-Down this time of day. You know Ricky has his car set up behind that kudzu wall."

"Dammit," Violet says. "He could at least sit on the interstate and catch tourists instead of locals. No offense," she adds to me. "Anyway, I need to grab some chocolate-covered Oreos before we go, if you have any. For Grams."

"Oh, that's right, your Grams..." Sophia trails off. "How is she?"

Violet shrugs. "She's okay. Better, now that school's out

47

and I can take care of her. Stubborn as hell, though. Won't move out of her house to live with my mama. Afraid she'll send her to that Live Oak old folks' home."

"Of course . . . you have to take care of her." Sophia shakes her head, as though she's tossing away some lingering question. "I don't have any Oreos made, but if you give me a minute, I can dip them for you."

"Thanks," Violet says. "If I came back without them, I'd be in trouble."

Sophia disappears to the kitchen, leaving me, Violet, and Jessie staring at one another somewhat blankly.

"So . . . is this place like Washington at all?" Jessie asks as we hear Sophia crinkling wrappers in the back.

"No," I admit. "It's much better, honestly."

"Even staying all the way out here? God, it'd make me nervous," Jessie says.

"It's nice. Quiet, but nice," I answer. If I could just forget about the forest, or get over it entirely, it'd be perfect.

"I don't know how Sophia does it," Violet says. "I mean, after the whole thing with her daddy, *I* couldn't do it. Maybe she finally cracked, and that's why she let two outsiders move in . . ."

My expression must give away my ignorance about whatever happened with Sophia's father — Jessie and Violet look at each other meaningfully. It's clear they think they've said too much.

"It's not a big deal," Jessie says, but I can tell by her voice that it is. I raise my eyebrows. Jessie chews her lip, then looks over my shoulder to see where Sophia is.

"Her dad," Jessie finally says in a whispered voice. "He got killed out here. In the house, about three years ago."

Death doesn't scare me. Disappearing, vanishing, being swallowed, yes, but death, surprisingly, doesn't affect me the way it does some people — I watched my mother die, then my father, and death is a lot easier to handle than disappearing. Still, I muster up a shocked expression when I ask, "How?"

Violet's eyes widen and she answers. "They think wild animals; someone said rabid dogs, maybe. Tore him to pieces. That's why Sophia had to move back to Live Oak — to handle his things and take over this place. I would've just shut it down, honestly. There's hardly anyone left in Live Oak to shop here anyway."

Now my eyes widen at the story, and I open my mouth to respond. But before I can articulate a single word, Sophia sweeps back in.

"Here you go!" She hands a bag of Oreos over to Jessie and Violet. Violet gives me a quick shrug, clearly not as paralyzed by what she's just told me as I am.

Sophia takes their money and drops it into an ancient red cash register. "Oh, and wait," she says. She reaches into the glass case and chooses three chocolate-covered strawberries, then puts them in a white box. "If Ricky gives you trouble, throw these at him and run for it." She grins. "Trust me, he can't help himself. He loves them."

"Thanks, Sophia," Jessie says, laughing as she takes the box. "See you later. Good to meet you, Gretchen." Violet waves as they push through the screen door. I lean back to see them through the window; they climb into an old Camry in need of a paint job. Sophia dusts her hands on her apron and moves back toward the kitchen.

I remember the look on her face this morning, the sad, wanting look. *Was it for her father?*

"Gretchen? Are you coming?" Sophia asks, and I realize she's holding open one of the saloon doors for me. I jump and realize I'd been staring at her, then follow her into the kitchen.

"So...what was that festival they were talking about?" I want to ask about Sophia's father, but I'm not sure how she'd react to questions. Besides, I'm an old pro at walking on eggshells for people.

"It's this thing I do toward the end of July. Big chocolate festival that I throw in the yard out back for all the Live Oak girls. I invite some out-of-town guys just for variety. That and the Fourth of July block party are the biggest events in Live Oak. Unless you count the Daughters of the Confederacy gala which...um...I don't, no matter how many mailers those old ladies send out," she says with a giggle. "They were right, though. You really should stay for it. I mean, I know it's, like...I guess a little more than a month away? But still, you'd have a great time."

A grin blossoms across my face. She really wants me not only to go to her festival, but to stay here for that long? I've never been invited to so much as a sleepover. I try to hide my smile—I don't want Sophia to know how alone I used to feel. I want Sophia to know the new Gretchen.

I slide back onto a bar stool in the kitchen. "Is that why

the old people don't like you? They blame you for ruining their gala or something?"

Sophia turns on the stove, and gas flames beneath a large cooking pot leap up.

"No," she says with a sigh. She drops a chunk of butter into the pot and swishes it around with the point of a knife. "Two years ago, the first year I threw the festival, a handful of the girls who came skipped town right after. And I guess that put the idea into the head of a few others, because last year another few left."

"How is that your fault?"

Sophia shrugs as the butter crackles and stares into the pot as though it has an answer for her. "I got unstuck once. Some people think I convince girls at the festival to leave— put the idea into their heads, give them some money, and send them away. After the first year no one really was mad at me, but then it happened again and people wanted someone to blame."

"That's ridiculous." I mean for it to come off casually, dismissive, even, but my voice is serious. I know what it is to be blamed. I know what it is to be Sophia.

"Where's your sister?"

They asked us questions. They wanted to know why we had let her go. What we last heard. What we last saw.

They didn't believe me when I said it was a witch. They didn't understand when I told them if it wasn't a witch, I didn't know what it was.

They wanted to know why we didn't help her. Why we let

her disappear. How could you leave her? How could you just let her go?

We wanted the same answers.

How could we just let her vanish?

I know what it is to be blamed for someone's disappearance when it isn't your fault. I know what it is to have eyes on you, to know people whisper, to at once both fear and long to vanish like her.

Sophia is still talking, and I pick back up midsentence. "...it's a long-standing Live Oak-ian tradition: graduate high school, grab your stuff, and take off before you end up barefoot and pregnant. Live Oak just has so few kids left; it's a bigger deal when a group takes off, I think," Sophia says, adding water to the pot. It steams up around her face and she stirs it slowly. "Plus they don't call or anything, so people suspect they really are missing and not just escaping this place. It kind of sucks, though, when people you've known your entire life — people you used to babysit for, even — start hating you for something you can't control. Something you can't help," she finishes, and hurt creeps into her voice.

"I understand."

Sophia looks at me, surprised, and then seems to remember what I told her yesterday about my sister and how they blamed us. She inhales, looks down, nods. When she looks back up at me, her eyes are wet, just like mine. We blink away the tears simultaneously and smile. I understand her, and for the first time, I think someone other than Ansel might understand me. Whatever the chocolatier's candy might do to make me happy, make me forget the forest, it's nothing compared to the glow of the knowledge that I'm not as alone as I thought. The knowledge that if Sophia can be brave and confident and happy, so can I.

When Ansel returns to the kitchen a few hours later, he's sunburned and sweating. There's a goofy grin on his face, though, and a hammer hanging from a loop on his jeans. I don't know that I've seen him so pleased with himself in ages—maybe Ansel is trying to start new here too. It's working.

"Roof is done," he says proudly.

"Really?" Sophia smiles at him, but it's not the smile she gives me—it's different, gentler, softer, and makes me feel as though I'm being left out of something between them. "I'm impressed. Let me get you something to drink," she says, swinging the freezer door open. The blast of cold air reaches me on the other side of the kitchen. She breaks apart an ice tray, pours Ansel a drink, then slides him a glass along with a few chocolates.

"Do you think you have time to fix that break in the fence? I meant to ask you this morning," Sophia asks.

"Of course. That'll be an easy fix."

"You're sure? You might have to stay another night," she says, glancing at me, as if I'm the one she really needs to convince.

"It's fine with me as long as it's fine with Gretchen," Ansel answers. He finds my gaze, pulls it away from Sophia. He looks pleadingly, longingly, and I can't tell if it's because the scent of the chocolatier has the same effect on him as it does me, or if it's Sophia herself that draws him in.

But the forest is still here, and it still frightens me—how long will Sophia's candies stave it off? Surely it will be only a matter of time till I'm back to being a little girl, ready to run, quivering when the leaves tremble. I wanted to start over at the ocean, but...

"How about this," Sophia says, watching my and Ansel's exchange carefully. "I've got to pick up some groceries. While I'm in town, I'll get a board for the fence—you know the measurements I need, Ansel?" My brother nods. "And you guys talk about it, okay? I don't want to split up siblings," she says with a grin, and for the first time I find myself wondering if she has that power. My stepmother couldn't, our parents couldn't, but could Sophia Kelly pull us from each other?

No, of course not.

Sophia offers Ansel a coconut cordial, gets the fence measurement, and then takes off for the store. It becomes very quiet, save the rustling of the outside world and the occasional slam of the screen door being opened and shut by the breeze.

"You don't want to stay here another night?" Ansel asks.

I think of the ocean for a moment, then shrug. "I guess. Sophia seems to like having us around." I pause, remembering how surprised Jessie and Violet were by our presence here. "Is that weird? She barely knows us."

"She's lonely, obviously," Ansel says, waving a dismissive

hand toward me. "Out here all alone? Wouldn't you want someone around?"

"Speaking of—Sophia's father was killed here, in this house. They say it was wild animals. Rabid dogs, maybe."

Ansel's eyes widen. "Right here?"

I nod.

"Poor Sophia," Ansel says, shaking his head. I can hear it in his voice—he wants to save Sophia. That's how Ansel works. Someone is in pain, and he wants to save her—he ran back into the woods after our sister, he became my rock. He didn't give up on our father, even when Dad became someone Ansel and I barely knew—it wasn't long after Mom's death that he started drinking, and once he remarried it got worse. He couldn't escape the guilt—over my sister, over our mother...Guilt ate him through the mouth of a bottle.

But something *actually* ate Sophia's father alive. Ansel's right—poor Sophia.

"I think this place is good for us," he says quietly. "I feel...I feel like maybe getting out of Washington is what we needed. To get away from her." It's not clear if he means "her" as in our stepmother, or "her" as in our sister.

I suspect both.

CHAPTER FOUR

❦

I don't know how two nights became three. Or four became five. I just know that by the fifth night of sleeping upstairs in Kellys' Chocolatier, everything seems normal, routine. I wake up to the sounds of Ansel working away on some new task Sophia found; I welcome the magic spell that is the chocolatier, the scent that deadens the presence of the forest outside. Luxe took to sleeping in my room by the third night; he makes it a habit of licking at my toes while I get dressed, then trots downstairs after me as I make my way to the kitchen. The Jeep is parked out front, repaired but used to haul things from the hardware store—neither Ansel nor I have mentioned the ocean in days.

Even when I planned to start over, I always pictured my future alone, or perhaps just with Ansel. Now I have to wait for Sophia to finish showering in the morning, and the bathroom smells like her pomegranate shampoo when she leaves.

I pass her in the hallways, see her and Ansel talking in the storefront. I talk to customers, even, the parade of people who seem to be coming as much to show their affection and support for Sophia as they do to purchase candies. The chocolatier feels a little like an island, a hideaway safe from witches and the glaring eyes of the rest of Live Oak.

I am a part of something, however small, however far out in the country. I am not an obligation to my stepmother; I am not the girl without the sister or father or mother; I am not the girl who is missing half of herself. I'm not even "Ansel's little sister." I am wanted. I am almost new.

That said, there isn't much to do here. Sophia claims there's even less to do now that I'm helping her sweep floors and do inventory. Most afternoons are just long pauses between customers—this one being no exception. We sit on the front porch, fanning ourselves and sipping on lemonade to stave off the climbing heat. Sophia talks casually, but I confess that I'm only half listening at this point. The temperature makes my mind fuzzy.

"So they split apart the cocoa powder from the cocoa butter, and then the way they blend the two back together determines what kind of chocolate it'll be," Sophia says. I lift my legs to set them on the porch railing between two seashells. There are seven seashells total—I know, because I've been playing made-up counting games with them all morning. I stir around the mostly melted ice in my glass.

"And…this is the most boring discussion ever, isn't it?" Sophia asks with a smile. The lavender bandanna holding her hair back is freckled with sweat; she kicks her flip-flops over the side of the railing, letting them plop into the grass below. This is casual, fun Sophia. I've noticed that there are two versions of her — the sweet, bubbly, happy version, and the other version, the one I catch glimpses of only when she thinks no one is looking — a sadder, heartaching girl. I suppose the second Sophia could be just a result of being blamed for missing girls, loneliness, maybe losing her father — but there's another layer to it, something I don't recognize. Something that seems to go to her core.

"No, no. Seriously, it isn't boring," I answer her, shaking my head and gazing up at the fan — it's not doing much beyond stirring the hot air around. "I only know book things. And I've never read a book on chocolate making."

"Your school was seriously lacking, then," she teases.

I shake my head. "I left school in eighth grade. Ansel finished, though, last year. I just wasn't... I wasn't cut out for school. I never fit in."

"You *left* school? What'd you do?" Sophia asks with alarm.

"Homeschooled. Kinda. Mostly me reading and my stepmother telling me I was turning the pages too loudly," I say, giggling.

"That's right, books! I'd blocked out the memory of how heavy your suitcase was," she teases. "I love reading. Probably should have studied English instead of philosophy."

"Why philosophy, then?"

"I like thinking. Nietzsche was my favorite — that's his quote on the wooden plaque by the door."

"The one about love?"

Sophia nods, a little somberly. " 'There is always some madness in love. But there is also always some reason in madness.' I love that quote." Her voice softens, the other version of Sophia coming through. "It explains everything."

" 'Everything' as in..."

Sophia shakes her head and gives a weak grin, then snap, just like that, back to happy Sophia. "Just...everything. Everything goes back to love. Even Live Oak can understand that, and believe me, they aren't philosophy fans. Those church ladies all think it's one step away from atheism."

"Which is unforgivable here?"

"Yep. Bible study Sunday mornings, tarot readings before bed. Somehow that's justified," she says affectionately. "That's Live Oak. Or how it used to be, anyway. Now everyone is just...angry, it seems."

"I noticed—everyone was glaring at us in the diner the first day."

"Yep. You've got to earn trust around here now. And once you've got it, god help you if you lose it," she says. She's trying to brush it off, but I can hear the hurt in her voice.

Sophia sighs and goes back to fanning herself with a folded-up piece of paper—a mock-up of the invitations for her chocolate festival. The real things are sitting inside, perfectly stamped and sealed like wedding invitations. Sophia said they were too important not to hand over to the mailman personally, so we've been waiting outside a half hour for him to arrive—even though she had no answer when I asked her what could possibly happen to them if we just left them in the mailbox. She takes her invitations seriously, it seems.

"I'm beginning to think he already came today and just didn't have anything to leave," Sophia mutters.

"We can catch him tomorrow." I shrug. It's not a question of if I'll be here tomorrow. Everyone was right about this place—it has a way of trapping you. The only difference is that I don't mind it. I lean down and grab a chocolate-covered potato chip and take a bite.

"Mail only runs three days a week here now. We'd have to wait till Wednesday..." Sophia looks through the screen door of the shop nervously. "I really wanted to get them out today, but...ugh, I hate driving into town."

"Do you...want me to go?" I hear myself say. It surprises even me—go into town, by myself? Where I go, Ansel goes, yet I want to go alone. I need to go alone. I take another bite of the chocolate-covered chips.

"You wouldn't mind? You could take my car. It kicks a little when it changes gears, but you won't break down on the interstate."

"Yeah, yeah, it's the least I can do. Why do you hate going into town?" I ask as we rise. I chug down the remainder of my lemonade while Sophia answers.

"Well, for one, I always seem to run into a member of the We Blame Sophia Kelly club—someone who gives me a mean look, then tells me I'm why their little girl left without notice," she says briskly, then continues. "And if I don't run into them, I run into someone who knows my family and wants to talk for ages... You know that sign when you first get to Live Oak, about the Acorns being the 1969 county champions?"

"Yeah, Ansel made fun of it," I rat out my brother. Sophia laughs.

"I can't blame him. My dad was the quarterback that year, though. So if people aren't talking to me about my grandmother, they're talking to me about him. It's not mean-spirited or anything, it's just that... sometimes I don't want to be reminded of things... I can't face them."

Once in the kitchen, Sophia scribbles directions down on the back of a receipt pad. They're weird, things such as "take a left at the big tree with the giant broken limb" and "go straight until you can see the sign for Judy's." I gingerly take keys and pause in the storefront, then walk around out back to where Ansel is visible on the roof, where he's methodically sawing dead limbs off the oak tree behind Sophia's bedroom.

"I'm going into town for Sophia," I call out to him, shading my eyes with my hand. I mean to sound strong, but my voice comes out meek and worried.

Ansel nods. "Give me an hour to finish this up?" He turns back to the tree.

"I don't think you need to come with me."

Ansel lowers his saw slowly, looks at me, as if he doesn't believe me. But he doesn't argue. Instead we stand and watch each other closely. There is a moment of silent communication, words exchanged in eyes and pressed lips: *I think we're safe here. It's okay for you to go alone. It'll be fine, don't worry. Don't be scared.*

Ansel and I have hardly ever been apart. And we've certainly never chosen to be—not like this.

"Be careful, okay?" Ansel says cautiously. "Please."

"I will. Promise."

So when I get in the car, I know that I have to do this. I know that I am ready to do this.

I leave all the windows rolled down—the AC in this car can't compete with South Carolina's humidity, and despite the temperature, the breeze is the most cooling thing I've felt all day. I drive just fast enough to keep the air flowing, and in spite of Ansel's confidence, my eyes are trained on the tree line. I look for what I always look for, what has become a habit more than a remnant of mourning—her hair, her hands, yellow eyes.

One time, a few years after she was gone, I walked into the woods. Alone. I didn't tell anyone I was going, I slipped out of the house barefoot, and I padded into the trees.

I wanted the witch to take me too.

That way I'd be able to understand. I'd know what happened to her, I'd be free of my parents' blame, I'd stop wondering. I would know.

I sat down in the trees for more than an hour, jumping at each crack, each pop, waiting to see the yellow eyes and finally know what kind of creature they belonged to. I figured that if it took me or killed me, I'd be with my sister—I'd join the other half of myself and finally feel like a real girl again, even if I was dead or lost in the trees.

It was selfish—I didn't think about Ansel. It didn't matter, because the witch didn't want me. I slumped back into the house, unsatisfied and just as uncertain about what had happened to my sister as I was before.

The trees here have as few answers for me as the trees in Washington. I speed up until they're a green blur, until they're nothing but scenery. *They're just trees, Gretchen. They can't hurt you, not here.*

Still, I feel better when the pines become pastures—most of which have SEE ROBERT E. LEE'S RIDING BOOTS signs posted on their fences. Those give way to houses, which give way to the tiny, forgotten-looking storefronts. Live Oak is laid out a bit like a bull's-eye, I realize—stores in the center, then houses in the next ring, then pastures. And then Sophia's chocolatier, so far away from the target that I'm surprised she even considers herself a Live Oak native, and not just someone surrounded by forest and sky. I guess Live Oak was the closest thing she could call herself a part of.

The post office would have been easy to pick out even without Sophia's directions. It's the only building on the block with the lights turned on and a car out front. I pull into one of the three gravel parking spots and walk inside.

"Hello," the graying woman behind the counter says, looking confused.

"Hi. I just need to mail these," I say, holding up the basketful of invitations. The woman gives me an uncertain look but takes the basket. She carries it to the back, and as my eyes follow her, they land on a row of photos lined up on the back wall. They're of girls, happy, smiling, tan and sparkly girls, and above each are the words "Missing Person Alert."

The chocolate festival girls, I realize instantly. My eyes widen; I scan across the names. Layla, Emily, Whitney, Jillian, Danielle, Allie, Rachel, Taylor—eight girls, eight people whom Live Oak—some of Live Oak, anyway—thinks Sophia made disappear. Now that I see their faces, I'm mesmerized. I keep hearing Jed's voice in the diner: "People think she's either the patron saint of candy or the first sign of Live Oak's end days."

He said she was the former, the saint. I think she's the saint. But it's hard to shrug your shoulders at eight missing-persons signs. Eight girls who vanished into nothingness. Maybe it was the witch. Did they see yellow eyes before they went? Were they scared? Were they chased—did someone let go of their hand?

But at least their families didn't insist their names be forgotten, their pictures be hidden away, their memory be trotted out only on holidays and birthdays. At least they aren't my sister. I stare at the posters carefully, memorizing the girls' faces, their features. The clothes they were wearing when they were last seen—party dresses, all of them: Whitney in a cardinal one, Allie in cherry, Taylor in rose. Their scars, birthmarks, tattoos.

I want to find them. The flicker of hope leaps around in my chest. What if I could find them, help them? I know it's stupid, I know it's ridiculous to even fantasize about being the one who solves the mystery, but it doesn't stop me. I used to dream about finding my sister, what I'd say to her, what I'd say to my parents when I walked inside holding her hand. How instead of blaming me, they'd hug me, kiss me, cry for joy.

What if I walked into Live Oak with a chain of eight girls behind me? I memorize their names, just in case my dreams come true.

Layla. Emily. Whitney. Jillian. Danielle—the one with the bird tattoo. Allie. Rachel. Taylor. I recite the names over and over in my mind till the words become a blur of sounds. *See? I won't forget you. I won't forget any of you.*

"You're the new girl!" a voice cries, startling me. I whirl around to see I'm no longer alone. A new customer, a woman in her thirties, is looking at me with a huge grin. A little red-headed girl sits at her feet, playing with a Barbie as the woman peels stamps off a sheet and sticks them onto envelopes.

"Um . . . yes," I say. "I'm the new girl."

"The one who lives in the candy house?" the little girl asks, looking up from her toy. My eyes widen in surprise that even the youngest of Live Oak know at least one thing about me. The woman nods, then pushes the envelopes back on the counter, where the postwoman will find them. I guess they aren't as precious as Sophia's invitations.

"Word spreads faster in Live Oak than a hot knife through butter, girly. Don't be scared, I ain't gonna be like those bitches down at the diner. So how do you and your brother like life with Sophia?" the woman asks, turning back to me as we both walk toward the door.

"It's great. I'm just dropping off the invitations to her chocolate festival."

"Ooh, lord, I wish I was young enough to be invited to that thing," the woman says. "This sprout is the only one in my family who'll be lucky enough to go someday," she adds, tugging on her daughter's ponytail gently as she holds the door open for me. "Unless her entire generation is outta Live Oak by then. People keep moving out, and it'll just be me and Ms. Judy!"

"Yeah, Jed said they might not even send a bus out here for school next year?" We pause in the parking lot to continue our conversation.

"I don't know about that—I think the great state of South Carolina might be required to truck out here for Live Oak kids. People are fools—a few girls make a break for the big city and suddenly families are moving out of Live Oak in droves. Like they expect Columbia or Augusta to be safer!" she says, rolling her eyes.

"Is that why so many stores are closed?" I ask, motioning to the ancient brick facades across the street.

She shrugs. "Hard to stay in business when there aren't any customers—"

"Can we go to the candy house?" the little girl asks, eyes wide.

"Ugh," the mother groans. "Not today." She gives me a polite wave and takes her daughter's hand.

"But I want candy!" the little girl cries.

"Yeah, well, people in hell want ice water too, honey. Bye, Gretchen!" The woman waves. I get into Sophia's car and crank up the AC. She knows my name. Maybe everyone here knows my name.

If I disappeared here, they'd put me up in the post office.

They'd have my name displayed there for everyone to see. My picture. Even if I disappeared into the trees, I wouldn't really vanish.

Layla. Emily. Whitney. Jillian. Danielle. Allie. Rachel. Taylor.

I back the car out of the lot and start toward Sophia's, past the ghost of a thriving town. Eight girls disappear, and people flat-out leave. Sophia really is the sign of Live Oak's end days, even though it isn't her fault.

I take a long time driving home—driving past the forest slowly is simultaneously punishing and empowering. If I can drive past it, could I walk past it? Walk in it? As the sun sets, the day cools off a little, and when I pull into Sophia's driveway a half hour later, the sky is streaked with violet and peach shades.

I'm about to open the chocolatier's screen door when something catches my eye. Something different—I turn slightly. On the far side of the porch is a seashell—a new one. I walk toward it, counting the others as I do so—there are now eight. The new shell is a conch shell, pale pink with perfectly shaped points spiraling around the larger end. I lift it, turning it over in my hand.

Something stirs in the woods.

My head shoots up, eyes scanning, old desperation and fear sweeping through me.

It's the witch. She's here. She's coming. I'm sure it's her. Is there even a recent photo of me to put on the post office wall? Yellow eyes—where are they? Hurry. I need to get to Ansel, I can't leave him—

An armadillo tumbles out of the underbrush, then hurries back into the forest.

I release the breath I'd been holding. My cheeks flush, embarrassed at my fear. Maybe everyone was right. Maybe there was no witch. Maybe I'm just a confused little girl. *Get it together, Gretchen.*

I turn my back to the forest and step inside the storefront. I inhale slowly for a few moments, until the fear fades entirely. The scent of vanilla, the low hum of Sophia and Ansel talking in the kitchen... *Relax.*

"What do you want to do eventually, then?" Ansel says lowly.

I hear Sophia exhale, and I grab the screen door before it slams shut. I'm not sure what's intriguing enough to warrant eavesdropping, yet I listen intently, peering into the kitchen through the slats in the saloon doors. I can see Sophia's back but not Ansel.

"It doesn't matter. This is what I do now. Besides, you already said you don't know what you want to do," Sophia says, voice light and giggly.

"The difference," Ansel adds, and I move close enough to see him lean over the counter, close to Sophia, "is that I know I want to do *something*. You aren't happy here, so what is it you want to do?"

Sophia puts down the spoons that were in her hand and is silent for a long time — I wonder what look she's giving my brother.

"I wouldn't mind making chocolate, it's just that things

are weird right now. But if I weren't doing that...I don't know. Maybe I'd write? Teach?"

"Was that so hard?" Ansel teases her. "And you'd be good at either."

"Yeah, yeah," Sophia says, and there's laughter in her voice. They're silent for a moment, so I use the opportunity to let the screen door go. It slams shut, and I see Sophia and Ansel jump and move away from each other. I take a deep breath and walk into the kitchen.

"I dropped the invites off. This woman at the post office knew who Ansel and I are. It's weird," I say to Sophia, sliding down onto a bar stool.

"Word travels fast here, I guess." She turns back to the pantry and gathers a jar of peanut butter and loaf of bread in her arms as Ansel refills his tea.

"Anyway," I continue, "they're all mailed. But hey— where did that new seashell come from?"

The peanut butter slips from Sophia's hands and thuds against the floor; the top pops off and the open container rolls across the kitchen, toward the screen door. Sophia stares at it; when she doesn't react, I finally jump up to grab it. Ansel stares, eyes flitting from her to me.

"You okay?" I ask as I pick up the lid and screw it back on to the peanut butter. Sophia's eyes look distant, as if she's not really looking at me.

"Sophia?" Ansel asks.

"Where is it?" she says faintly.

"The shell? On the porch," I say, taking the bread from

her fingers and putting it on the counter. I've barely done so when Sophia brushes past me, pushing through the saloon doors and then the screen. Ansel and I follow.

It takes Sophia only a heartbeat to see the new shell. She inhales slowly, then walks over to it, as though she's afraid she might frighten it away. She lifts it delicately, running her fingers over the points and tracing the spiral with her nails.

"Sophia, are you okay?" Ansel asks, voice strong, demanding an answer.

"Oh." Sophia snaps out of her daze, back to her happy version. She smiles and sets the shell down. "Yeah, I'm fine. Someone must have dropped this off...Guess they didn't have enough time to come in." She pulls her hair up as she holds the screen door open with her hip.

"I didn't see anyone pull up," Ansel says as we head back inside.

"Might have walked."

"Sophia, you live in the middle of nowhere—" I say.

"Maybe they biked, then. People bike here sometimes," Sophia snaps.

My eyes widen and I take a step backward—she's never used that tone before, and it startles me, scares me, almost. Ansel's eyes flicker between me and Sophia, waiting for one of us to make the next move.

"Sorry," Sophia says, her voice sincere. She takes my hand. "Sorry. I'm just worried about the Fourth of July block party and the chocolate festival. It's a lot to handle."

"It's okay," I say slowly. "Want me to make you a sandwich or something?" I add, nodding to the bread and peanut butter on the counter.

"Yeah. Yeah, please. Thanks, Gretchen," Sophia says, and gives me an apologetic look. "I'm going to go get some fresh air. Maybe have a drink and some of those hazelnut pralines . . . I'm sorry, seriously."

"It's okay," I say, shaking my head. Sophia nods; as she passes Ansel, she lets her hand rest on his shoulder for a moment, then folds her arms over her stomach and continues on outside.

"What was that all about?" I mumble when she's out of earshot.

"I don't know," Ansel says, popping his knuckles. "Maybe she's just mad whoever left that thing didn't come in to buy something? Should I look around, make sure no one is here, hiding or something?" His eyes scan the yard.

"Maybe . . ." I hesitate. "You haven't heard or seen . . . *anything?*" I ask cautiously.

Ansel gives me a hard look. "Nothing. Did you?"

I shake my head quickly. "No."

If Ansel isn't afraid, I don't need to be afraid. I glance out the back door, to where Sophia rocks back and forth on the bench swing, biting into a praline. I can almost see the relief flooding through her as she swallows it, as if it's calming her. I should have one too.

Anything to make the fear fade.

CHAPTER FIVE

❦

A week later, I take my books out of my suitcase. I slowly, carefully line them up on top of the dresser, putting them in order by the cover colors. I handle them delicately, as if they're photos or mementos instead of paper and cloth. When I finish, I step back and stare at them for a moment. They look as though they belong here. I spend a few minutes arranging and rearranging them, flipping some on their side, remembering the first time I read them. Thinking about how I'll read them again in this beautiful new place.

I smile and walk to the bedroom door, then gently open it.

I yelp and clasp a hand over my mouth.

"Sorry, sorry!" Ansel says quickly, trying to hush me. I groan and shake off the surprise.

"Why are you lurking outside my bedroom?" I grumble at him, embarrassed at shouting.

"Um, well…I'm going to…" Ansel shuffles his feet on the hardwood. I raise my eyebrows and fold my arms. Ansel finally spits out the rest of his sentence. "I'm going to ask Sophia to dinner."

"To…dinner…what?" I try to suppress the smile emerging at the corners of my mouth.

"I just…it's like she makes me feel comfortable. Normal, I guess. I don't know. Stop making that face!" Ansel says, cheeks reddening.

The laugh escapes my lips. Ansel rolls his eyes at me and turns around to storm down the stairs.

"Hey, wait, wait," I say, chuckling a little. "Sorry. I get it, I get it. She makes me feel that way too. I'm just not asking her out. But where are you going to take her?"

"I was thinking that Italian place? The guy who owns the hardware store said it's the only date place left in Live Oak. That is, when he wasn't laughing at me." Ansel sighs. How long has he been planning this? I bet he hasn't given the forest a second thought. It's been on my mind more and more lately, as I recite the eight missing girls' names over and over in my head. The scent of the chocolatier seems to have worn off, and old fears are fighting to win me back.

I pause a long time before answering. "She doesn't like to go into town, and people in town don't always like us anyway. You should make something here."

"Here?"

"Yes, here," I say, waving my arm at the living room. "I mean, just go to the grocery and get stuff for sandwiches and drinks and have a little picnic in the living room."

"That doesn't sound as nice as a dinner out," Ansel says skeptically.

"Trust me. It's the little efforts that count. Anyone can take a girl out to eat." Ansel frowns but nods. Good. He should listen to me—I mean, I've never actually been on a date, but years of studying romantic leads in books and watching couples while still in school taught me a thing or two.

"Anything else I should do?" he asks, and I laugh. It's odd, giving him advice—I feel as if I'm the protective one suddenly. It's not a bad feeling.

"Be yourself, Ansel. You'll be fine," I tell him.

"That's the most vague advice ever," Ansel grumbles.

"Trust me."

For most of the day, I help Sophia mold chocolate-shaped acorns in white, dark, and milk chocolate; we even make a few with white chocolate bodies and milk chocolate caps. She's in a fantastic mood—three RSVPs for the chocolate festival came in. The way Sophia gazes at them pinned up on a corkboard by the kitchen door, you'd think they were diamond studded.

Between the two of us, work goes fast, and by dinnertime there's nothing left to do. I make myself a peanut butter and jelly sandwich and head for my room, thinking I'll eat there, read a magazine, and go to bed early. In the living room I pass Ansel, who is busy spreading out his array of fine Piggly Wiggly–brand delicacies—a huge plate of fried chicken, tub of potato salad, biscuits, and half a pecan pie.

"What do you think? The guy in the deli said this was good date food," Ansel says nervously.

I shrug. "Your guess is as good as mine, but it looks delicious to me. I'll be in my room," I say, nodding toward my bedroom. Ansel leaps to his feet.

"What? No. You can't be...right there."

I fold my arms and lean against the door frame. "And why not?"

"Because I can't be on a date with Sophia Kelly while my sister is seven feet away," Ansel says, eyes widening as if I've missed the most obvious thing in the world. "It'll be...um..."

"What am I supposed to do, then?" It's one thing to ask Sophia on a date; it's another thing entirely to throw me out in order to do so.

"I don't know. Go read downstairs or something."

"In the kitchen. You're throwing me out and telling me to go hang out *in the kitchen*."

"Or the porch. I don't know. Come on, Gretchen." He shakes his head, eyes pleading and serious. "Just this once. Please. I'll owe you big."

I groan and finally nod. Ansel grins and proceeds to throw open the windows behind the couch. I duck into my bedroom and grab a magazine, and Ansel elbows me softly as I head downstairs.

"Seriously, Gretchen. Thanks," he says.

"Be quiet. I'm trying to think of how you're going to repay me for this."

Sophia is stocking orange caramels in the storefront. "Reading the latest on makeup styling from"—she pauses to peer at the magazine in my hand—"ooh, six years ago. I should throw those things out—not like we have those fancy stores that carry the models' clothes out here anyway. Or I could find you a book, if you want? Surely you've finished all yours by now."

"Don't worry about it. Besides, with hair like this," I say, motioning to my rainbowed tips, "advice from six years ago is probably better than none at all."

Sophia laughs as she pulls out a candied lemon and takes a bite. "My grandma said these give you courage," she explains with an embarrassed chuckle. "It's a southern thing. We love our food."

"Understandably. But if that gives you courage, maybe you should take a few to Ansel," I tease her.

"Trust me, I haven't been on a date in...I don't know. And then it's *Ansel,* and I just...You really don't care? I'm scared you care and just aren't telling me," Sophia says so anxiously that I understand why she needs courage. "I don't want you to be mad. If it makes you mad, I won't do it. Really."

I smile—a little forcefully—and shake my head. "No. It's fine."

"It's just...he asked me out and I was afraid that if I said no, he'd leave and *you'd* leave and I just…I kinda freaked out. I mean, I like him and all, I just…" She chews her lips nervously.

"It's fine, Sophia. I'm just going to read for a while, I guess. Care if I drink that last can of Coke, by the way?" I ask as I dip into the kitchen.

"Nope, help yourself," Sophia answers. I hear her shut the glass display case and the creaking, groaning sound of the stairs as she walks up to meet my brother. I grab the Coke from the fridge and coat myself in bug repellent, then head to the porch to slide down into one of the rocking chairs.

The yard is brightly lit from the porch lights that stream out over the grass and fade to darkness where the forest begins—I keep my eyes away from the trees. I've been practicing being close to the forest without panicking, but at night it's scarier, trickier to convince myself that those are fireflies and not yellow eyes looking back at me. I can hear the murmurs of Ansel and Sophia talking, voices drifting down from the upstairs windows. If the date goes well, what happens if they eventually fight? Break up? Stop talking?

I peer through the screen door and up the stairs. The steady rolling sound of the rocking chair on the wooden porch, the gentle clicking of the fan, the cries of locusts, swarm my senses. I gaze through the yard, between the trees. The fear in my chest spikes, but I smash it down, stomp it deep into my heart.

I don't have to be this way. I don't have to hide anymore.

77

We didn't have a choice before, my sister and Ansel and I. We didn't know the witch was really there, didn't know it would chase us, didn't know *it* would get a choice: which of us to take forever.

I shut the magazine.

I have a choice now. The words are half joy, half sigh. I have a choice now, and I need to make one.

I rise and set my magazine down on the porch floor. I am not Layla, Emily, Whitney, Jillian, Danielle, Allie, Rachel, or Taylor. My name is Gretchen, and I am starting over.

There is nothing in the forest to scare me, to make the remaining half of me vanish. There are no witches. I duck into the chocolatier, open the display case, and snatch a lemon peel from inside. I chew slowly, focusing on what I want to do, while the tart flavor explodes along my tongue. I hope Sophia's right about the courage.

I slip into the kitchen, where I rustle around in a junk drawer for a flashlight. I flick it on and off a few times to be certain it works, then whistle sharply for Luxe. The dog bounds into the kitchen and looks up at me eagerly.

"We," I say quietly, "are going on an adventure."

The first step from the front door is the hardest. Then the next, to the front of the porch. Down a step, another step, another step. *There are no witches, there are no witches,* I mentally chant. I step gingerly across the lawn; Ansel just cut the grass, and my sandals flick the clippings up against the back of my legs. I ignore the itching it causes—I have to keep moving forward because if I stop, I know I'll run back to the safety of Ansel, the safety of the chocolatier, of Sophia.

The forest seems to begin with two large oak trees; their branches arch overhead like cathedral doors. I hold my breath as I step through them. My feet crunch against the ground as soft grass is replaced with fallen leaves.

And then I'm in.

Luxe bounds forward, nose to the ground and tail in the air, as I shine the flashlight through the trees. I duck under low-hanging branches and the limbs of saplings. The chocolatier's lights grow smaller, broken apart by trees until they're scarcely any different from the fireflies that blink on and off around my head.

It's cooler in here, under the canopy of leaves, though the heat of the day seems to rise from the damp ground below. Luxe trots back toward me with a pinecone in his mouth, and my nerves calm. There is nothing in this forest—nothing but the fireflies, Luxe, and me. *Maybe a squirrel,* I think as I hear something clatter around the trees ahead. Raccoons, possums. The other half of me is not here, nor is the thing that took her.

It is safe.

I take a right turn, with newfound confidence in my ability to decide where to go. I hear the trickling of a creek ahead and use it as my guide—I'll go to it and then return to the chocolatier. Mosquitoes ignore the repellent and nip at my arms and ankles, and I struggle to pull my hair off my neck. The noise of the creek grows louder, until it manages to overtake the sounds of the trees, the insects, and the crunching of leaves under my feet and Luxe's.

I finally reach the creek. Moonlight pours down into the little crevice that the water carves through the forest. It's serene, beautiful; I carefully lower myself to sit on a patch of mossy ground beside it. The moss is like fabric against my bare legs, and I feel drowsy. I inhale the night air, then lift my eyes to gaze at the stars above.

Luxe barks, sharp and bold against the peaceful wood. I shush him without even looking his way, letting one of my feet dangle into the chilly creek water. It's freezing—far, far colder than I would have anticipated given the dense southern air.

He barks again. I whirl my head around to glare at him for interrupting this moment of solitude.

His fur is on end, his front feet braced against the forest floor, his teeth bared. I tap a hand on my leg, concerned, and Luxe slinks toward me, tail between his legs. When he reaches me, he curls up against me, pressing his body against my calves.

He's shaking in fear.

Suddenly the creek seems deafening as I rise and strain to listen to the forest. Something is out there, something to scare Luxe, but I hear nothing. I turn in circles, eyes scanning the trees. The rational part of my brain tries to convince me that it's something harmless and that Luxe is just a wimp, but no—I sense something, something no amount of lemon peel will let me ignore. Dread creeps up from my feet and begins to overtake my body; my hands tremble and my throat tightens.

Luxe peeks his head through my legs. He lets out a low, dark growl. Something rustles, something large enough that I hear it over the creek's rapids. I blink hard and stiffly turn to see whatever it is that Luxe is growling at. Whatever it is that's moving. Whatever it is that's waiting for me on the other side of the creek.

It's a man.

And he has yellow eyes.

"Oh, hi," the man says, smiling. Perfect white teeth, sweeping blond hair that's only a shade or two darker than mine. "Didn't mean to frighten you."

He's just a man—I want to believe he's only a man— and yet the *eyes*. Those are the witch's eyes. They stall my breath and make my fingers tremble. My chest aches, as though my heart is pounding so hard that the skin may tear, and yet I can't run. I can't run now.

The man in front of me is the witch. And I can't run from him again.

"Miss?"

"Where is she?" My voice is hoarse, and I can't believe I'm speaking to the witch after all this time.

"I'm sorry?" he asks, and now he sounds different, part-way between a growl and a mutter. He takes a step toward me, and I catch his scent. He smells like something dead.

"My sister. What did you do with her?"

He

just

smiles.

The witch jumps for me, long arms outstretched. My brain reconnects with my legs. I dash through the forest. The flashlight slips from my sweaty fingers. Trees fly by me, limbs slice at my face ruthlessly, I feel as if I'm a little girl again. Lost in the woods without a trail of candy and running running running. No hands to grab on to, no hands to let go of. Luxe dashes ahead, a golden ball of fur that cuts under brambles and around trunks faster than I can. I stumble. Twigs and branches cut into my palms, sting and grind, but I ball my hands into fists and keep going. I look behind me.

He's there, only not. The man is different now, his shoulders hunched forward and his jaw too long for his face. Teeth break out of his gums like bloodied white mountains, his fingers are curled and ragged, but his eyes—his eyes are the same, golden suns in the darkness, watching me, chasing me, toying with me—

Did she see his eyes before she died too?

Run. My chest aches, begging for water or rest, and my legs tingle and weaken. I don't remember walking this far. The lights—I should be able to see the lights from the porch. But all I see are fireflies, and Luxe is gone, far ahead of me. The witch—the man—the monster—says something I can't hear over the wind whistling through my ears.

Faster, Gretchen, faster.

I stumble again, and this time my head slams against the trunk of a tree. Everything swirls and the corners of my vision go red. I hear his feet getting closer, an inhuman gait. I use the tree to haul myself to standing.

"Now, now, miss. Let's not be careless," he says, the final sound a groan. I blink, trying to stop seeing the same man three times, and my vision clears. His blond hair is gray and brown, dungy and matted. Skin mottles with bits of fur, and he takes another step forward. His nails break off his fingertips, and claws ooze out of the skin.

I grab the wound on my head, feel sticky blood, run. My feet move, but I can't see—wait, I can see. There's moonlight ahead, intense moonlight. The backyard of the chocolatier. Which means the windows will be open, Ansel and Sophia will hear me...

The witch laughs, and suddenly the sound of two feet on the forest floor becomes the sound of four. Get to the backyard, get to Ansel, get to my brother. I don't want to be a girl on the Live Oak post office wall.

My feet hit pavement.

It's not the backyard; it's a road. A road with no cars, no houses, no anything in either direction.

I swallow hard; my body refuses to continue running. I turn around, trying to stop the trembling that ripples through me.

There is no man behind me. Just a monster. Head slung low to the ground, teeth jutting up through hanging black lips. His ears are plastered back on his head. Each time he

83

takes a small, careful step toward me, his claws click and scratch at the pavement. The yellow eyes are locked on me.

The monster's breathing grows more labored, hungered; he extends his nose toward me and inhales. He's close now, so close that the stench of his body suffocates me. He circles me, eyes running up and down my body, surveying his catch. I hear him lick his lips, sloppily and hungrily.

Something in the woods crashes.

The monster and I both snap our heads toward the sound. Another witch? Ansel, maybe? It doesn't matter—the monster is distracted. I force my deadened feet to move. Anywhere, any direction. *Go, go, faster.* My sandals clip against the pavement, my arms pump, air flying behind me.

I hear the claws. Walking, running, faster and faster. I keep moving but lock my shoulders, bracing myself for impact. Where will he bite first?

Please don't let me disappear.

And then the shot screams out.

The claws stop, and I hear flesh hitting the pavement. My body keeps moving, keeps running forward, but I dare to glance behind me. The monster is on the ground, slumped over a heap of fur and blood. Someone emerges from the woods—a man. A *real* man. He trudges forward slowly, as though he's not worried that the creature will spring to life.

The stranger stands over the witch's body, fiddling with something on what I realize is a gun of some sort.

And then the monster explodes into darkness. Shadows dance away from the pavement, terrified of being exposed

84

over the asphalt. They skip off into the forest, leaving nothing but the bare moonlight and a puddle of blood.

I should feel relieved, but I can't—I can't feel anything. Too many emotions, and my body has shut down. Where was the man with the gun twelve years ago? Why did he save me, and not my sister?

Why do I get to survive?

"You!" the man's voice cracks through the night. I snap my head up. "Who are you?"

He lifts the gun and aims at me.

CHAPTER SIX

I'm not scared.

Maybe I should be, but after I'm nearly killed by a witch, a man with a gun doesn't scare me.

"I'm Gretchen? Gretchen Kassel?" I say raspily—my throat is dry and my lungs ache. The stranger walks forward, sure-footed, confident steps that make me feel queasy. As he nears, the shadows on his face lessen and I make out his features. He's young and wearing a stained blue T-shirt and jeans. He slings the gun over his shoulder from a strap as his feet thud against the pavement in heavy leather work boots. Recognition hits me—the guy from the diner our first day in Live Oak, the green-eyed boy who hates Sophia.

"Are you okay?" he snaps, seemingly irritated.

"I'm fine," I answer, coughing. I rub my throat, touch the cut on my head, and wince.

He gives a curt nod and then, without stopping, breezes past me.

"Who are you?" I ask.

He turns to face me, and I take a step backward. His eyes pierce me, judging, perhaps, evaluating, darkening more each moment they stay on mine. I look down, trying to escape the glare.

"Samuel Reynolds," he answers. His voice is gruff, carries the weight and sorrow of a much older man. "Come on, you need to get out of here. There could be more of them."

"More?"

Samuel takes forceful strides, daring something to leap from the woods and take him. I run after him.

"There are more?"

"Of course there are more," he hisses. He suddenly ducks off the road, toward the tree line, and pulls a motorcycle from its hiding spot in the grasses. He pushes it along the road, dusting bits of dead leaves off as he walks.

"What are they?"

My voice stops him, though I'm not sure if it's the question or the fact that it sounds so much smaller than normal. But he has the answers. He clearly knows about them. He knows what they are, and after all this time I'll finally know what it was that stole my other half. I hold my breath in anticipation.

He turns, gaze shooting through the night and startling me once again. "They're monsters. Werewolves. And there are more out there, but I'm going to guess you want to be behind locked doors at that candy store before they show up and I start shooting. So if you could not attract them by shouting stupid questions, it'd be great. Doesn't do a lot of good to keep the bike quiet if you're going to shout like an idiot."

He turns back around and continues to walk. My feet won't move.

Maybe I should be afraid. Maybe I should be angry, or I should cry, or I should scream because this means that my sister didn't vanish—she was slaughtered. The same teeth the monster snapped at me were in her skin—skin that looked and felt just like mine.

But instead, all I feel is warm, flooding relief. Because my sister didn't really just vanish.

And now I know what the witch is.

"Are you stupid or something? I said, *come on*," Samuel mutters, eyes glancing off the trees that frame the road.

"I thought they were witches."

Samuel freezes midstride. He turns toward me and raises his eyebrows. The act changes his entire face—the hard lines vanish, the deep-set eyes become interested instead of foreboding. It lasts only a moment, and then the intensity returns full force. "The *Fenris?* You've seen them before?"

"Yes," I answer, touching my forehead. "When I was little. It—*one* of them—took my sister." How many are there? How many yellow eyes waiting in the forest?

Enough to take eight Live Oak girls, I realize, and I grimace as their faces run through my mind, trailed by my sister's face, the last terrified expression I saw in her eyes.

"Your sister..." He shakes his head, and I'm afraid he's going to yell again, but then it seems as though he can't remember what he was going to say. The chocolatier appears in the distance, an oasis of light beside the road.

It's another moment before I answer. "I thought they were witches," I repeat, defeated. I feel as if the fear is draining from me now that I know the face of the monster, and it leaves me raw and unfinished — it turns out I'm not sure who I am without the fear. "But werewolves — I don't..." I look up at the moon. There were werewolves in the book my sister had used to help us find the witch, in other fairy tales. Full moons, silver bullets, red capes —

"They have nothing to do with the moon," Samuel says, rolling his eyes at me. "They're monsters. Don't overthink it." He turns and continues walking, facing away from me; I can barely hear his words over the sound of locusts crying. "Besides, Sophia Kelly is the only witch in Live Oak. I've been trying to convince everyone in Live Oak the Fenris exist for the past two years. All it's gotten me is a reputation for being a lunatic."

"Sophia isn't a witch," I argue, though I'm not sure why that's the point that struck me.

"Whatever," Samuel says, waving a hand at me. "Just remember that I warned you to stay away from her."

"What does Sophia have to do with the...Fenris?" I ask. I don't like the term. It makes them seem like an animal, a dog or a cat or a bird, instead of something that might devour me, instead of a werewolf. I can't believe the witch is another monster entirely. We stop in front of the chocolatier, and I fold my arms, unsure what to say.

"You're here. Go inside and stay out of the woods."

"Obviously," I mumble, brushing my hair back over my head. I hesitate, glancing at Samuel. I feel as if I should say something. Thank him, maybe, but he doesn't seem like the type you thank—he seems like the type I should run from. I shuffle my feet until Samuel gives me an impatient glare.

"I'll…um…see you later. Thanks," I add, just for good measure. Samuel shakes his head, turns the bike, and walks back down the street.

I climb the steps to the chocolatier silently. Luxe waits for me on the porch, a tired look on his face.

"Some protection you are," I tell him. I look over my shoulder to see Samuel still walking away. He strides as though he's protesting something, storming the street to tell it off for existing. He eventually fades into darkness. I wait until I hear the distant grind of the motorcycle before ducking inside.

I keep my eyes off the forest and lock the chocolatier's front door.

As if a dead bolt could possibly keep the witches—no, the *wolves*—at bay.

CHAPTER SEVEN

My dreams are mostly nightmares—the witch charging, transforming into a hundred thousand werewolves. Then Samuel, stepping out of the darkness, followed by my father. But neither raises a hand to help me as the werewolves close in, and Ansel is nowhere to be found. At the very last moment my sister arrives with a rifle in hand, a shadow of a girl who steps out of my body and looks just like me; the werewolf turns and runs when it sees her. The dream repeats itself—I wake up at the end, then drift back to uneasy sleep only to dream it again.

Maybe Ansel's lack of presence in the dream is why I don't tell him about the witch the following morning—or maybe it's because claiming to be chased by a werewolf is as unbelievable as claiming to be chased by a witch. My brother is in the storefront messing around with some of the shelving; our eyes meet very briefly.

I should tell him.

No. He survived. He moved on long ago. Don't send him backward, don't make it like you're kids again. I feel guilty — Ansel has spent so much of his life trying to keep me safe, and here I am, keeping it a secret that danger is right outside.

But I still can't do it. I can't watch his face when I try to explain to him that the witches are werewolves and they're real. I can't handle what he'll say if he believes me or, worse, what he'll say if he doesn't. I love my brother too much to tell him.

So I nod at my brother, an understated "good morning," and make my way into the kitchen with my secrets intact. For now.

"What happened to your head?" Sophia asks in alarm, slamming a mortar and pestle down on the counter and hurrying toward me. I cringe — I thought I'd swept my hair far enough over my forehead to cover the mark left by falling in the forest, but apparently no such luck.

Think, think fast. Sophia pulls my multicolored hair away from my face, eyeing the wound with a look of dismay. "It was stupid," I say quickly. "I was playing with Luxe last night in the yard and fell off the front steps." Ansel, who'd been coming in to see what the problem was, returns to the storefront through the saloon doors when he hears my explanation, shaking his head teasingly at my apparent clumsiness.

"Why didn't you come get us?" Sophia asks, looking

almost hurt. "I bet that'll leave a scar! Hang on, I have some Neosporin, I think…"

"It's not that big a deal—"

"Are you crazy? You're way too pretty to have a big scar right on your head," Sophia says, rolling her eyes. She dives into a drawer and pulls out a basket of medicines. Before I can stop her, she's slathering ointment on the mark. "Seriously. You should have come and gotten me."

I laugh nervously and go to the refrigerator. "I was told not to interrupt the hot date." Sophia blushes a little and turns to the stove, where she stirs a double boiler filled with slowly bubbling chocolate.

"Want to help?" Sophia motions to the chocolate and rows of empty molds. "It's not as boring as regular mold filling. I'm making shells for the truffles I serve at the chocolate festival, since a lot of the Fourth of July stuff is already made—except those toffee bars. Don't let me forget those. Anyway, the truffle ingredients should come in today, so I thought I'd get a head start on the shells. That way things aren't *too* frantic. Just…*mostly* frantic."

"Sure," I say, happy to see the way my answer makes her smile. "What do I do?"

"Take these," Sophia says, digging through another drawer until she emerges with what look like two small paintbrushes, "and just paint along the insides of the molds using what's in the boiler."

"I can do that," I say, nodding. She's right—it isn't as boring as filling. It's satisfying, covering the inside of the molds with milk chocolate. Sophia pulls out a mixing bowl and stirs crushed almonds in with some of the chocolate. She's making something similar to her specialty, the gingerbread chocolate that made me feel so safe.

I think back to last night, the lemon candy, how they were supposed to give me courage. *No more,* I decide firmly. *If there are witches here, and the candy is what made me brave, I can't keep eating it. I have to be focused.*

"You okay?" Sophia interrupts my thoughts, and I realize I've been staring at a truffle mold for several long moments.

"Yeah," I say quickly. "I'm fine. Sorry. Spaced out."

"It's the thing about me dating your brother, isn't it?" Sophia says with a grimace. "I knew it would bother you. I'm sorry—"

"No, no, not that. Seriously, Sophia, I just blanked. Besides, if I'm bothered about anything, it's worrying that you'll decide you're done with my lame brother and kick us out," I tease, loud enough so that Ansel can hear. He sighs in response from the next room.

Sophia grins and shakes her head. "Tell you what—if I decide I'm done with your lame brother, I'll just kick him out. You *have* to stay. There hasn't been another girl in this house for a long time. I have to confess I've missed it."

I laugh as I put the double boiler back onto the burner for a moment to soften the chocolate a bit more. Sophia nods approvingly. "Who was the last girl that was here?" I ask, leaning against the counter.

Sophia studies one of the molds intensely and pauses before answering. "Just my mom. That's all. She had cancer, died a long time ago."

I move another finished tray over, think about our mother dying. It was the grief—the doctors said it was a myriad of things, but I know it was the grief. She watched the forest like I did, waiting for the missing half of her daughters to stumble from the trees, until she faded away.

But I didn't die. Not in the forest, not after, even though I was afraid. Terrified that the witch would come for me, terrified of vanishing. Terrified the exact thing that happened last night would happen.

And it did. But I didn't die.

Images flash back to me: Samuel shooting, Samuel taking down the wolf with a bullet. He didn't run from the monster— *he walked up to it.* And shot it. That's all it took to destroy everything I've been afraid of for twelve years, everything that could make me disappear.

I've never fired a gun before—never even considered it— but what if I could? I lean over to look with awe at the gun mounted over the fireplace mantel. I wouldn't have to be afraid anymore. I wouldn't have to be afraid of anything ever again. I swallow guilt that has strangely bubbled up in my throat—guilt over wanting to defend myself when my sister had no choice. I feel as if I'm cheating somehow, figuring out yet another way to survive when she's gone. Now that there's a potential solution to my fear, being afraid feels like the only thing that connects me to my sister. The moment in the woods so long ago, when we were both running for our lives, scared.

But still. I want to learn. I don't want to be scared. *It doesn't mean you don't love her, just because you want to change. Staying like this, being the victim—that won't bring her back.*

There's only one person I know that could teach me.

In bed that night, I try to shake from my mind the idea of shooting werewolves, loosen it from the corner of myself that it's wedged into. *He'll never agree to it. He'll never teach you. He hates Sophia, for whatever reason. He thinks she's the witch.*

But then, he hates the werewolves too. And I'm the only one he's met who knows about them, who believes they exist. Surely there's some desire, some longing, to talk about the monsters. To have a kindred spirit. To help someone. His eyes are as lonely as Sophia's, as lonely as mine—it's just that they're rimmed in bitterness instead of self-pity. He'll help me.

The idea itself feels ridiculous—Samuel Reynolds doesn't strike me as the type to long for epic conversations. I turn to face the empty side of the bedroom and picture the conversation I want to have with him playing on the blank wall, as if I'm watching a movie.

"Hey, can you help me learn to shoot a gun? I want to protect myself," imagined-movie-me says brightly.

"Sure! I'd love to!" Samuel says with a grin. Or at least, what I think would be his grin—I've never actually seen him smile. I sigh.

I can't be afraid any longer. I *won't* be afraid any longer, won't wait for the next time I see yellow eyes in the trees.

The only solution is to ask him.

CHAPTER EIGHT

The problem with wanting to ask Samuel to teach me doesn't begin with "he'll probably say no." It begins with "where the hell is he?"

Every time I run errands for Sophia—which I confess has become a little more seldom, since now I know for certain what's waiting in the forest—I scout out Live Oak, waiting to see his motorcycle parked outside one of the open stores. People still treat me as a stranger—but a few talk to me. Unfortunately, it's mostly totally unhelpful. The clerk at the drugstore scoffs and asks why I'd want to "find that jackass anyway." I can't exactly blame her—if Samuel is as charming to the rest of the world as he was to me, his attitude leaves something to be desired.

Five days after I was attacked—and four sleepless nights in which I was sure I heard a werewolf's claws on the front door—I head into town for groceries. I stall at the Piggly

Wiggly, hoping to see Samuel in the cereal aisle or at the checkout counter. No such luck, though.

I wheel my cart toward the only open checkout lane—the others must be seldom used, because they're piled high with broken buggy parts or dented cans. The elderly cashier smiles and waves to a man in overalls as he exits the store, then turns her eyes toward me. The lipsticked grin fades, and what I thought were warm brown irises now look brittle and cold. I give her a feeble nod and begin unloading the groceries.

The old woman—Dorothy, according to her name tag—manhandles my purchases into plastic bags and punches in a code on the register so intensely that you'd think the machine had personally insulted her. Just when I thought a few people were starting to come around to me.

"Seventy-three twenty-two," she tells me.

"Okay," I answer, and hand over Sophia's credit card. "I'm living with Sophia Kelly," I explain quickly. "She gave me her card to use."

"I know who you live with," the woman says bitterly. "And you can tell her my granddaughter got her invitation, and we threw it straight into the garbage."

"So . . . she's not going?" I ask, unsure how else I'm supposed to react.

"I won't have that woman convincing my baby girl to leave her family. Giving her money and God knows what else—who the hell knows what she puts in that chocolate, what kind of witchcraft she uses. I don't care if Sophia's grandmama *was* my friend—two years in a row is enough to convince any sane person to lock their little girls up tight the night of her party," she says.

"She doesn't... she isn't giving them anything." I stumble over the words, unsure how to even begin defending Sophia to someone clearly insane—especially now that I know without a doubt that it's real witches, real monsters, who took those eight girls, not Sophia. Their names tear through my mind again, shouting at me, desperate not to be forgotten.

Dorothy puts her hands on her hips, daring me to argue more. "Don't think you can just show up and understand how things work right off the bat. Secrets sink into this town and get stuck way down deep, deeper than some outsider can know in a couple of weeks. You want to stay in Live Oak, sweetheart, you'd best align yourself with a better crowd."

My mouth opens, but no words come out. Dorothy sniffs unhappily in my direction as I begin to load the groceries back into my cart; a bag boy finally comes over to help. He rolls my cart out to the car and accepts a dollar tip graciously.

"Watch out when you leave," he calls back over his shoulder as he walks away. "Ricky is set up behind that big sign. He's pretty much gotta pull over everyone in Live Oak to meet quota. Newcomers are easy targets—no one'll get mad at him for pulling you."

"Thanks." I climb into the car and hesitate. Dorothy seemed so normal. A perfectly normal, kind lady, who suspects Sophia. Do the people of Live Oak really just need someone to blame that badly? I frown and back the car out of the parking spot.

I nod congenially at Ricky as I drive past the massive SEE ROBERT E. LEE'S RIDING BOOTS sign—he looks disappointed, then goes back to his newspaper. I take a right, down a residential street. If I can get off this strip, I can get out of Ricky's sight and speed back up. Antebellum houses line either side, most with For Sale signs stuck into the lawn, followed by freshly mowed pastures and, finally, the start of the forest.

They're in there, in the trees, somewhere...I watch the edge of the road, plan what I'll do if a werewolf emerges. Watch the breaks in the trees, wonder if the paths are worn by humans or—

I slam on the brakes. Throw the car into reverse.

On the edge of the road is an overgrown gravel drive, so narrow that I'm not sure a car could make it down without hitting low-hanging branches. The drive itself isn't anything notable—there are dozens like it. But just inside the drive, sitting in the shade of the trees, is a motorcycle. Samuel's motorcycle.

I inhale. I pull the car off the road, onto the grassy shoulder. Slowly get out, stare at the drive that seems to disappear into the trees. Samuel is back there. He has a gun—it'll be fine even if there *is* a witch. Besides, if he isn't afraid, why should I be?

Before I can talk myself out of it, I trudge down the drive, keeping my eyes straight ahead; if I look into the trees on either side, I'll get scared again. Gravel crunches under my feet and I sidestep a few old puddles, then finally emerge in a large, paved clearing.

Wait, no, not just a clearing. The paved area is the size of a baseball field, with a steplike formation — every fifteen feet or so the concrete drops down lower. On either end is a giant white billboard-type screen, both graying and partially collapsed. Encircling the whole area is the forest, the tree trunks like cell bars, locking us in.

And in the center of it all is Samuel.

He's sitting at the edge of one of the steps, staring at a screen with a lost look on his face. He looks different in the sunlight, or maybe it's because the hard lines of his cheeks and eyebrows are relaxed. I take another step forward, accidentally sending a rock skittering across the asphalt.

Samuel leaps to his feet. Hard lines return, fists tighten. He looks ready to fight me for a split second, but then when he realizes who I am, he exhales and relaxes. He rolls his eyes at me and turns away, shoving his hands into his pockets.

"Hi," I say firmly, as though I'm completely assured of myself. I walk toward him.

"Hey," he answers over his shoulder, tone withering.

I stop a few yards from him, rocking back on my heels. His back is still to me, and I'm not sure what to say. I glance at the screens, fiddle my hands. "What is this place?"

"Once upon a time," Samuel begins sarcastically, "this was a drive-in movie theater. The only drive-in theater Live Oak's ever had."

"Oh." I've never seen one in person, but now concrete steps and screens make sense — stadium seating for cars. "So, um . . . why are you here?"

"To think. Clear my head. Why are you here?" he says, finally turning around. It's doubly clear I've interrupted something, now that I can see the dark look in his eyes.

"I, um . . ." I shake my head as a breeze rustles the forest, and a small piece of one of the screens tumbles to the ground. "I want you to teach me to shoot," I finally say, as though it's a line rehearsed for a school play.

"No."

The answer is confident, in a not-to-be-argued-with tone, and Samuel brushes past me toward the drive. I blink, trying to analyze what just happened, as Samuel storms away. I shake off my frustration and hurry after him.

"Why not?" I shout; my voice is loud and invasive in the quiet of the drive-in, and I feel guilty, as if I've been disrespectful. When he doesn't answer, I repeat my question in a normal voice.

"I don't teach people," he answers from the mouth of the drive. I jog to catch up to him before he makes it back to his bike.

"Just one lesson," I beg.

"Why?" he asks without turning to look at me.

"Because I want to be able to defend myself."

Samuel stops so quickly I almost run into him, then turns to face me. His eyes look even greener when he's framed by so many summer trees.

"You think taking aim at a Fenris isn't a faster way for you to die? Right now you're just a meal to them. If you've got a gun, they'll kill you quick. No chance to run like last time," Samuel hisses.

"I don't care. I don't want to be afraid anymore."

"Is this about Sophia Kelly?" he asks. "Did she tell you to ask me this? Is she trying to make me look stupid?"

"Of course not. I'm just sick of feeling helpless. I'm sick of thinking I'll end up like my sister or the girls who disappeared here."

Samuel studies me for a moment, as though he's trying to find something in me. He tries to hide the loneliness, tries to push it to the back, but it doesn't work—not on me. I try to pull it out of him, try to appeal to it. *Come on,* I mutter to him silently. *Please. Don't pretend there are loads of people asking to spend time with you.*

Samuel grimaces and bites his tongue. "Fine," he finally says. "I'll teach you. Once, maybe twice. I don't have time to be your own personal gun tutor."

"When? Where?" I say. I manage to stop the excitement from bubbling into my voice but can't prevent myself from bouncing up on my toes.

"Nowhere anyone will see us," he mumbles. "There's a field off Old Eighteen. You can see it through the trees if you're looking for it—used to be a tobacco farm before the Mitchells foreclosed. It's walking distance from the candy store. Meet me there tomorrow at, say, two o'clock."

"Walk there? Past the woods?" I instantly curse at myself

for how fragile my voice sounds, but it's hard not to think of the wolves in the trees.

"You managed to get into the drive-in just fine," Samuel says, waving a hand at the trees that surround us.

"Okay...do I need to bring anything?" I ask as he turns and hurries to his bike.

"Yeah," he says without looking at me, swinging a leg over the seat. "My sanity, if you can find it."

CHAPTER NINE

I used to read to escape.

No matter what the characters in a book were going through, their stories had a final page. A conclusion. I knew the mystery and adventure would end, and it was so much more appealing than the constant wonder about my sister, the constant fear, the constant worry.

But right now? I'm reading to kill time. Because the only thing I can think about is learning to shoot. My mind fills in the rest of my story a hundred different ways: I learn to shoot, and then a witch comes for me and Sophia and I kill it. I learn to shoot, and I trek into the forest and pull my sister out. I learn to shoot and walk up to a witch, instead of running from it.

On top of that, reading is a nice break from watching my brother and Sophia. It's not that I mean to stare, it's just that I've never witnessed the breathy, floaty look of first romance in person before. But that's clearly what it is—I recognize all the signs from books and movies. Hands brushing against one another, conversations that end with long stretches of eye contact, the sweet, soft way they talk to each other. I am mesmerized, though I'm not sure if it's in a good way or not.

When one thirty finally rolls around, I lie: I tell Ansel and Sophia I'm going for a walk, lace up my tennis shoes, then take off down the road. They don't argue, and I suspect it's because they either are tired of me staring or are happy to be alone for a little while.

I walk quickly—I'm afraid to run. Running feels as if I'm being chased. I stare down the trees as though they've offended me. Samuel wouldn't have suggested I meet him here if the wolves were around, right? At least, that's what I say to try to convince myself.

I finally reach Old 18, a former highway that is identical to almost every other street in this part of Live Oak. The motorcycle is parked off the road, and Samuel is walking away from a small hill that has a target with a gray man shape taped onto it. He reaches down and grabs some sort of rifle off the ground and slings another over his shoulder as he storms toward me—well, not storms, I suppose. That seems to be his normal walk.

"Okay, this is the gun you're using today," Samuel says with such immediacy that I'm startled. I begin to take it from his hands, but he pulls it back. There's no loneliness in his eyes now—just challenge. Determination.

"Wait. This is the safety," he says, pointing to a little

lever near the trigger. "Flip it this way, it's on; the gun can't fire. This way, it's off. Unless you're aiming, keep it on."

"Right. Safety," I repeat. Samuel sends me a contemplative look, green eyes searching mine for something, as if he's expecting me to make a joke out of this whole thing. I'm not sure why — there's nothing to joke about when you might find yourself moments away from being eaten.

"Come on," he says, tilting his head toward the middle of the field. I walk along beside him until we reach a point not too far away from the target. There are a few small cardboard boxes on the ground, labeled with terms I don't understand: hollow point, 36 grain, copper plated. Samuel hands me a rifle.

"Load it like this," he says, twisting a cylinder near the top. He grabs a handful of bullets from one of the boxes and drops them into the gun, then closes it up.

"Got it," I answer, though I could honestly use another demonstration. I follow suit clumsily.

"Rules," Samuel says. "Don't aim it at a person. Ever. Count the number of rounds you put in the gun. Don't put your finger on the trigger unless you're ready to fire." He swings his own rifle back over his shoulder, then pauses. "And don't ever, ever fire at a Fenris until it transforms. Just in case your instinct is wrong and it's actually a person."

"Right," I mutter. I notice the rifle he's holding is far bigger than my own. "Isn't this a little small to kill a witch?"

"Fenris. Wolf. Why are you still calling them witches?" Samuel asks, voice exasperated.

I blush, fight to find words. "That's what's always scared me—the witch."

"And a Fenris doesn't scare you?"

"I know what a Fenris is. Besides, it seems weird to call the witch something different after all this time."

Samuel doesn't seem to understand—he shakes his head as though it's not worth arguing with me. "It's not too small to kill a witch or a wolf or a Fenris or a serial killer or whatever else it is you are or are not afraid of. It's all about your aim," he answers.

"How good is your aim?" I ask, eyebrows raised.

Samuel shrugs. "My father and his father and his father and all my brothers are woodsmen. Some are good at building things, some are good at carving, some are good with an ax...I've always been a good hunter. Anyway, lift it like this," Samuel says, raising his own rifle up to his shoulder.

I try to mimic him.

"Push your left elbow in farther, so it's right under the rifle. Right. Okay, and then the stock of the gun should be right..." He swings his gun back around his shoulder and moves around me to adjust my position. He touches the rifle whenever possible, avoiding my skin as if it might poison him. "There," he finally says.

Samuel points to a tiny circle at the end of the rifle. "So to aim, you're going to line this circle"—he moves to point to a little v-shaped piece of metal that rests on top of the rifle, just a few inches away from my face—"up with this V. Close your left eye; look at everything from your right."

109

"Okay," I mutter, struggling to line everything up—the moment I get it all in order, I shake or the wind blows or I breathe and everything is out of whack again. Samuel continues to adjust my shoulder and the rifle itself, which doesn't exactly help. Every time he gets close, he brings with him a strange scent, something bright and forestlike that lingers on his skin, like the smell of fresh leaves.

"Wait. There—perfect," Samuel says. He raises his hands and backs away slowly, as though he's steadying a vase. "Okay, flip the safety off...good. So, you want to squeeze the trigger—not yet! Christ, give me a second to explain. You want to squeeze the trigger, not yank it. Separate your finger from the rest of your hand."

"Is it going to kick back?" I ask, keeping my right eye locked on the target. The wind sweeps my hair around my face, but I make no move to brush it away—I'm not sure I'll ever be able to hit a position that Samuel considers "perfect" again.

"No. Just squeeze—"

"Are you sure?" I cut him off, thinking about the way guns always slam back into the shooters' shoulders in movies. I should have worn something more substantial than a tank top...and what if it kicks and I shoot into the air or into Samuel's head or something?

"It won't kick," Samuel says testily.

"Maybe you should do it first—"

"Squeeze with your finger—no, don't say anything else.

You're talking yourself out of it. Just shoot the damn gun, Gretchen," Samuel says.

I inhale slowly, and as I exhale, I squeeze the trigger so lightly that I'm not sure I'm doing anything at all. I think of my parents. I think of Ansel, I think of my sister. I think of releasing Ansel's hand in the forest twelve years ago, and how the witch could have chosen me instead of her to make vanish.

I squeeze a little harder.

It fires—a sharp, shallow sound that ripples through my ears. One shot, two, three, each separated by long pauses so I can adjust my aim and take another breath.

Ten total—but I forgot to count. The rifle clicks but doesn't fire as I try for shot eleven. I exhale.

"And there you go. Put the safety back on," Samuel says, his voice lighter than normal.

I don't move.

"Put the safety on," Samuel repeats.

I inhale and raise my head, gazing down at the rifle. I shot it—I know how to shoot it. Somewhat, at least. I can aim, I can shoot, I can protect myself from the wolves.

"Gretchen," Samuel says sternly. He takes a step toward me.

"Sorry, sorry." I snap out of the daze and flip the safety over. Samuel steps in quickly to take the gun out of my hand and set it on the ground. He raises an eyebrow at me, but I ignore him and start toward the target. I want to run, want to spring forward and find I'm victorious, that I've hit the gray man square between the eyes. The urge to leap across the field nips at me; I have to breathe slowly to control it.

As the gray man grows closer, I try to imagine him as a werewolf—as the blond-haired monster from last week. Would I have hit him? Saved myself?

Actually, no, I realize as I reach the target. I didn't hit it once.

"Not bad," Samuel says, frowning as he pulls a blue marker out of his jeans pocket.

"Not bad? I didn't even hit him," I complain, folding my arms. All ten shots are clustered closely together in the upper right corner of the paper on the white part.

Samuel shakes his head as he reaches forward with the blue marker and puts a slash through all ten shots. "But you were consistent. Same area all ten times. It just means you need to take the overall aim down and to the left."

"But I—"

"Are you going to pout?" Samuel says, eyeing me, "or are you going to try changing your aim and starting over?"

I stare at Samuel for a moment—bright eyes looking *into* me, eyes that make my heart beat faster and mind leap excitedly, a feeling that comes without the scent or taste of candy, and is all the sweeter for it. "I'll try again," I answer firmly.

And, for the first time since I met him, Samuel smiles.

CHAPTER TEN

When I get home, Sophia's car is gone and Ansel is using a hammer inside the shop. Luxe is sitting outside, looking profoundly irritated with all the banging going on.

"How was your walk?" Ansel asks, looking up at me from under a display case when I come in.

I try to wipe the grin off my face, the one I've been wearing ever since I left the lesson. "Fine," I say with a shrug. Ansel nods, looks down, but doesn't go back to hammering.

"I can go with you next time, if you want," he says.

I shake my head. "I'm okay," I answer, and I'm surprised to realize I really mean it.

Ansel smiles and shakes his head. "Wow."

"What?"

"I just...you were walking. Past the forest. By yourself," he says.

I nod, but now that he says it, I'm hyperaware of how

odd it is. Does he suspect something? Will I have to tell him that the witch is here?

"I'm just impressed, that's all," he responds to the look on my face. I exhale and he continues. "This sounds weird, I know, but I feel like...I had to mourn our sister, then our parents, and the whole time it felt like I was mourning you too. Even though you're here."

He pauses a long time, and I open my mouth to apologize. He waves his hand to stop me. "I'm not trying to make you feel bad. I'm just saying—if I'm not mourning you anymore, then...that means we're *both* finally out of the woods."

I smile automatically at the sincerity of my brother's words, emotion that's mirrored in his eyes. We're both free.

Even though the witch is closer than ever, we're both free.

"Can you do me a favor?" he asks, sliding farther under the glass display case with the hammer and breaking the tenderness filtering between us.

"Sure."

"I left a few wrenches by the door of the shed. Grab them for me?"

I cut through the kitchen—Sophia has rows and rows of truffle molds laid out, ready to be filled—and out the back screen door. I hurry toward the three wrenches that are resting just outside the shed and swipe them off the ground.

I drop them instantly—the silver metal is so hot from the late June sun that it's scalding. I curse at them, make a basket out of the front of my shirt, and toss them into it. I'm about to turn to go back inside when my eye catches something—the shed door is slightly ajar.

On closer inspection, I realize why: the chain that I assumed locked up the shed is actually just wound loosely around the handles with no padlock whatsoever. I press my face against the gap in the door and try to peer inside—this is the only part of Sophia's property I haven't seen. Would Sophia mind that I'm curious? It's not locked—the chain seems to be more to keep the doors shut than to keep anyone out. I cradle the wrenches with one hand and use the other to unwind the chain. The doors swing open easily.

There's not much inside. A lawn mower, some spare pieces of wood, a few boxes labeled "Hanukkah Chocolate Molds." But then, in the back, below an upper level that spans half the shed, I see something different—something covered in dust and dead leaves, as if it's been in there a long time. A row of cardboard boxes, each tightly taped up. Beside those, a bed and a lavender dresser that match the furniture in my room exactly. I turn to look up at my bedroom's window and remember how the room's design so perfectly reflects itself—no wonder it feels strange. Half of it is missing, stuffed into the shed. I take a step closer, and my foot accidentally hits an open box, spilling its contents onto the floor.

Seashells. Five of them: beautiful, flawless conch shells wrapped in cloth that's come loose with the box's motion. I kneel, rewrapping them and placing them back into the box, only to realize there's an identical box beside it with three seashells inside. Something about them strikes me as

115

disconcerting, worrisome. They're just seashells, but I remember the way Sophia reacted when one appeared on her porch a couple of weeks ago, and I can't help but be curiously wary.

Sophia's car pulls up. I jump up and dart to the door, hurriedly relooping the chain around the handles. I rush back inside with the wrenches, trying not to look too out of breath.

"Thanks," Ansel says, taking the wrenches from me just as Sophia reaches the screen door. She smiles at me.

"Wow," I say, looking at her armful of boxes. "Need help?"

"If you're offering," she says, just as a box topples off the top of her stack. "There are a few more in the car—"

"I'll get them," Ansel says quickly, and before we can stop him, he's out the door. Sophia and I manage to wait until he's out of earshot to giggle at each other over his enthusiasm to help her. I grab the box Sophia dropped and take a few others out of her hands.

I read a mailing label as we move to the kitchen. "From Brazil?"

Sophia grabs two pairs of scissors from a drawer, and we go to work opening the boxes. "Most of what I put in the truffles has to be ordered. You can't find it in Live Oak."

I tear open the box I was holding—Brazil nuts—and then unpack containers of anise, Madagascar vanilla, pear brandy from Oregon, chilies from Venezuela.

"I try to make more exotic things for the festival," Sophia says with a shrug, opening a packet of huckleberries. "Everyone wants to get out of Live Oak...I think they like having things they can't normally find here."

"How..." I shake my head, then look at her. "How do you afford all this, Sophia? No offense," I say, motioning toward a bottle of raspberry Chambord.

Sophia frowns. "I admit, I'm kind of draining my inheritance down to zero—I can't believe how much I've burned through in three years. It's just...it's just money. There are things that are more important." She shakes off the sadness I see beginning to creep over her.

"If it helps," I say, "I'm pretty sure Ansel will work for free forever, if you want him to."

Sophia laughs and shakes her head. "He asked if I'd go to a movie with him, earlier today. While you were gone."

"There's a movie theater in Live Oak?" I ask, surprised, thinking of the run-down drive-in.

"Sort of—there are three screens. And most of the seats are covered in duct tape. But it exists," she says. "And there are a few in Lake City, anyhow." She pauses, chews her lip. "Is it okay with you still? That I go out with your brother?"

"Yes," I answer, faster than I expected. "As long as you two remember I exist," I tease.

Sophia laughs. "I promise. And thank god you said yes—I've been living in fear that I'm going to get so desperate, I start dating Live Oak guys again. That's how it starts—you get a boyfriend here, then one of you can't or won't leave, so you get married, and then suddenly you're fifty and you've barely left the state."

117

"But...if you were that scared of getting stuck in Live Oak, why take over the shop? You could just close it, sell it, that kind of thing, right?"

"It's what I'm good at. I need the chocolatier, and it needs me."

"But it's not what you want?"

Sophia shrugs. "I'll never have what I really want, Gretchen. So I might as well have what I can do well." She says it with a sense of finality, but I'm too curious to stop there.

"What do you mean?"

"Hmm?" Sophia says, looking up at me.

"You can't have what you really want?"

Sophia looks at me a long time, and I can almost see her deliberating between giving me a carefree, fake answer and the real one. "I want things back the way they were before my dad died, I guess. Back to when things were easier."

My heart pangs and I feel guilty for my question. Of course, I know exactly how she feels. I want my dad back too. I want it back to the way it was not only before he died, but before Mom died, before my sister was taken. When everything was simple and beautiful.

Or at least, that's what I used to want. But I can't go back to that day in the trees; I can't go back in time and hold on to my sister's hand tighter, I now realize. And so I want to fast-forward. To a future where I know how to shoot, how to kill them. How to keep myself and other girls from vanishing.

What would Sophia fast-forward to?

I change the subject, ripping open a package loudly to

break the heavy silence in the room. "Did you ever date Live Oak guys then? When you were younger?"

Sophia shrugs, and the happy version of her pops back into place. "A few, I guess. Most of them were actually Lake City boys, though. I've mostly lost track of them."

I pause, but I have to ask. "Did you ever date a guy named Samuel? Samuel Reynolds?" Maybe that's why he hates her so much — she broke his heart.

Sophia's eyes rocket to mine fast, so fast that I momentarily think she's going to yell at me. Instead, she shakes her head rapidly. "No, not at all. Why do you ask?"

"Someone at the grocery store mentioned him," I say, trying to be casual enough that Sophia will relax. Her face softens a little, but the tension remains.

"Samuel Reynolds isn't from Live Oak — he showed up a few years ago and started dating this girl. She left him after my festival. He's one of the people who thinks it's my fault — though I guess he isn't exactly on the side of those old ladies in town either. He kind of has a reputation for being the town lunatic."

"Lunatic? Why?" I'm unable to entirely process the idea of Samuel Reynolds in love — that doesn't exactly seem like an emotion he frequents.

Sophia shrugs, but her voice sounds odd — nervous, almost? No, that's not it. Hesitant? "After his girlfriend left him, he stumbled into a bar drunk, started talking crazy. I don't know. I tried to stay out of it."

"What was her name?" I ask, crushing an empty box with my foot.

"Layla," Sophia answers with a shrug.

Layla.

Layla. Emily. Whitney. Jillian. Danielle. Allie. Rachel. Taylor. Layla was the girl with the dark hair and the Spanish eyes. Chipped nail polish. Last seen on Main Street.

I swallow. No wonder he's angry at the world. He knows what really happened to the girl he loved. I can feel my face paling and am immensely grateful when the mail truck pulls up and interrupts the concerned expression on Sophia's face.

"Oh, yay, mail time!" Sophia says excitedly. Luxe bounds out the back screen door while Sophia rubs her hands on her apron and springs into the storefront. She grabs a bag of milk chocolate mouse-shaped truffles as she cuts through the shop and onto the porch.

I can hear only her half of the conversation with the mailman: "For Jenny! I know—she said she loved the kitty-shaped ones so I thought I'd give these a go with her. Oh, yes! Thanks, Paul. Have a good afternoon!"

Sophia walks back in, flipping through the mail in her hands. I lean against the glass cases and take a long drink of lemonade. "How many?" I ask.

Sophia blushes. "Three. Just three..." She sticks them up on the RSVP board beside the others. Sophia gazes at them. She runs her hand across them and I see a flicker of unhappiness cross her face before she steps away. Yet another secret Sophia keeps that I still don't understand.

CHAPTER ELEVEN

hen I come downstairs the next morning, Sophia and Ansel are bowed over the sink. The water is on full blast.

"Why didn't you take it off?" she scolds him.

"Because I never take it off! And didn't think I'd need to—you're going to rip the skin off my knuckle if you keep doing that. Twist it or something."

"I can't twist it—your finger is too fat." Sophia laughs.

"And who's the one handing me candy all the time—"

"What's going on?" I interrupt. Sophia and Ansel turn to me; the front of her apron is soaked. The scent of lemon dish soap drifts to my nose.

"My class ring," Ansel says, nodding to his finger. "It's stuck." Sophia has one hand wrapped firmly around my brother's wrist and tugs on the enormous ring with the other.

"Maybe lay off the chocolate-covered potato chips," I

tease him, trying to ignore the fact that he looks a little less than pleased that I interrupted them. I pour myself a cup of coffee as Sophia and Ansel continue to wrestle. Finally, with a yelp from my brother and a victorious cry from Sophia, the ring slides off.

Ansel rubs his swollen finger while Sophia cuts off the water, then turns to me. "I made eggs!" she proclaims, pointing to a frying pan of scrambled eggs that look overcooked. I raise my eyebrows. "Don't judge me." She pouts. "Candy is different from real food."

"So if you could douse eggs in chocolate, you'd be golden?"

"Probably so. We're going to a movie today, to a Lake City theater. Want to come? Tuesday matinees are cheap!"

She seems genuine. I think she really wouldn't mind if I went with them and crashed their date. But I don't even have to look at my brother's eyes to know he'll do anything for me to say no, to guarantee him alone time with Sophia.

"I'll stay here," I say with a shrug. "Driving from Washington to South Carolina was enough of a road trip to keep me away from long car rides for a few years."

"Okay, but I was thinking that I could teach you to make that Coca-Cola gingerbread later tonight? Or tomorrow, maybe?" Sophia says.

"I'd like that," I say, and she grins.

"It's a secret family recipe. Seriously secret. People used to come from Lake City to buy it from my grandmother—I think it has some sort of 'come and get me' magic power. You have to promise you won't let anyone in Live Oak know I shared it."

"Then why share it with me?" I ask. "And how much do you think they'd pay for it?"

She laughs. "A lot, probably. I don't know—I don't have any other family in Live Oak. You're all I've got," she teases, poking me in the ribs. It's such a quick phrase—it bounces from her lips as though it's nothing—but I smile. We are family now, I suppose, in the oddest way. Sophia is like my sister.

Well. My *other* sister.

A few hours later I watch Ansel and Sophia drive away; Luxe chases their car down the drive. I lock the door behind them and convince myself to read a few pages of one of Sophia's books while waiting for two o'clock to roll around for lesson number two. My second and last lesson. I haven't learned much, but I guess it's better than nothing.

Not even *Little Women* can keep me engaged enough to ignore my anxiety for the upcoming lesson. I look at the time. I'll walk slowly—I have to get out, have to move; the excitement is too overwhelming for me to sit still. I tie my hair up, lock Luxe inside the house, and trot down the front steps. My mind races through everything I learned yesterday.

As I get close to the field, I'm surprised to see Samuel is already there; I'm sure I'm early. I wave slightly as I approach, but he hardly acknowledges it and begins speaking as soon as I'm within talking distance.

"We'll do the same thing as yesterday," Samuel says without looking up. "Only this time, I won't tell you what to do."

"I can handle that," I say, hoping to sound more confident than I feel.

Samuel hands me a rifle, and I go through a mental check-list, flip the safety on, and begin dropping rounds into it. Samuel watches me carefully—he doesn't seem quite as imposing today. Something about the light makes the shadows under his eyes disappear. I realize that when you're a part of the task at hand instead of getting in his way, he doesn't seem nearly as irritated with you. I close the chamber and look up at him for approval.

Samuel nods. "So," he says, waving at the rifle, "do you actually have a gun?"

"Well...no," I say. "Not exactly. But...I thought I could get one eventually. When I have money—I don't have any at the moment. And if not, there's one over the mantel at Sophia's. It was her dad's, so I don't think I could really practice with it, but...it's there."

"Better than nothing," Samuel says, though he looks annoyed that I didn't mention this before. He pauses. "Then again, they don't go into houses. Not here, anyway—unless you count Sophia's father."

"You think werewolves got him?" I hadn't questioned the story about the wild dogs and now feel stupid for not making the connection.

Samuel shrugs. "I'm not sure what to think. It doesn't make sense that they would go into Sophia's house, kill a man, and never come back. I can't explain it. I think it really might have just been a freak accident."

I bite my lip, aim, and fire. "Why come here, then? If they aren't going to attack people unless they tromp through the woods looking for them?"

Samuel stares at the target ahead as though he's reading off cue cards. "I have a theory."

He pauses until I put a hand on my hip.

"I think they wait. Until after Sophia's chocolate festival. Girls go and get the idea to leave town—I don't know if they get it on their own, or if those people in town are right and she convinces them—but either way, they sneak off in the night after the festival and in the nights following...and the wolves pick them off as they leave town, one by one."

It's suddenly very quiet, as if everything has stilled for my curiosity, my pity. I lower the gun to look at Samuel. "So you think that's what happened to Layla? She was last seen on Main Street—she was leaving town, and they..."

Samuel's face darkens and the world's noises pick back up, flocks of crows and grasshoppers screeching in discord. "Who told you about Layla?" he demands, with the same forceful tone he used with me the first time we met.

I swallow. "Sophia—"

"You told Kelly about us?" he snaps.

"Calm down!" I answer defensively. "I didn't. I just thought maybe you two had dated and had a bad breakup or something, so I mentioned your name. She said you blame her for Layla and went into some bar drunk..." I drift off, unsure what kind of answers I want from him.

Samuel shakes his head and looks down. "They always leave after her festival. They go and see her, and then they sneak off without telling anyone, without...saying good-bye. I tried to tell Kelly about them. I tried to tell *everyone*

125

about the wolves—I just made the poor decision of trying to tell them in a bar. All it got me was a reputation for being crazy, even when other people started to suspect Kelly."

"No one believes you," I say softly. It's a statement, not a question, and a sentiment I know all too well. No one believes a little girl about witches; why would they believe a boy about werewolves?

"Of course they didn't believe me. But belief in the Fenris or not, Kelly knows the girls disappear. Even if she doesn't know about the wolves, even if she isn't convincing girls to leave, they still vanish without a trace. And Kelly doesn't care."

"She does. Really," I answer defensively. "Sophia acts happy and bubbly most of the time, but she's sad—I mean really, genuinely sad—about something. I think part of it is that girls keep disappearing and people are blaming her."

"Then why keep throwing the festival?"

I don't know what to say—Samuel is right, but then, I still can't bring myself to blame Sophia, to think she's the first sign of Live Oak's end days. Sophia can't know about the monsters—she wouldn't live alone in the forest if she did. She must really think the missing girls are just skipping town. She has to be innocent.

No one just lets girls vanish. At least, not on purpose.

I grimace and fire nine more times.

"Better. Kind of. Try again." His voice is still angry.

I reload the gun and aim, but end up shaking my head and lowering it. "Someone I love disappeared too."

Samuel scowls at me. "What?"

"My twin sister. I'm just saying, I'm not asking about Layla because I think you're crazy. I'm asking because I get it. One day my sister was there, and the next she wasn't, and I never even knew why until that wolf chased me here. I just knew there was something with yellow eyes chasing us, and then she vanished."

Samuel looks at me, as though he thinks I'm tricking him into giving up something. "What was her name?"

The question startles me, throws me off balance. We don't say her name. *It upsets your mother—just don't say her name.* Though in the end it didn't matter—not saying her name couldn't keep our parents alive. But still. We don't say her name.

Layla. Emily. Whitney. Jillian. Danielle. Allie. Rachel. Taylor. They all get to keep their names. Some little part of them, however small, never fully disappears. But half of me is forgotten.

I've hesitated too long; Samuel sighs and looks away, and it tugs at something in me, anger and sadness at once.

"Look, I don't want to go home thinking you're all mad because I found out about Layla," I say, trying to sound bold.

He folds his arms. "Why do you care?"

"Well"—I stumble for words—"I just...I don't want you to be mad at me." Samuel is the only one in Live Oak who knows about the monsters. The one who saved my life in the forest. The one who believes me about witches when even my brother doesn't. I don't want that person hating me.

Samuel meets my eyes for a long time, as if he's hoping to

find more information. He sighs and takes the rifle from my hands.

"I'm not mad," he grumbles, checking the gun to make sure the safety is on.

"Promise?" I say, shoving my hands into my shorts pockets.

"Sure," Samuel says sarcastically, but then continues in a gentler tone. "Besides, it's hard to be mad at someone with clown-colored hair."

I exhale and smile a little as we walk toward the target. Samuel pulls out his marker and circles the bullet holes.

"Not bad. Three odd shots," he says, motioning to three bullet holes on the bottom left of the target, "but the rest of the group isn't bad. Close to the center, anyway."

"Better than yesterday?" I ask.

"A little. You might as well start aiming for the head now, though," he says, drawing a line through the bullet holes.

"The head?" I look at the small gray space between the gray man's line-drawn ears. Far smaller than the center of his chest, where I'd been aiming.

"That's where you have to hit them. Square between the eyes."

"To kill them, though, right? Can I slow them down if I just manage to hit them?" I ask as we walk away from the target.

"Not really," Samuel says, shaking his head. "They hardly even notice. Maybe if you managed to get your hands on some sort of machine gun, but last I checked, those were a little out of your price range. Your best bet is to aim perfectly and hit them on the first shot."

"Between the eyes."

"Yep. That's why I use a rifle. I can aim best with a rifle. Aim is worth more than size."

"Great," I mutter as we approach our starting spot. I pick up the gun and prepare to fire—Samuel reaches forward and adjusts my arm. Ten more shots, aimed between the gray man's ears. I already know I did a lousy job before we even go to check it out—one hit him, and not even centered. I groan and start to complain, but Samuel shuts me up and I try again.

In a few hours, I haven't improved—I think the prospect of hitting such a small target is psyching me out. I glumly gather my things and prepare to start back toward the house.

"Monday, same time?" Samuel asks as we cut through the field.

I look at him in surprise—he had said one or two lessons. I thought I was lucky to get the second lesson out of him, much less a third. I'm not stupid enough to point that out, though, so I nod and pretend as if a third lesson isn't unexpected.

"So," I ask, because I want to change the subject before he remembers the two-lesson promise, "are you going to the Fourth of July block party?"

"Me?" Samuel looks surprised. "No. I went once with..." He stops, and I silently fill in the name: *Layla*. He sighs and continues. "But not anymore. I told you—everyone in Live Oak thinks I'm a lunatic. You're going, I assume?"

129

"Yeah. Sophia does a booth or . . . something. I heard it's a big deal," I say, feeling a little guilty.

"It is," Samuel agrees. "The tourists love it. People hit up Live Oak on the way to the beach; it's all small-town feel with fireworks and American flags on all the storefronts. They try to make the town look like something out of the fifties instead of mostly abandoned."

"Do you at least watch the fireworks?" I ask.

Samuel shrugs. "Yeah. But from the roof of a building near my house. It's just as good a view without the snide remarks from Live Oak's finest. But have a deep-fried Snickers bar for me."

I'm not sure if I should feel bad for Samuel or not—he's not exactly the most welcoming person I've ever met. I imagine some of his reputation is warranted.

But then, the same people who hate him are the ones who aren't killed by monsters because of him. And if he's right about the monsters killing the missing girls, he fights them only to watch the festival happen again and again, girls happily skipping to Sophia's house to eat candy while monsters lurk. No wonder he's so angry. I watch him, looking for any indication of self-pity, but he walks with self-assuredness, solid footed, eyes straight ahead. I'm not afraid of him, but I understand why some people are.

We reach the edge of the field and Samuel turns and walks away, toward his motorcycle, without saying goodbye. Just like last time.

CHAPTER TWELVE

S ophia is hanging on to an oak tree limb.

Luxe is not pleased about this.

She's perched near the top with the confidence of someone who has climbed this particular tree many, many times before, but that doesn't make me any less nervous. Or Ansel — he paces below it, ready to catch her if she falls. Luxe is running in circles around the tree, golden hair flying, barking angrily at Sophia to get down.

"Okay, Gretchen, can you tighten that wire?" Sophia calls between Luxe's rants.

"What do you mean?" I ask, squinting into the sunlight that looms behind her.

"Just run toward that corner of the yard with it," she says, swinging off the branch. I think she's going to fall, but no — she's completely sure-footed, even twenty feet off the ground.

I take the wire to the far corner of the yard as Sophia

reaches the bottom of the tree. Ansel moves to help her down, but she just jumps, landing squarely in the dirt right beside him. She jogs across the yard toward me, dog at her heels. She's fully dressed—I'm still in pajamas that are now covered in morning dew. Apparently all this setup is easier with more people, and Sophia woke me by bounding onto my bed and begging for help. The festival is still about a month away, but Sophia seems determined to make sure she's well prepared—the more she gets done now, the less she has to do the week of the festival, according to her.

"There's a hook on that tree...somewhere," she mutters as she arrives at a birch tree and scans its trunk. "Here!"

"So this is for...?" I ask.

"Lanterns. Paper lanterns," Sophia says with a breathless grin. "Because I put a table right at that tree, so it's like the lanterns are sliding into the table."

"No expense spared, huh?" I ask, struggling to come up with an enthusiastic response. It's hard to be excited about the chocolate festival after hearing Samuel's theories on how it relates to the missing girls.

Sophia shrugs. "It's fun. I don't get to do all the things most girls do, you know? Like...I don't expect I'll ever get to plan a wedding. So instead I plan this."

"Why do you say that?" I ask as Ansel ducks back into the storage shed to get another loop of wire. I bend down to scratch Luxe's belly when he flips over and wiggles in the grass.

Sophia smiles a little. "I don't know. Who'd want to marry me?"

"Says the girl who's dating my brother," I remind her. Sophia blushes.

"In the end, he won't want me," she says softly.

"Don't be stupid," I say, nudging her gently. "Any boy would want you."

Sophia laughs it off, though the humor doesn't reach her face. "Yeah, yeah. But your brother is different from any boy."

"He's more annoying than the rest of them combined?" I tease.

"Nah. He's serious. I mean, I think he just thought I was a pretty face at first, but now it's like...he wants to help me to *help* me, not to get closer to me. I don't know that I can explain it."

"I think I get it," I say. "But keep in mind I've never had a boyfriend. So I know nothing."

Sophia laughs. "Seriously? Never?"

"Not one. I was too...preoccupied to date. And I was always the weird girl who used to have a twin..." I drift off, and Sophia gives me a gentle look.

She twists the wire around her fingers, chews on her lips. "You're way more than just a pretty face too, Gretchen. You just have to find someone who knows that."

"How very motherly," I tease her gently, and Sophia laughs and finally meets my eyes again.

"Yeah," she says, "I'm contractually obligated as the oldest person here to say things like that to you. But I'm good at giving advice! You should believe me!"

"Here," Ansel says, stepping out of the storage shed. My mind flickers to the extra bed and the seashells in there, and I wonder about mentioning them to Sophia, but before I can say anything, she's off, sprinting toward another tree. Ansel watches her, grinning.

"You're staring," I tell him.

"Yeah, well," he mutters, face turning dark red even underneath his tan. "Can you blame me? She... gets me. She gets you too. Most people don't understand either of us, much less both."

"True," I agree, and turn to run the wire to the opposite end of the yard. I manage to find the hook on another tree without Sophia's help, and before long, Ansel, Sophia, and I are standing in the middle of the yard, staring up at the X the wires make above us.

"Well, that's done," Sophia says. "This is all a million times easier with help, just so you know. It usually takes me twice the time."

"You know we're happy to," Ansel says.

"Well, then," Sophia says, dusting her hands on her pants. "More to do, more to do. If I show you those tables from last year, will you help me refinish them, Ansel? Although I really should make sure I've got enough solid milk chocolate bars for the Fourth of July first..."

"Sure," Ansel says, springing up. "I bet you're dying to help, right, Gretchen?" he adds, tugging my ponytail.

"I'd love to, but I have some very important hair washing to attend to," I joke.

We enter the chocolatier and Sophia immediately busies herself with checking on how a tray of truffles is setting. I hurry to my room to kick off my pajamas—blades of grass cling to my legs and fingers when I try to brush them off. It's hard to appreciate hot showers when the air outside is so warm, so I run the water on nearly cold and get out as quickly as I can.

The sound of Ansel and Sophia's grappling with some new task outside rises to my ears as I dart to my bedroom. I tug on shorts, then grope around inside the top dresser drawer for my brush but come up empty. Holding my hair into a ponytail, I hunt around—and then see it. In Luxe's mouth.

"Luxe...here, boy," I call, patting my free hand on my leg. Luxe takes a step forward...then two steps backward, tail wagging.

"Luxe, come on, bring it to me," I scold. Luxe prances, then crouches, his body tense. I dash for him; I've barely moved before he's bounding out the doorway. He takes a sharp left into Sophia's bedroom, already inside before I've even made it to my own door. I groan and round the corner of the dark room.

It's always the same, almost as if she doesn't actually sleep or change or *anything* in here. Bed made, pillows fluffed, thin shades drawn, and the oak tree's branches casting crazy shadows across the floor. I see Luxe's tail twitch, sticking out from under the dust ruffle of Sophia's bed. I creep across the hardwood floors, then dive.

Luxe thrashes and kicks as I grab his hind legs and drag

135

him out from under the bed. He wiggles happily, licks my hands, then bounds off again—without my hairbrush. I roll my eyes and duck under the bed to find it.

Naturally, Luxe dropped it almost dead center under the queen-size bed; I lie flat against the floor and stretch my arm as far as it can go before my fingers finally grasp the handle. As I'm inching it into my palm, I raise my head a touch too far and ram it on the bed frame. I wince and withdraw, rubbing the stinging on the back of my head just as something under the bed clatters to the floor.

Eyes watering from the sharp pain, I duck down to see what part of the bed I've broken. To my surprise, what fell is actually a picture frame—it lies facedown on the floor, as though I've killed it. I reach down and gingerly lift it, cringing as I hear bits of glass clink together. I turn it over—the glass is shattered.

I scoot away from the bed and hold the photo up to the pale sunlight. It's two little girls who look almost identical— I'd believe they were twins were it not for one appearing a few years older. They both have dark blue eyes and soft brown hair, and they're crouching over a sand castle at the beach with silly, happy-little-girl smiles on their faces. The youngest one waves an orange shovel at the camera; the older clasps her sandy hands together at her chest.

The older is Sophia. The fact hits me suddenly, and even though this photo was taken long ago, I've got no doubt it's her. Something in the eyes. And the younger one? I have no idea.

"What are you doing?"

Ansel's voice startles me, so much so that I almost drop the frame all over again. I shake my head and stand.

"Luxe ran under her bed with my hairbrush. I knocked this down while I was getting it, but..." I trail off as Ansel steps over to look at the photo in my hands. He grimaces and looks away.

"You broke it?" he asks.

"The floor broke it. I was just chasing a dog," I argue. "Who do you suppose the little girl is? Cousin, maybe?"

"It's..." Ansel shuffles his feet and then sighs. "It's her sister."

A forgotten sister, a girl without a name. I swallow as I think about my sister, and from the look in Ansel's eyes, I can tell he's doing the same. I shake off the memories.

"Sister? Sophia hasn't ever mentioned a sister," I tell him.

"I know. She told me about her only a week ago."

"So what, one afternoon she just said, 'Hey, Ansel, did I mention this secret sibling?'" I try to suppress the hurt that Sophia would tell Ansel something she kept from me, that my brother would keep her secrets—they know *everything* about me. I told Sophia about my sister the first day I met her. I try to keep the pain from my eyes, but it doesn't work. Ansel gives me a pitying look.

"Well, not exactly," Ansel says. He starts to sit down on the edge of Sophia's bed but seems to remember he's sweaty and dirty at the last instant. "One night she came into the living room and woke me up, crying. Then she asked me about you, weirdly enough. Said that I would understand because of you. Actually, she said I *had* to understand and that I was the only one who could."

"Understand what?"

Ansel frowns. "I'm not sure, to be honest. It was weird. She told me about Naida and then after a few moments seemed to snap out of it. Told me she was just emotional because her sister's been at college in Charleston and never comes home to visit. She's been gone three years, I think— she left right after their dad died."

"Just in Charleston? That's two hours away, tops. Why wouldn't she come home from Charleston in three whole years?"

"I asked the same thing," Ansel says. "I even offered to go pick Naida up, bring her back here. But Sophia said no. Something about not wanting Naida to get stuck here again, like she is."

"Why didn't you tell me?" I ask, and am frustrated to hear the hurt that has seeped into my voice again.

"It just...it feels so much like *her*," Ansel says, shaking his head. "When she disappeared and Mom pretended everything was okay when it wasn't. You've been doing so well here—you're a whole different person than you were in Washington. I didn't want to upset you."

He's right. It does feel like her. It feels exactly like her— the charade, the pretend smiles, the hope that one day the girl who disappeared from the forest will disappear from your heart too. Does Sophia hate herself, the way I sometimes hate myself, for wanting her gone?

Ansel clears his throat and continues. "Look, I'll tell her I broke it—chasing Luxe, right? But don't tell her you know about Naida. She...trusted me."

"Why cover for me? I'll just tell her I broke it—"

"No," Ansel says hurriedly. "I don't want it to cause any problems. Besides, it isn't really a big deal—she says her sister is in Charleston, and I don't see any reason for her to lie to us. It's just a little odd, but it's not...it's not worth..." But he never completes the sentence to tell me what Sophia's secrets aren't worth.

"Okay..." I sigh. "Okay." Ansel trusts people. When people told him there was no witch in the forest, he believed them. When Sophia told him her sister is just in Charleston, he believed her. No matter what his gut tells him, Ansel goes with his head. With reason. With the people he trusts.

My brother walks away, leaving me with nothing to do but wander back into my bedroom. I sit on the edge of the bed and focus on the empty space across from me. The wannabe-symmetrical bedroom—I get it now. The bed in the shed—it must have been on the other wall. This wasn't Sophia's childhood bedroom, it was *their* room. Sophia and her own sister.

Yet now, all traces of Naida are hidden under mattresses or shoved into the back of sheds. Not like the other girls of Live Oak—her picture isn't up at the post office. I don't have her name and date of birth and last-seen location memorized. She truly vanished, just like my sister did. I count back years—if Naida left three years ago, it means Sophia started throwing the chocolate festival the year after her sister vanished.

Maybe she's just lonely, a voice in my head argues. *Maybe she throws the festival to have people over, because Naida is gone.*

Maybe.

But try as I might to convince myself, I know that *something* isn't adding up.

CHAPTER THIRTEEN

ou're late," Samuel says when I finally arrive Monday afternoon, but he doesn't sound mad. He smiles at me.

"I'm sorry, I'm sorry," I say hurriedly. "But only by, like... five minutes. Sophia is freaking out over making enough cookies for the Fourth of July thing this weekend—"

"Right." Samuel cuts me off, shaking his head and rising. "So, this is a slightly larger rifle. Go ahead and aim, but don't fire just yet."

"It's heavier—why am I trying this one? I just got used to the other one, the twenty-two or whatever it is."

"Because it's good to see what gun you're best on."

"Sure, sure," I murmur, trying to peer down the rifle. The added weight keeps it from rocking around so much, but I know I won't be able to hold it up for long.

"Check your hands," Samuel warns. I move my left hand

back a little and push my elbow under the rifle. "And get your head down lower," he adds. I oblige.

I fire. Seven, eight, nine, ten times, while Samuel covers his ears.

"Not bad," Samuel says. His face seems lighter now, less intense, but I can't tell if it's because that's actually the case or if I've just stopped noticing the harsh lines and bitterness that I saw before.

"So what am I supposed to do with a moving target?" I ask as I set the gun down. Samuel and I weave through the long grasses toward the target to circle my hits.

"Planning on shooting at me?" Samuel asks, smiling as he pulls the marker out of his back pocket.

"Maybe." I grin. "But actually, I'm just thinking—nothing that wants to hurt me stands still."

"You just move your aim. Quickly." Samuel shrugs, sweeping his hair out of his eyes as he circles my shots. They're not bad—a few crazy outliers, but most of the group is together, clustered around the gray man's head.

"How am I supposed to practice that?"

"We'll get there, trust me," Samuel says. "It takes practice. Maybe we can give it a try tomorrow."

"How much practice did it take you?"

"I…" Samuel frowns. "I don't know. It was just something I was good at and then just got…better at with time."

"So." I pause. "Do you hunt nonwerewolf things? Deer, rabbits, raccoons?"

Samuel looks down. "Not exactly."

"All this, it's just for witches—Fenris?" I correct myself.

"And target shooting. It's fun."

"So why not other things?" I ask as we turn and trudge back to where we were standing.

"I don't like it," Samuel says gruffly. "I had other people to handle that, my older brothers and father."

"You just"—I suppress a small smile—"you just don't like shooting at cute things?"

"No, I don't need to shoot those things. Besides, there are Fenris to kill."

"Why not go home, then? I mean, there are werewolves there to destroy, right, wherever you're from?" I ask as I flip the safety off, then carefully aim. I try to imagine long, sharp canines on the gray man—it helps. I fire three rounds, then pause to readjust. In the silence, Samuel answers.

"Well, I...she..." He drifts off. Layla—that's why he's still here, I realize, and there's a strange pang in my stomach. Samuel kicks at the dirt and sits down.

"She's been gone two years, right? Since the first chocolate festival?" I ask delicately, trying to hide the odd feeling of envy that comes with Layla's name.

"*Almost* two years. It's not that I expect her to come back," he adds quickly, though I'm not sure I believe him. "It's just...someone has to protect everyone else. Where I'm from—Ellison, in Georgia—they have people to fight the wolves. But Live Oak...if I go..."

I gaze at Samuel, then look down at the gun in my hands. I understand. I don't want just to not vanish—I want to keep other girls from vanishing. No, not just vanishing—from being killed. From being stalked, from being a monster's prey. I say the names of the eight Live Oak girls silently, tacking on Naida Kelly's name at the end.

Naida. Should I tell him? Am I pushing him too far? He's just a few meetings shy of being a stranger...but still, I need to ask. "Did you know Naida Kelly?"

"*Naida* Kelly?" Samuel asks, raising an eyebrow. "Who is Naida Kelly?"

"She's Sophia's little sister," I answer.

"I didn't know she had a sister."

"Me neither. I found a picture under her bed. Sophia told Ansel that Naida has been at college in Charleston for the past three years and doesn't want to come back."

"From Charleston? That's just a few hours. And that's also the story half the town has about their missing daughters or sisters or girlfriends, all the people that take off after the chocolate festival," Samuel says bitterly. "The people who don't want to admit those girls are gone for good, when you can tell they know it's true, that they're in mourning. But they still don't want to hold a proper memorial or anything." He spits the last sentence out, and I can tell he's talking about Layla's family.

I hesitate, trying to find an appropriate response, when something occurs to me, something I can't believe I didn't notice till Samuel talked about Live Oak in mourning. "She's not dead." Samuel looks at me, confused. I continue. "The others might be dead, but Naida's not."

"What makes you say that?" Samuel says, and he sounds a little disappointed—as though if Layla is dead, Naida should be too.

"Sophia isn't mourning," I say slowly. "I know mourning. I'm practically a pro at mourning. I watched our parents mourn our sister, then my father mourn my mother, then my stepmother mourn my father...and Ansel and I mourned everyone. Sophia isn't mourning."

"Just like she isn't canceling the festival," Samuel answers darkly. "She's..." He stops himself, starts anew. "She doesn't care about those eight girls. And she clearly doesn't care about her own sister either."

I ignore him—whatever Sophia may be guilty of, whatever she's kept secret, I can't see her as a witch. "But why Naida? Why Layla? What's so special about those nine?"

Samuel gives me a cold look.

"Not like that," I say with a sigh. "But why not Sophia or Jessie or Violet? Why not every girl in Live Oak?"

Why not me? It's a silly question, but one I'll never stop turning over in my mind. Two little girls, mirror images of each other, two halves of the same person, and the witch chose her. Why her? Why the others?

"Tell me about Layla. Please. Maybe we can work out why it's them and not girls like Sophia." The words fall from my mouth before I've thought them through, and I cringe at the look Samuel gives me as he shakes his head. Part of me is relieved, I admit—I don't want to hear about her. I don't want to know about the girl he still aches for. The girl who vanished, whom—I know from experience—he still probably sees if he closes his eyes long enough.

But I have to know. I have to know why Layla was special, because maybe knowing means no one else has to vanish. Maybe knowing means I can help stop girls from fading away. I can make up for letting go of my sister's hand in the forest.

I inhale. "Maybe we can keep other girls from vanishing, Samuel."

He looks up at me. He bites at his lips and drums his hand on the side of his pants for a moment.

"I told you about my brothers," Samuel begins slowly, "about growing up with them. Everything was a competition, and then my dad got sick, and then...it was all too much. Some of my brothers moved far away, across the country. But I wasn't quite that bold, so I just trekked around the southeast. I ended up in South Carolina one day, and I met Layla."

He stops, and for a moment, I think he's going to try to get away with ending his story there. Instead, Samuel takes a deep breath and continues affectionately, nostalgically. "She was with her friends at the drive-in you found me at, watching some stupid girly movie on the opposite screen as me. Brown eyes, brown hair, blue jeans, and an orange shirt—I never liked orange before that moment. And..." Samuel shakes his head. "I had to know her. I followed her around Live Oak for hours before I got up the nerve to talk to her, and when I did...I can't even explain it." He looks over at me. "Have you ever met someone and just known that somehow, everything you do in your life is going to have to do with that person? Even if you don't know how yet?"

I shake my head and try not to look too distraught about it. That sort of certainty, that sort of knowing, isn't something I've ever experienced. Until Sophia, I hardly even had a friend, much less a soul mate.

"She told me about living in Live Oak, how everyone here is stuck. And I thought about my brothers scattering across the country, about my dad's Alzheimer's getting worse, and for some reason...a place where you get stuck, where everyone you love gets stuck...that seemed sort of like a paradise. So I stayed. She and I started dating; we..."

"Fell in love?" I offer when Samuel doesn't say anything for a moment too long.

"Yeah," he says. "We fell in love."

Samuel rubs his temples, and I see where the dark lines on his face come from: the expression he's wearing right now. Worry, fear, concern, dismay.

"Sophia Kelly had just gotten back from college the year before and taken over the chocolate shop after her old man died. I'd only met her a few times—I didn't think as much of her as everyone else did, but then, I only had eyes for Layla. But Layla and all the other girls in town were excited to go to this chocolate festival that Kelly was going to throw.

"The party was on a Saturday night. Layla came by afterward and..." He stares at the ceiling before continuing. "Spent the evening with me. And then she was gone. People saw her leaving my house, walking down Main Street holding her shoes. That was it. She was gone."

Vanished. People probably asked him. People probably blamed him. I know how it works. I know the look they give you when they think somehow, someway, it's your fault.

Where's your sister?

"Are you still in love with her?" I ask Samuel, though as soon as the words leave my mouth, I realize that I don't really want an answer.

I can't blame him if he is. When people are gone, they're perfect—like my sister, the daughter I could never live up to, no matter how much I looked like her. If he loved Layla that much in her life, of course she's even more wonderful, more beautiful, in her death. Yet still, I hope he isn't. I selfishly, greedily want him to say he isn't.

Samuel's lips tighten and he hesitates. Just as I think the answer is about to emerge from his mouth, he rises sharply. "We'll talk about it later. You need to get back to Kelly's."

CHAPTER FOURTEEN

M y brother has been invited to play football with a
bunch of the Live Oak guys—I guess our quarantine
as strangers is over. According to Sophia, they're some of the
Lake City football team's ex-stars, kids good enough to be
Live Oak heroes but not good enough to get scholarships out
of town.

"Seriously. Plus, Ansel is, like, four times the size of most
of them. I have a feeling it'll be him pummeling them, and
then we'll go get ice cream if Dairy Queen is still open,"
Sophia says.

I look away, press my lips together. Technically, I'm supposed to be meeting Samuel today for another lesson. But
based on the way he looked at me when I asked him about
Layla, I wouldn't be surprised if he isn't there. Besides, I feel
guilty skipping the game—Ansel hasn't played in ages and
Sophia wants me to go...

"It's not a big deal," Ansel tells Sophia. "She's seen me play a million times before. And besides, when Gretchen wants to finish a book, that's all she talks about anyway," he teases me. It's the line I fed them—I'm so caught up in a book that I want to stay home and read all day.

He's probably not even going to be there. Just go. Go with Sophia and Ansel. Don't think about monsters or Naida or your sister for a little while. That's what you always wanted; that's the new life you wanted to start.

The voice in my head is very, very convincing.

But not as convincing as the desire to stop girls from vanishing.

So Ansel and Sophia leave, and I start out toward the field. I pick dandelions as I walk, trying to keep my mind on finding bigger and bigger blossoms instead of worrying about whether or not Samuel will be there.

I reach the field. Samuel isn't anywhere to be seen. A lump forms in my throat, half frustration and half self-pity. Of course. I knew I should have kept my mouth shut.

I let out the breath I've been holding when I hear the rumble of the motorcycle engine and Samuel rounds the corner. He edges to a stop beside me. I try to control the grin that wants to slide across my face.

"Hey."

"Hey."

Samuel raises an eyebrow. "Are you okay? You look..." But he can't seem to find the word. I can fill it in for him easily: *relieved*.

"I'm fine," I answer.

Samuel shrugs, then turns around to grab a silver helmet off the back of the motorcycle. He holds it out for me.

"Come on. Field trip time," he says sarcastically.

"Um ... what?"

"You want to know more about Naida, right?"

I nod.

"Well," Samuel says, shaking his head, "I know someone who knew Naida. Probably did, anyway—she knows everyone. And if you're willing to sit through an hour of Civil War stories, she's happy to talk."

"But ... now?" I ask.

"Yes," Samuel says in a tone of defeat. "If Naida and Layla and those other girls are special, I want to know why as much as you do. Please, Gretchen."

I swallow, then take the helmet and pull it down over my head. It's a little too big but better than nothing, I suppose. Samuel's muscles tense when I grab on to his shoulder and hoist myself onto the back, and he doesn't relax until we're moving, cutting through the thick heat.

"Sophia and my brother are out at a football game somewhere in town," I yell over the noise of the bike.

"We can avoid them," he says, and I think I hear reluctance in his voice. He revs the motorcycle forward. The motion brings me closer to him, and before I know it, my arms are tighter around him than I intended. Underneath the leaflike scent is the aroma of sandalwood.

We're approaching downtown Live Oak when Samuel

suddenly takes a sharp turn; instead of cutting down the main road, he goes to the opposite side of the block, where the remaining stores' back doors are located, most of them covered in graffiti. He keeps his eyes firmly locked on the road ahead of him, but I can feel the change in his body once we enter town; he stiffens, his back muscles knitting together. We seem to go around the outskirts of town, then dart back in for an instant—just long enough to pull into the drive of a massive antebellum house. Large columns line the front porch, and the driveway is shaded by sweet gum trees.

"I need to duck into my house first," Samuel calls back to me. He cuts the engine and balances the bike as I slide to the pavement. I pull off the helmet and shake the sweat out of my hair.

"You live *here?*" I ask in amazement as we walk through the enormous house's shadow. The porch is dotted with rocking chairs, one of which contains a dozing calico cat. The wind blows gently, and the scent of peaches stretches from the remains of an orchard to my nose. This house looks...loved. It doesn't match the rest of Live Oak, as if it's proud to be sitting here instead of a forgotten bundle of wood and concrete.

"Expected a tent in the woods?" Samuel says with a cocky smile.

"Not exactly," I answer, avoiding his eyes.

Samuel laughs. "I don't live there," he says, nodding to the house. "I live there." He motions toward a building I thought was a shed, mostly hidden behind the peach trees.

It's held up on a stone foundation, and the windows are cloudy with age.

"It was the slave quarters," he says as we cut through the trees; the buzz of Japanese beetles roars around my head. "Rent's cheap enough that I can pay it by doing odd jobs around town instead of breaking down and applying to the Piggly Wiggly. It'd be hard to hunt Fenris from the produce section."

Samuel's house looks as though it might fall over in a strong breeze, but I don't think that's why I'm nervous as he sticks a key into the door and pushes it open. He hurries me inside and shuts the door behind him.

"Sorry," he says quickly. "I don't have AC. If you can trap the cool air inside, it's not so bad, but if you leave a door open and the hot air gets in, it stays in."

"Right," I say, as if I've heard of such a thing a thousand times before. My eyes scan the room—a bed, unmade and lacking a frame, rests in one corner. A single chair, beaten shag rug, a stack of worn magazines...and that's it. Very bachelor-esque. Samuel ducks into a doorway and lets the door drift almost shut behind him.

I hear the sound of water running, drawers opening and shutting. Just as I'm considering snooping in what I assume is a kitchen around the corner, he emerges. His hair is smoother than normal, and it looks as though he's washed his face. I raise an eyebrow.

"My landlord is particular. Trust me, you'll understand

when you meet her," he says, face reddening a little. "Here, brush your hair."

"What?" I ask, offended.

"Seriously," he says, passing me a comb. "If you don't brush it, she'll say something."

"Fine," I mutter, blushing, although when I catch a glimpse of myself in the bathroom mirror, I realize the helmet wasn't exactly kind to my hair. I run the comb through it and return to the main room.

"Better?"

Samuel nods and, before I know what he's doing, strips his shirt off. He drops it onto the floor and kneels down to a dresser drawer. I don't mean to stare, really, but I find myself doing just that. Samuel isn't especially muscular and has a farmer's tan where his T-shirt lines hit. But his skin is smooth and the muscles create soft lines around a tattoo of a family crest on his back, a shield shape with a tree in its center and the name *Reynolds* beneath it. The entire thing seems a little raised, as though if I ran my finger across it, I could read it like Braille—

Samuel turns around, yanking a newer-looking T-shirt over his head as he does so. I frantically search the room for something to stare at.

"Ready?" he asks.

"Yes," I answer eagerly. I follow Samuel out the front door and toward the antebellum. The house's back porch is lined with rocking chairs and citronella candles; pink hydrangeas are planted around the edge. Samuel darts in front of me to rap sharply on the back door.

Nothing, save the screech of the Japanese beetles.

Samuel raps again, harder this time.

"Goddammit, I'm coming!" a voice shrieks from inside the house. Samuel gives me an apologetic look. Behind the door is a series of thuds, a few sounds of cats yowling, and finally, a key in a lock. The door flings open to reveal a short, bent-over woman. She's covered in age spots and her limbs look like a pile of glued-together matchsticks. The walker she's leaning on has tennis balls stuck on its feet, and she's wearing a long turquoise muumuu and a neon pink head scarf.

"What? I got your rent check already," she says, eyeing Samuel as if she's ready to clock him with her walker should he try to enter.

"I know, Ms. Judy. I actually had a question?"

"No. No discounts. I don't care how long you've been renting." Her hazel eyes move to me appraisingly. "And no shacking up. Not in my backyard. But Christ, Reynolds, if you're gonna take a lady friend, at least wear something better than that old T-shirt."

"Of course, Ms. Judy, you're right," Samuel mutters. A white cat flies around her feet and dashes out into the backyard before Samuel can continue.

"Dammit, Noodles!" Ms. Judy screeches, shouldering past Samuel and me to the back porch. She bangs her walker on the boards angrily. "Fine, then, go eat mice! I'm not putting your dinner on the porch again just so the raccoons can get it!"

Ms. Judy spits down the porch steps and slowly turns around. When she sees us again, her face falls, as if she'd hoped we would have already disappeared.

"And who the hell are you?" she asks me, putting a hand on her hip.

"Gretchen Kassel," I answer quickly, dipping my head a little. "I—"

"And what do you want?" she cuts me off, pushing past us again. She bumps along with her walker back into the house. When she leaves the door open yet keeps moving down the hall, Samuel shrugs at me and steps in after her.

The inside of the house isn't exactly a reflection of its owner—it's spotless, perfectly decorated, and beautiful. It looks like something you might see in one of those old-house-turned-museums: pictures of old Confederate soldiers on the walls, vases of silk flowers, elegant furniture, and long, heavy drapes.

"We had a question about a girl, actually. One who used to live in Live Oak? We thought you might remember her—"

"Oh, I see how it is," Ms. Judy says, waving a fragile arm around. "I should know everyone 'cause I'm so old, right? 'Cause I've been here longer than dust?"

"Uh, no," Samuel says, and I see his eyes flicker to the ground. "Because you know everyone. Ms. Judy owns the diner off the interstate," Samuel explains to me. I open my mouth and nod, as if this is the most amazing thing I've ever heard. "It's the most successful business in Live Oak."

156

"And we sponsored the Acorns the year they were county champs," Ms. Judy says. She's not quite smiling but looks rather pleased with herself. "In fact, only reason Live Oak exists is because of my great-great-great-grandfather." She wiggles her walker toward an oil painting over a small end table. It's of a rather cranky-looking white-haired man in a Confederate general's uniform. "He started this plantation. Most successful rice plantation in the state at one time!"

Ms. Judy gazes at her great-great-great-grandfather with a misty sort of reverence. "Course, we lost it all in the war. But my family didn't leave. We built back up. We Blakes are survivors! You know why? 'Cause we ain't afraid to work! Ain't afraid to make money! We built Live Oak back up after the war, and we'll prolly be here still building even after every other shop on Main gives up."

"Right," Samuel says. Ms. Judy turns and hobbles around a grand staircase to a formal sitting room. There's an ancient piano against a wall and several fancy-looking chairs facing a coffee table with a silver tea set on its top. She wheezes and hacks as she slowly lowers herself into one of the chairs—I'm almost certain her entire body is moments away from breaking in half.

I'm a little afraid to sit down—these are the kinds of chairs that our stepmother filled our house with, and Ansel and I were allowed to sit in them only if we promised to be very still. But Ms. Judy gives me a fiery look, so I carefully drop into one, crossing my legs at the ankles. Samuel sits up very straight, looking phenomenally out of place.

"We were just wondering," he says politely, "if you know anything about Naida Kelly."

"Ooh," Ms. Judy says. "Naida Kelly. Haven't heard that name in a piece."

"So...you know her?" Samuel asks.

"Hell yes, I know her. It's the Kelly girl, the little one. One that run off after the incident with her father."

"Ran off?" I say breathlessly.

"Are you dumb? That's what I just said." Ms. Judy smacks her lips for a moment. "Left that older girl all by herself. Rumor from the diner has it you're living with her," she adds, nodding at me.

"I am, but she never told me about a sister. And no one ever mentioned a sister to Samuel. So...we were curious about her..." I choose my words carefully.

"Yeah, yeah...that's the thing you outsiders have to know about a place like Live Oak," Ms. Judy says, nodding slowly. "All our secrets are family secrets. You don't just go blabbing to strangers about tragedies and murders—"

"She was murdered?" I gasp before I can stop myself. Ms. Judy's eyes rip to mine and silence me.

"I didn't say that. In fact, I believe I just told you that we keep our secrets around here," Ms. Judy says sternly. "But," she adds, eyes lightening a bit, "what the hell do I care? I'm one foot in the grave already, and like I said, I ain't afraid to make money..." She frowns and studies her nails for a moment, waiting for something.

Samuel sighs. "I can't afford to pay you for information, Ms. Judy."

"Oh, no, child! Of course not!" Ms. Judy says, looking appalled. "I couldn't take your money. But see, I was just thinking—I pay that fat boy from town to come mow my grass every Sunday. And it just pains me, *pains me,* to see that lump trying to move around my yard."

"I..." Samuel grits his teeth. "I'd be happy to do that for you, Ms. Judy."

"Oh, would you?" Ms. Judy cries. "That would just be lovely, Samuel. Also, Noodles—poor kitty hasn't had a bath in ages. I just can't handle him anymore, you know. Energy of a kitten."

"I—and Gretchen," he says, glaring at me, "will certainly help you give Noodles a bath."

"Oh, that's just excellent. You're lovely children, really," Ms. Judy says, nodding. "Well then, let's see... Jacob Kelly, the little girls' father, one who ran that candy shop, *he* was murdered one night about three or four summers ago. Brutal. Police report said it was wild animals, dogs or something, since he was all tore up— 'shredded' was the word they used, 'shredded.'"

I suppress a shiver. "That's why Sophia came home from school," I say aloud, quietly. "To take over the chocolatier because he died."

"Well, if you knew all that, why the hell are you bothering me?" Ms. Judy says, glaring at me. She harrumphs and continues. "But yeah, she came back to attend to her family's land and all that. And then it weren't but about three, four months later that the younger Kelly girl up and left town. Older girl said she went to college, but . . . yeah, sure she went to college. Hasn't been seen or heard from since, and whenever anyone asked the older girl about her . . . well, it was pretty damn clear she didn't want to talk about it. And then, next thing you know, girls are taking Naida's lead and just up and running from Live Oak. Like that brunette one you were hot for!" Ms. Judy exclaims, nodding at Samuel as if he should suddenly realize Layla is among the disappearances.

She continues. "Slipping off in the night like a horde of bootleggers . . . Here's the thing they don't understand — the thing no one understands. Being stuck in Live Oak is like being stuck in a barrel of molasses. You're only stuck if you struggle. If you'd just relax and wait for someone to hand you a tree limb, you'd be able to slip right out. And now people are taking off right and left, thinking this place is dangerous, calling in the government cronies to look for their girls . . ." Ms. Judy makes a sour face. "For what it's worth — I don't think the older Kelly has anything to do with it. Families just want someone to blame when their kids choose a life grander than their own."

"So . . . was there anything about Naida that was . . . different?" I ask carefully.

Ms. Judy presses her thin lips together thoughtfully. "She was a sweet girl. Shy. Terribly shy. Waitressed at the diner for me a few summers, and dammit to hell should a man ever say anything to her other than his order. She had colored hair

160

like yours for a while, only instead of lookin' like a rainbow she looked like she dunked her head in toilet bowl cleaner."

"I'm sorry?" I ask, confused.

"Blue. She dyed her whole head blue. Only girl in this town with colored hair till you came along. I don't know what the hell is wrong with you young people. If the good Lord Jesus wanted you to have purple hair, he'd have given you purple hair."

"Oh," I muster, sinking back in the chair a little.

"And sit up straight," she commands; I snap back up. "Anyhow, girl was troubled. Nervous. Something about Live Oak didn't sit well with her, I guess, though I can't imagine her out in the big world without her sister. Sophia was protective of that girl; so was her father. But that's all I know on her. Sad family, that is. Mother had cancer, father murdered or killed or who knows, one daughter gone, and the other a beautiful tragedy. Livin' out there all alone. It true she's courtin' with your brother, by the way?"

"Something like that," I say.

"Good for her. Pretty girl like her needs to get knocked up 'fore she gets too old."

"Ms. Judy!" Samuel says over a laugh.

"You laugh, honey, you laugh. But it's a sad day to wake up and find the baby makers aren't making nothin' no more," Ms. Judy answers sharply. "Anyhow, I'm tired. Is that good enough for you people?"

"Yes, Ms. Judy. Thank you," Samuel says sincerely. He rises and we wait as Ms. Judy heaves to her feet.

"Now, how about you darlings come by another day for poor Noodles? Maybe 'round the end of the month? He always starts digging in the fire ant piles 'round the end of July. He'll need a bath then, I reckon," she says as we walk back past her great-great-great-grandfather.

"Happy to," Samuel says with a groan he's unable to hide. This seems to please Ms. Judy even more. She lets us out the back door and we trudge back toward Samuel's.

"Well?" Samuel says as we near his front door.

I shake my head. "I don't know what to think. So she had blue hair. Why does that matter?"

"What about the fact that she was the first?" Samuel suggests, leaning against the side of his house. "Maybe she started it all—the girls disappearing. She disappeared *before* the chocolate festival. She was special."

"But why?" If she started it, there has to be a reason. I sit down on Samuel's front steps.

"Okay, well, in that case, how about the fact that Naida sounds way more like you than she does any of the other girls who vanished?"

I open my mouth, but I don't know what to say. He's right. She does sound like me—down to the hair dye. But I didn't disappear, and she did, so...it's just a coincidence, right?

"Come on," Samuel says, and offers me a hand up. "If we wait to leave, we'll run into people leaving the game. You think people glare at you now—wait and see what they do if they catch you on the back of my bike."

I duck my head against his shoulder as we rumble through Live Oak — in this direction, I can see a crowd ahead, near the abandoned high school. Their backs are toward us, but I can see coolers and lawn chairs set up around a field that clearly used to be for baseball, not football. The small crowd cheers, and among the people I catch sight of a few of the players — I don't see my brother, but he's there. So is Sophia.

They are able to move on, able to forget girls who vanish. But I guess in the end, I simply am not.

CHAPTER FIFTEEN

Sophia wakes up so early on the Fourth of July that it's borderline insulting. The sun is barely up, and a layer of frostinglike mist is settled on the field behind her house. Ansel's eyes are droopy, but he's doing his best to look awake and eager to help. I'm more awake, but not because I'm excited for the party—because I can't get Ms. Judy or Naida out of my head. Because every time Sophia walks into a room, I jump, feeling as though she's caught me doing something. As if she's caught me thinking about her vanished sister.

"You think this is bad? You should see me before the chocolate festival. I'm up at four in the morning," she says as we fill picnic baskets. "I just want everything to be perfect." Sophia hurries to ice what looks like five thousand cupcakes—icing them ahead of time makes them crunchy, she explains. I try to help her, but cupcakes aren't exactly my forte; it's just a few moments before she suggests I help with stuffing the truffles into coolers instead.

"Hey," Ansel whispers at me, calling me into the bathroom a few hours later. He's wearing a blue shirt, but there's a black one and a yellow one laid out across the shower curtain rod. "Which shirt should I wear?"

"Are you asking me for fashion advice?" I ask, confused.

"Sophia said we should look nice. I just want her to know I…um…tried."

"You're weird. The blue one is fine."

"Fine good? Or fine okay?"

"Ansel, you're starting to worry me," I say, rolling my eyes and walking away. But even I double-check the clothes I've laid out before we load up the car later. Because even with Naida, even with the chocolate festival, even with the secrets, I still want to make Sophia happy. She's the first one in years to be kind to me; how could I throw that back in her face?

Can't one girl who's lost her sister forgive another a few secrets?

It's amazing that Ansel will need to make a second trip back to the chocolatier, considering the amount of stuff we cram into the car to begin with. A giant table hoisted onto the roof, the trunk open with an array of baskets and covered trays tied down with twine and bungee cords…I have just enough time to shower and leap into the front seat before we take off.

Sophia talks fast and with her hands, two things that

make the ride into Live Oak terrifying—she ponders if she made enough dark chocolate, and next thing you know, she's yanking the car back onto the road just moments before it would have landed in a ditch. I let out a long-held breath as we approach town and she plants two hands firmly onto the wheel.

Downtown Live Oak looks like a scene from a movie, some war epic where the hometown decorates in red, white, and blue. American flags adorn the sides of the buildings, and thick-bulbed Christmas lights are strung across the street, a zigzag of wires in the daytime. The SEE ROBERT E. LEE'S RIDING BOOTS signs are everywhere, hanging on buildings with arrows pointing to the storefront that apparently houses them. Vendors are setting up tables and booths, and there's a giant cooler of beer in the center of the downtown square, just beneath the Confederate soldier statue, from which everyone seems to be pulling cold bottles. All the closed-down shops and rusty signs are covered with Americana, making Live Oak look like a bustling small town instead of a mostly abandoned piece of history. It's eerie—like seeing someone in a costume that covers his face. I'd rather see the Live Oak I know than a pretty version of one I don't.

Sophia's name echoes across the square as she slows and pulls through the street at a snail's pace. She waves out the window and grins as people regale her as though the queen of Live Oak were riding through—and in a way, she is, I suppose, complete with political adversaries. I see a few people glare at her, then turn away from the car. I think Sophia simply didn't see them, until I catch her eyes when she stops the car. She looks scared.

"I can do this," she mutters. Sophia reaches behind her and fumbles around in a box, then emerges with a candied lemon peel. She swallows it almost whole, as if the need for courage is overwhelming her.

"You'll be fine. I promise," I tell her, though I suspect I might be lying.

"They're convincing more and more people that it's my fault, but..." She shakes her head and smiles sadly at me. It pulls at my heart, flashes me back to the way Ansel and I were when everyone quietly whispered about us, pointed at us, not-so-secretly thought it was our fault our sister was gone. I squeeze Sophia's hand gently, and then she opens the door.

She barely makes it out before someone brings her a beer from the cooler and an older lady wraps her up in a firm hug. Sophia smiles and waves and sparkles as though she's never met someone she didn't love.

"You know my boyfriend? Ansel?" she says, ushering Ansel over. *Boyfriend*. Of course he's her boyfriend. I knew that—still, hearing her say it is different. Ansel's ears are pink but he hurries over to shake hands with a trio of sun-aged men who give him a hard time about dating Sophia, how they'll come after him should he wrong her. Ansel looks happy—really *happy,* in a way I haven't seen him since we were little.

"And this is...hey, Gretchen! Get over here," Sophia says through a grin. I raise my eyes over the car and slink around the side. Sophia wraps an arm around my shoulder and squeezes me to her.

"And Gretchen, who is like my right hand. Seriously. I've never done inventory so fast," Sophia says, and I laugh because if I don't, the guilt cocooning around my body will surely show through.

"Well, pleased to finally meet you both," one of the men says, clapping Ansel and me on the shoulders simultaneously. "Sounds like you're doing Sophia a lot of good. And she deserves it," he says seriously, meeting Sophia's eyes. "She really deserves it. Glad to see you're finally opening up to people, Sophia. Even if it is out-of-towners!" He laughs loudly.

"Oh, Mike," Sophia says, looking at the ground and twisting her feet in something resembling modesty, though the emotion in her eyes is closer to guilt.

"Well, it's true, honey. Your daddy would—"

"Can you help us set up the tent?" Sophia cuts him off.

"Sure thing—hang on, I'll get the rest of them," Mike says. He turns and whistles sharply, and before I know what's happening, a crowd of people swarms the car. The table is pulled off and set up, and portly ladies begin lining it with the trays. "Do these need to stay out of the sun?" "Nothing out of the coolers yet, I imagine." "Oh, sweetie, what pretty cakes!" "You make sure you send them to my booth!" are the chorus of the crowd. Shade blooms over me as Mike and his friends erect the tent.

"And Ansel, you're going back for the second trip?"

Sophia calls over the fray. Ansel nods but looks reluctant to leave Sophia behind so long as she's introducing him as her boyfriend. Nonetheless, he gets into the car and edges it out of the square.

The crowd slowly fades, a few old women being the last to leave and return to their own booths. Sophia looks at me and exhales.

"Still alive?" she asks with a grin.

"Barely," I answer, collapsing into a chair and propping my feet up on the table. "You're okay?"

Sophia takes a long sip of her beer. "I'm fine. I'm glad Mike and his friends showed up. It helps."

Sophia slides the free candy a little closer to the edge of the tent. She's giving away so many free samples that I wonder why she's even bothering to charge for the rest — and if any amount of free candy can help her reputation. Her eyes float to the empty vendor stall next to her.

"Who will our neighbor be?" I ask, nodding toward it.

Sophia frowns. "It's usually a guy who does woodworking — little statues, whistles, ashtrays, that kind of thing. He's got a daughter a little younger than you, Emma, and I heard he... well..." She twists the beer bottle around in her hands. "I heard he isn't showing this year. Didn't want the tent next to me and won't let Emma out of the house the night of the festival. I guess it doesn't matter — she's so young anyway," she finishes in a mumble.

"There's an age limit?" I ask.

"Oh, no," she says quickly, voice a little panicked, though

I'm not sure why. She continues. "Just...she's so young, she has more time to come to them. Maybe her dad will relax."

"Probably," I say, though I'm not entirely sure I mean that. "Besides, maybe he's just pissed off that you sell way more candy than he does ashtrays."

Sophia laughs a little and gives me an appreciative smile. The sun is going down slowly but surely—it looks as though it's resting on the roofs of the tallest shops in downtown Live Oak. People are beginning to arrive with blankets and lawn chairs—they tape the blankets down with silver duct tape so no one can steal their spots while they socialize.

"Oh, look!" Sophia whispers sharply. She points to a large black woman with a table tucked under one arm. She's wearing long, wispy blue robes, and her hair is piled up on her head. She drops the table in a spot underneath a gnarled oak tree, then heads back to where she came from, thick earrings sparkling in the waning sunlight.

"What's she selling?" I ask curiously.

"Fortunes," Sophia says with a grin. "Miss Nikki—she reads tarot cards. Been doing it forever, always at the Fourth of July festival under that tree. It's a telling tree—slaves told stories under it, according to the Live Oak historical society. Which, oddly enough, is made up of stuffy white people."

I laugh. "Have you ever gotten your cards read?" I ask her.

Sophia shrugs. "I used to—I haven't been recently. I guess I'm not too interested in knowing my future anymore. She's predicted all sorts of Live Oak stuff with those cards, though—she's the real deal, I think. You should go tonight!

Wait till just before they do the fireworks—the line is always low then."

"Only if you come with me," I answer. "Because not only should you get your cards read, but it'll be hilarious to watch Ansel try to manage customers."

Sophia laughs loudly, a sound that turns smiling faces her way. "Deal," she says, eyes sparkling.

The tourists start to filter in. I didn't think I'd be able to tell them apart from the locals, since I don't know everyone in Live Oak despite their knowing every detail about me, but it's so, so obvious. The tourists have bathing-suit tan lines and take pictures of the Americana and yell loudly over the crowd. The locals are low-key—not quiet, necessarily, but practiced; they've done this all before, and they'll do it all again.

By the time Ansel returns with the second carload of candy, Sophia and I have already refilled the free samples of chocolate-dipped peaches and almost sold out of cinnamon truffles. I'm so caught up in the whirl of filling bags and making change that the sky is pale lavender before I know it.

"Ooh, I want an early taste of the chocolate festival—which I *am* coming to, by the way," a teen girl squeals as she eyes the array of candies. Sophia grins and I see relief on her face.

"Take one of these—new truffle recipe. I was going to try it out on unsuspecting tourist guinea pigs, but you'll do, Sara," she says.

Sara eagerly reaches forward and takes the truffle, then

171

bites it in half. "Good god, Sophia. The devil is gonna steal you to be his pastry chef."

"Good, then?" Sophia asks. "It's a raspberry center..."

"Amazing," Sara answers. "I'm so excited about the festival, you don't even know. I got two red dresses when we went into Lake City a few weeks back. One's a sort of tunic dress, and one has ties like the one, um, Jillian wore last year." She pauses, Jillian's name hanging heavily in the air, then shakes her head, as though that'll run the name off. "Which one do you think would look better?"

"Um...oh..." Sophia looks down, busies herself tidying up the counter space. She swallows hard, as though the answer hurts her. "The tunic one, probably."

"That's what I thought! My grandpa said it was trashy, but whatever. He spends all his time watching over those Robert E. Lee boots in the museum—what would he know about party dresses, right? I just hope it's the right shade of red..."

"Oh, there is no right shade, don't worry," Sophia says. Her voice cracks a little; Sara doesn't notice, turning back toward her family.

"Oh god, speaking of, I think Grandpa has moonshine in that flask. Ricky is gonna smell that from a mile away."

"Ricky would never throw your grandpa in jail," Sophia says reassuringly, snapping back to the happy version of herself so quickly that I shake my head in disbelief. "He's afraid to mess with Live Oak's elders."

"Hell, I'm not afraid he'll jail him," Sara says, hiking up

her sundress and starting toward an old man in white shorts with a silly grin on his face. "I'm afraid he'll drink it. Ricky drunk on moonshine and cop powers is not pretty!" she finishes, calling out to us as she rushes away. Sophia watches her go, then sighs. When she turns back to me, she's smiling again.

"Speaking of, Gretchen, do you have a red dress?"

"It has to be red?"

"Everyone who graduated the May before the chocolate festival wears red—it's the color of the old Live Oak high school. Kind of a 'hey, look, I'm one of the people who didn't drop out and get knocked up instead of graduating' thing. I guess you could call it tradition," Sophia says.

"Well, technically, I didn't graduate from Live Oak. In fact, I didn't even go to high school," I remind her, and she laughs before turning around to face my brother.

Ansel, clearly exhausted from hauling half the chocolatier into town, is planted in a lawn chair toward the back of the booth. "Ansel?" Sophia asks in a sugary voice, and Ansel narrows his eyes teasingly at whatever she's about to request. "Would you watch the booth for us for a few minutes?"

"Why?" Ansel asks, but he's already kicking his legs off the cooler and rising.

"Your sister and I are going to go get our fortunes read," Sophia answers, biting her lip excitedly as she looks toward me.

"Oh, come on," Ansel grumbles, but he takes Sophia's place behind the counter. Sophia chuckles and kisses him on the cheek so swiftly that he seems confused by it, and we skip off, leaving my brother touching the spot on his face where Sophia's lips were.

"That was cruel," I tease her. "He'd do anything for you, even sell truffles to people in fanny packs."

Sophia looks over her shoulder as she links her arm in mine. "He'll survive. Besides, he shouldn't fall in love with me anyway."

"Too late for that," I say, raising my eyebrows. Sophia frowns, but at the same time her cheeks flush hopefully.

The bulk of the audience meanders back toward their blankets now that it's nearly dark, making it difficult to move in the opposite direction. Sophia forges ahead, fingers wrapped in mine, toward the blue tent. The line isn't short, but it's died down considerably. We take our spots in the back, behind a duo of middle schoolers with tricked-out cell phones and belly shirts.

"So what are you going to ask her?" one says, twirling her hair.

"If I should go out with Cody or Sean," the other says. They launch into a conversation that's entirely too fast to follow.

"She should go with Cody," I whisper to Sophia.

"Yeah, all the Seans I've known have been asses," she replies. "And Miss Nikki hates it when girls ask about boys. Says it sets feminism back a hundred years."

The line draws closer, until finally the middle schoolers duck inside, one at a time. The sky is blackening, and people are staring up as if they expect the fireworks to appear from nowhere. Sophia points out a group of men on the roof of the hardware store twisting wires and moving things around, preparing for the show.

The first girl emerges looking bored, followed by the second, who looks bitter. Apparently the reader told her to date neither Cody nor Sean, and they complain about the inaccuracy of tarot cards loudly as they walk away.

"Wish me luck," Sophia says, and her voice betrays the grin on her face — she sounds worried, as though this is much more than just a block-party card reading. Then she disappears under the dark blue fabric into the booth. I shove my hands into my pockets and rock back and forth on my heels, unsure where to look now. I glance toward the sky, letting my eyes run across the stars and down to Live Oak's rooftops. Samuel is up there, somewhere. I wish I could find him among the chimneys.

Sophia emerges, looking something between irritated and sad, though she does a decent job of hiding it with a bright smile.

"Your turn!" she says cheerily.

"What did she say?" I ask.

Sophia falters, then shrugs. "Nothing exciting. Oh, wow, I need to go help Ansel..." She points through the crowd. I can just barely see him, scrambling to make change and turning over boxes of wax paper and toothpicks. Sophia laughs and brushes past me as I duck into the blue unknown.

CHAPTER SIXTEEN

The inside of the tent almost makes me forget that there's a festival going on outside. There's a single table covered in purple cloth with a lamp on it. The lamp's red shade casts the room in pink and creates dark, heavy lines on the card reader's face. She gathers Sophia's cards and looks up at me.

"Ah. The Washington girl," Miss Nikki says as I enter. She leans on one elbow, tapping her pointer finger against her cheek in undisguised judgment.

"Yes. Gretchen," I say quickly, lowering myself onto a tiny wooden stool. "And, um...Miss Nikki, right?"

"Not exactly—it's the full name tonight. Tourists don't pay for Miss Nikki. They pay for Miss Zuelika," she says, slumping back in a peacock chair that's seen better days. She fiddles with a deck of tarot cards for a moment while I drop three dollars into the fishbowl on the table's edge. Miss Zuelika smiles and sets the cards down in front of me.

"Cut the deck, sugar," she instructs me. I reach forward and split the deck into two uneven halves; the cards are worn and don't lie flat.

"Now shuffle 'em, thinking about what you want to know," Miss Zuelika says. I do so, struggling to keep the cards from flying off the table.

I can't think of a question.

I shuffle as slowly as possible. I mean, there are a thousand things I want answers to — most involving Sophia and witches. Question, question . . .

I don't have any questions.

No, that's not true. I have questions — I just don't know how to put them together.

Layla. Emily. Whitney. Jillian. Danielle. Allie. Rachel. Taylor.

Naida.

My sister.

There's the question — the one I've always wanted the answer to. Why my sister, and not me? Two little girls, exactly alike, and the witch chose her. She vanished, and I didn't.

Why her, why those Live Oak girls, why Naida, and why not me? Are they special, or am I?

The cards pop and snap together as Miss Zuelika takes them from me and drops them onto the table. I sit up straight, inhale. Miss Zuelika rubs her palms together and lifts the deck carefully, then draws out three cards.

"This is you," she says, dropping a card featuring a

mermaid holding a single oar out of the ocean. The Ace of Wands, according to the caption.

"This is the other—the thing? Person?" she asks as she lifts another card.

"Um...person," I say meekly. People?

"This is the person your question is about. Ace of Chalices." The card has an elegant hand wrapped around a pink conch shell that reminds me of the shells on Sophia's porch and in the back shed. "And this," she says, pulling the last card, a grin spreading across her face, "is your solution." She drops the card onto the table.

The Devil. The card displays a large, sinister-looking merman with angel's wings looming above two kneeling mermaids wrapped in chains.

I cringe. My stomach twists around in my gut.

"Oh, calm the hell down—don't act like a tourist," Miss Zuelika says, rolling her eyes. "Devil card don't mean you're doomed. Wait for the damned reading first."

I nod and try to relax, though the twisted feeling in my stomach doesn't go away entirely.

"So you, hon," Miss Zuelika says, tapping the Ace of Wands with a long, painted fingernail. "Ace of Wands. Undertaking a new endeavor? Something bold, something you've never done before?"

"Yes," I say, surprised.

Miss Zuelika continues, "You've got the power, got the skill. But you have to give it direction, honey, or all that talent is gonna burn right out. A hot flame can only stay lit for so long 'fore it fizzles. Gotta choose your path wisely so you don't burn right out of this world."

She taps the second card, the Ace of Chalices. "The mirror of your card, if I say so myself. This person, they're just like you. Pure potential, pure skill, pure love, pure peace. They've got the same problem as you—have to make a choice before all that potential vanishes. You and this person, you're the same. Same problem, same choices, same future, same truths."

The Live Oak girls, my sister, Naida. We're the same.

"You're both held captive by the same thing. Same force, holding you both down, chaining you both up. That's why you gotta make the right choice, hon—to get away from this, this darkness," she says, waving her arms around with a frown. "You and this other, you have the same destiny right now. You gotta look the Devil in the eye and shake free of the chains holding you down. Look at their hands." She points to the card, to the mermaids at the Devil's feet. "Those chains aren't attached to them—but they believe they are, and that's enough to hold them there. Be strong, fight back, or the Devil'll burn your potential right out."

"What if," I say, and my voice is hoarse. I swallow and continue. "What if they're already burned out?"

"You asking if that means you'll burn out too?" Miss Zuelika says, glancing toward the Ace of Wands.

I nod.

"Depends on what you do next. Right now, you're headed down the same path as them, same dangerous road. Like I already said, you and them are mirrors. It's no easy task to break free of your reflection, but you gotta do it."

I stare at my cards, burning the images into my mind so that the mermaids' faces are replaced with my own and Naida's.

Naida started this in Live Oak. And my fate is to mirror her, to vanish, unless I break free. All this time, all this surviving, learning to shoot, learning not to be afraid, and I still have the same destiny I feared when I was a little girl. I can still disappear.

"Anything else, hon?" Miss Zuelika says, raising her eyebrows. I can feel the color draining from my face and shake my head weakly. "Right, then. Next!" she barks loudly. I rise to my feet shakily and make my way to the tent door.

I think I'm going to be sick. The shuffling of the people outside and the weight of my thoughts make me dizzy. I want out of the crowd, out of the lights and movement and the scent of stale beer. I glance at Sophia and Ansel, who are standing so close that, from this distance, they blend into one person. Sophia is eating lemon peels, Ansel is picking at chocolate potato chips. They look happy, carefree, as if there's nothing to Naida's disappearance or Live Oak's distrust or the chocolate festival.

As though everything is okay, when in the post office just across the street there are eight pictures of missing girls. And under Sophia's bed, there's a ninth.

I hurry away from the Confederate soldier statue, toward an alley between two storefronts. The Live Oak girls' names race through my mind, images of their faces, of witches coming... When I make it into the alley, I keep walking, letting my fingers trail across the brick. The deeper I go, the darker it gets, and it helps me breathe, helps me think.

I have to break free. I can't vanish; I don't want to vanish. Make a choice, do something different, something to escape...

I shake my head, unsure what exactly I'm talking myself into. There's movement at the deeper, blackened end of the alley I'm headed toward, light scuffling of what I think are cats fighting over Dumpster scraps. I try to breathe as I hear something else: footsteps. They're somewhere near the mouth of the alley, following me in. I gulp and prepare my speech for whomever is coming—probably Ricky.

Of course, what will I really tell him? That I'm scared? Afraid of a witch—no, a werewolf—in the forest? But even more afraid that I'm bound to a destiny I thought I'd finally escaped.

I guess I could just tell him that I'm a scared little girl. The exact thing I was years ago, when I was running with my brother and sister through the trees.

I stop walking and turn around to face Ricky as he approaches. *Breathe, Gretchen, or he's bound to think you've been drinking moonshine too.*

As my head clears, the fog that was surrounding my thoughts floats away. And I now realize the footsteps aren't coming from the mouth of the alley. They're coming from the black end.

I turn to look.

A dark figure emerges. He lumbers toward me with slow, long strides. My mind scatters; a scream lodges in my throat. Already? The witch is coming for me already? I turn to run—but where to? I can't take a monster into the crowd, can't watch him feast on girls on their summer vacation. My feet scramble to find direction as the figure nears—I can hear him breathing, hear some noise from his throat, the scent of sweat—

Think. Think, Gretchen, think. I take off down the alley—I can run away from the festival once I get out. He'll follow me, I think, I *hope*. The girls out there will be safe for now. I hear feet behind me. Dirty water splashes up around my legs as I run through old puddles in the near blackness. *Go, faster, go*—

The monster hits me, slamming his body into mine and trapping me in his arms. I scream, but his hand clamps down on my mouth. I bite down; he yanks his hand away and roars but doesn't release me. I thrash, try to yank away. The monster is yelling, shouting, grabbing my wrists and squeezing them so tightly that I feel the blood vessels popping.

"*Christ, Gretchen, stop,*" a voice hisses angrily at me. I flail once more before finally allowing the words to connect with my brain.

That scent—leaves and forests and fresh rain—cuts through the darkness and winds around my head.

"Samuel?" I ask, scared of what the answer might be.

"Who the hell did you think it was?" Samuel snaps, lightening his grip on my wrists.

"I..."

"You bit me. I can't believe you bit me."

"S-sorry," I stammer. "I thought you were a witch. Are you hurt?"

"You mean, did getting *bitten* hurt? Yeah, actually. Believe it or not," he says in the darkness. I wince as he releases my wrists, then rub the skin tenderly.

"Are you okay?" he asks with a sigh.

"Yeah, I just...there was this thing and then my sister and..." I struggle for words. How to explain myself without sounding crazy?

A sharp light flicks on at the mouth of the alley, shining directly into our eyes.

"Hey! What the hell do you two think you are doin'?" barks a voice. I squint in the light and Samuel and I both raise our hands to block the glare.

"Nothing, Ricky," Samuel says, though I imagine he must recognize Ricky's voice—god knows I can't see anything but spots at the moment.

"Hey, now," Ricky says, voice suspicious. He lowers the light a little, till I can make out his beetle-shaped eyes staring at me. "You okay, Washington? This guy didn't hurt you, did he?" Ricky gives Samuel a hateful glare.

"No, no," I answer quickly. "I'm fine."

"Fine, huh? Then what were you doing with him in an alley?" Ricky asks, hitching his pants up. Samuel grits his teeth next to me, shakes his head angrily. I glance from him to Ricky, then take a step closer to Samuel.

"Really, Ricky, I'm fine," I say, looping my arm through Samuel's. I feel Samuel's muscles tense and his eyes dart from the ground to my face. I ignore him, staring at Ricky. "We were just after some alone time."

Ricky snorts, then laughs heartily. "Oh, darlin'. Of all the boys in Live Oak...he's the one you oughta be afraid of."

"I'm not afraid of him," I answer shortly, and my words have more bite than I expected.

Ricky raises his eyebrows. "Whatever you say, honey. Now move on outta here." Ricky gives a curt nod, then flicks the light off, casting us both back into utter darkness. I hesitate for a moment, and then Samuel and I pull our arms apart.

"He hates me," Samuel mutters.

"He's *afraid* of you, if you ask me," I say, rolling my eyes.

"And you're not at all?" he asks, voice serious.

I pause. I wish there was at least a hint of light down here so I could see his eyes. "No," I answer.

Samuel laughs, a faint, light sound I wouldn't recognize as laughter if I didn't know him. "I might be afraid of *you*, Gretchen," he answers, then breathes out loudly. "I saw you from the roof. You looked freaked out."

"I was." How close are we to each other right now? It's hard to tell—I dare to stretch out a hand and my fingers brush across his T-shirt. I pull my hand away as Samuel inhales.

There's a moment before he speaks again. "You want to go back out there?" he asks. "The show is about to start."

"Not really."

"Come on," he says, and I feel his fingers close around my right wrist. I pull away — it's tender from where he had to hold me back earlier.

"Sorry," he says, yanking his hand away. "It's just hard to find in the dark, if you don't know the way."

There's a long pause; I focus on the sound of Samuel breathing, trying to figure out what he's thinking. He reaches forward, finds my wrist in the black again, but this time his hand runs down to my palm. He folds his fingers over mine; I instinctively grip his hand tightly.

Neither of us says anything, but there's a second, a tiny moment, where we stand in the darkness, hands intertwined, and I know he's as fully aware of my skin on his as I am.

Samuel inhales again. He turns, tugging me along behind him gently. He leads me farther down the alley, then slows to a stop, lifting my hand to a ladder rung.

"Climb straight up," he says. I gaze upward, where the ladder emerges from the darkness to a rooftop. I pull myself up, focusing on one foot after another and not the fact that we're getting scarily high off the ground. I finally heave myself over the edge of the roof and crawl away from the side, then stand. Samuel hops up with practiced skill. I find his gaze in the pale yellow glow from the lights that are strung off the roof's edge.

He looks at me for a long moment, as though I'm someone

185

he hasn't seen before, then drops his eyes and walks over to the edge of the roof. I follow, afraid to get as close as he is. A guy with a bullhorn is blasting out instructions, that the show will begin in three minutes and everyone should find seats before the lights are turned off. I can see Sophia and Ansel settling down together in front of the chocolatier's booth and Miss Zuelika's tent by the telling tree. Samuel follows my gaze.

"So what happened?"

I turn to him and exhale. "I had my cards read."

"By Miss Nikki," Samuel says, nodding. He shoves his hands into his pockets and sways slightly.

"Yes. And she told me that me and the other eight girls and Naida and my sister . . . we're the same. We're mirrors of the same person. And we have the same destiny."

Samuel raises his eyebrows. "Miss Nikki told you that?"

"The cards did. I mean . . . that was my question. I wanted to know why they disappeared and why I didn't. I thought either they were special or I was. But she said we're mirrors, and I have to make a different choice than they did to break free." The bullhorn guy gives a final warning to sit down. "Is that stupid, though? To think I'm destined to be like my sister because of a tarot card reader at a Fourth of July party?" I want him to lie to me so badly.

But that's not how Samuel Reynolds works. He shakes his head and lowers his voice. "She's been reading cards a long time. People here believe her; tourists don't always."

"I know," I mumble, looking away when I catch a glimpse

of Sophia leaning in to kiss my brother. I should warn Ansel. Warn him about what, though? That she's keeping secrets? That she's hurting? That something is wrong, and I can't tell if it's with her or with Live Oak or with witches?

"What's the choice, then?"

"What?"

Samuel looks at the sky. "You have to make a choice. What is it?"

How do I make a choice when I don't even know what I'm choosing between?

You know. You've always known. Vanishing or not.

So simple, so easy, yet so complicated at the same time. But I know what I choose. I'm making a choice not only for myself but for all the girls sitting below, the eight fading girls of Live Oak, my sister, Sophia's sister, Sophia herself.

I will not vanish. And I will not let anyone else vanish either. I know how to use a gun. I know what the witch is. I know what to do to kill it. I can't keep being afraid, can't keep reliving that moment in the forest with my sister. I can't sit here with a gun, waiting for the witch to find me.

I just . . . can't. I can't be the scared little girl. I won't.

The lights flick off, leaving us in moonlight. I turn to Samuel, find his eyes as the crowd below hushes in anticipation. "My sister's name is Abigail."

His eyes widen; he inhales. "Abigail?"

"We called her Abby," I whisper. "And I don't want to pretend anymore that she wasn't real. I don't want her to disappear, or Naida, or Layla, or the rest of them. I want to help."

Samuel's green eyes flick to mine just as there's a popping noise from the other side of the square—the first of a few fireworks shooting toward the sky. "I'll help you," he says as the fireworks erupt into a shower of gold sparkles and the speaker system gears back up. Patriotic music blasts over the square; I take a few steps forward to stand beside Samuel and watch the spray of light above our heads.

CHAPTER SEVENTEEN

Samuel leads me back down the ladder and bids me a short good-bye. I feed Sophia and Ansel a line about sitting down near Miss Zuelika's tent to avoid getting caught in the blackout; I'm not sure if they don't question it because it's a good story or if they don't question it because it allowed them alone time.

It's well past my definition of *late* by the time we've packed up and gotten everything back to the chocolatier. I ignore the feeling in my chest, the gnawing hurt that comes when I look at Sophia as we unpack the car. When I see her, I think of Naida, of all Sophia's secrets, of the eight Live Oak girls. I think of Abigail.

I'm too exhausted to actually analyze it any longer; images of the missing girls just rotate around my mind. They continue long into my sleep — in fact, when I wake up, I can't tell the difference between my last few hours of unloading and my first few of dreaming. Same images, same fears.

I can't stay in bed any longer. I have to get my mind off Naida, how we're the same...I look at the clock in my room. I've had only a few hours of sleep, but it'll do. Not surprisingly, Sophia's door is still shut, but Ansel seems to be awake; the couch-bed is in disarray. He's standing by the kitchen's screen door sipping on coffee when I come in.

"Wow," he says. "You're up early."

"So are you," I note. I don't like coffee, but I want the caffeine, so I pour myself a cup. As I head to the fridge to load it up with milk, he nods to the field outside. It's packed with deer grazing in the early morning mist, shooting their heads up to eye the chocolatier suspiciously when I shut the noisy fridge door.

I lean on the opposite side of the door and watch them. For as hot as South Carolina is in the afternoon, it's almost chilly in the morning.

"I'm worried about Sophia," Ansel says in a low voice. I raise my eyebrows and take a deep breath. Something washes over me—relief? Camaraderie? He's worked it out; he knows Sophia is keeping secrets, that something isn't right, no matter how beautiful and wonderful she is. It's not just Samuel and me—it's Ansel too.

"I'm worried about her too," I say almost breathlessly.

"Really?" Ansel says, and he looks as relieved as I do.

"Yes. For a while now," I say, stepping closer to him.

Ansel nods and continues. "She misses Naida and her

dad. And then all the stress about the chocolate festival...
people blaming her..." he says, avoiding my eyes.

The balloon in my chest deflates and I bite my lip. My
brother and I aren't of the same mind after all.

"Anyway," he continues gruffly as he tops off his coffee,
"I don't really worry about *anything* here, weirdly enough,
but this thing with Sophia has started to get on me. I was
thinking she needs a break. I've been trying to convince her
to take a day to herself, but she won't listen to me. I thought
maybe she'd listen to you."

"Over you? I doubt it."

"You're kidding, right? Sophia talks about you like you
hang the moon in the sky. She's always talking about how she
needs you, how she's worried you're going to leave. She'll listen to you."

I hang the moon in the sky. Sophia thinks that of me, yet
I *know* she's hiding dark secrets from the world, from Ansel,
from Live Oak. Why do I feel as if I'm betraying her by knowing at least a fraction of the truth? Guilt stalls me for a
moment, so I buy myself time by turning to pull two eggs
from the refrigerator.

"What did you have in mind?" I ask as the fridge door
drifts shut.

"Like a girls' day or something. Nails and hair," he suggests, waving a spoon at me before swishing it around in
his cup.

"What is this, the 1950s?" I say, rolling my eyes. "But
fine. Maybe later this week?"

"That sounds good. And then...I was thinking..." He looks down again, as though he's afraid to say whatever it is he wants to. I wait. "I was thinking," he finally continues, "that maybe after the festival, we can leave."

"You and me?" I ask, and it's only a beat after speaking that my mind jumps to Samuel. What about him, how can I leave—

"You, me, and Sophia. I mean, if we could convince her to. It's just that leaving Washington was so good for you; I was thinking that maybe it'd be good for Sophia to leave Live Oak. This place is dying anyway."

I inhale, calm the worries that are leaping up inside me. There's plenty of time to deal with the prospect of leaving.

"Maybe. Let's get through the week first?" I ask my brother.

"What's going on this week?" a voice breaks toward us from the storefront. Sophia emerges through the saloon doors, looking exhausted. "Oh, thank god, coffee. Gretchen, would you be opposed to injecting it straight into my veins?"

"Not if you do me a favor," I say as Ansel nods emphatically at me from over Sophia's shoulder. Sophia is normal, casual. Of course she is. She doesn't know about the card reading.

"Oh yeah? I have to inject it into yours first?" she teases.

"Nope. I was thinking," I say, fingering the colored tips of my hair, "I need to go get my hair cut—or rather, get this cut out. You know, so I don't look like Skittles for the festival. Want to come with me?"

"Me? I usually just cut my own..." She studies the ends of my hair for a moment. "If you want to go, though, I'll pay for it."

"Wow—my hair looks that bad?" I ask, pretending to be offended. "Come on, we'll go together. It'll be fun."

Sophia laughs. "When were you thinking of going?"

"I don't know—this coming week sometime?"

"I haven't been to Kool Kutz in years. But..." She pauses and looks at me intently. "Okay. I'll go. Just...maybe late in the day? So it won't be as busy?"

"Yeah, sure," I say. "It'll be fun. Girls' day out."

"Okay, Gretchen, hair is one thing, but if you start suggesting we film a shopping montage, this 'girls' day' will come to an abrupt end," she jokes, and I laugh.

Thank you, Ansel mouths over her shoulder. I shrug. Truth is, he didn't have to ask me to hang out with Sophia. Because despite everything, I still like her. I still want her to like me.

She's still the first real friend I've ever had who hasn't disappeared.

"By the way," Sophia says through a yawn, "I meant to continue the conversation with you yesterday after I talked to Sara about her dress—*do* you have anything to wear to the chocolate festival?"

I shiver, thinking about what Layla was wearing, what the other girls were wearing, but try to appear casual when I shake my head.

"I was thinking you could borrow a dress from me, if you want," Sophia offers.

"That works."

"In fact…come on," Sophia says, and walks out of the kitchen, toward her bedroom. I grab my coffee and follow, unsure what else to do. By the time I catch up with Sophia, she's reaching into the back of her thin closet that's packed with clothes hangers.

"I have this one that's a little too small for me. I was thinking it might look good on you," she says. I set my mug down on her nightstand and sit on the bed, painfully aware of how Naida's photo might still be beneath me. "Here it is."

Sophia yanks out a sundress that's a washed-out red with a few ruffles around the skirt. It's very much her style, and I can tell by looking at it that I won't be able to fill it out the way Sophia can. But I tug off my pajamas and try nonetheless. Sophia zips me up and opens her closet door wide, revealing a long mirror on the inside.

I look ridiculous. The dress is hanging off me, as though I'm a little girl playing dress-up. Sophia giggles and I can't help but join her.

"I mean, could we take it in or anything?" I ask, pointing to the mass of fabric hanging around my chest.

"Do you sew? Because I've never sewn anything in my life," Sophia says, uselessly attempting to tighten the dress via the straps.

"I don't sew. Maybe we could pin it or something…" I suggest.

"Maybe…" Sophia says, but it's soon very clear that no amount of pinning will make it fit. "We could always go buy you something in Lake City," she offers.

"I don't want you to have to pay for that," I argue. "Do you have anything else that might work?"

"I..." Sophia gazes at her closet for a long time, then sighs. "I think so. Hang on, I'll be right back."

Sophia disappears, and I rise, then twirl around in the dress, rolling my eyes at the way it fits. At least I could hold a gun with it—the straps allow for plenty of motion. A flitter of movement catches my eye out the window. I peer through the translucent curtains and see Sophia unwinding the chain around the shed handles. She disappears inside for a moment, and when she emerges, she's holding a red dress with flowers on it. She holds it delicately, as if it's either horrible or precious. The screen door slams shut, and I hear her footsteps on the stairs.

"Maybe this one will work?" she says, and she smiles. The expression doesn't reach her eyes, and I know why.

That's Naida's dress. I'm sure of it.

I don't want to put it on—I really, really don't want to put it on. I nod weakly, unsure what to do. Admit I know about Naida? Refuse to wear something that was hers?

"Where'd it come from?" I ask.

Sophia exhales and puts the dress on the bed. "It was mine when I was younger." The lie would have worked if I didn't know about Naida, I suppose. As far as Sophia is aware, I don't—and she clearly isn't planning to tell me about her sister anytime soon. "Go ahead. Try it on."

I nod, trying not to move too stiffly, and remove Sophia's dress. The new red one smells like summer from years of sitting in the shed. I cringe as I pull it over my head and the material falls down around me.

It fits me. Perfectly, almost, as though it's always belonged to me. I stare at myself in the mirror, unable to move. Of course it fits me. Naida and I are the same. I try to imagine the girl in the reflection with blue hair and Sophia's eyes, but it frightens me and I finally look away.

"That one is great," Sophia says when I find her gaze. She's trying to swallow the quiver in her voice, but it doesn't work. "It fits you."

"Are you sure?" I say, and although I'm not clear on what exactly it is I'm asking, I know I'm seeking answers beyond the dress.

Sophia hesitates, and finally a tear slips through her eyes. "Sorry, sorry. It's just that you look really pretty. I'm glad you're here." Before I can speak, she swoops forward and hugs me. Her heart is racing, and I can tell she's crying pretty hard even though she's managing to keep her tears silent.

I don't understand her. I don't understand her secrets. I don't understand the festival.

And when Sophia hurries downstairs to check on something in the fridge, I realize I won't be able to lift a gun if I wear Naida Kelly's party dress.

CHAPTER EIGHTEEN

W hat's that?" I ask.

"One of the few expensive guns I haven't pawned," Samuel confesses, looking at it a little sadly. "I've just got the three rifles and this one now."

"So it's a…superspecial gun?" I tease, raising my eyebrows as I sit down in the clover beside him. I spin the tips of my fingers around the soft leaves. The night on the rooftop seems years ago instead of three days ago, emphasized by the space between us.

"Shotgun." He glances up as he corrects me—his eyes are the same color as the clover stems. "You've seen it in movies— see the pump?" He grabs my hand and, before I can react, puts it on a wooden part under the barrel of the gun. He wraps his fingers around my palm and slides the piece forward and backward, creating a clicking sound that echoes around the field.

"Right," I say, though to be honest I'm more astounded

by Samuel's calloused hand over mine than I am at the gun. A moment goes by, a long moment, and then Samuel inhales sharply and releases my palm.

"Anyway," he says aloud, so quickly that I know he must have been surprised at himself as well. He reaches into his bag and pulls out a box of red plastic cylinders. "I thought you might as well give it a try. Maybe you'll like it better than the rifles. It has a different kind of ammo; it sprays tiny BBs."

"Sure." I stand up and brush off the back of my legs as thunder rolls in the distance.

"It's not supposed to rain for another few hours." Samuel nods toward the sky.

"I think you've been lied to," I answer, staring into the clouds. I lower my eyes back to his.

"Here," Samuel says. "So you drop the shell into this little section, like this…and then you have to pump it. And that loads it. Safety is right above the trigger, the little bar that slides back and forth."

I take the gun from Samuel, readying it at my shoulder. "This right?"

"Almost. It's a little different; you need to slide your right hand. No, wait, your other right. Hang on," he says, and swoops in behind me. He puts his arms around my shoulders, sliding my hands accordingly. But all I can focus on is the fresh leaf scent coming from his skin.

Snap out of it, Gretchen! I shout at myself. *This is Samuel.*

"There. That's it. It'll kick a little, by the way," Samuel

says quietly, then steps away. I wiggle my shoulders to slide the straps of my shirt up and take aim. I inhale slowly as I pull the trigger.

The gun fires, a bright, sharp sound that's louder than the rifles. But I barely notice the noise because the shotgun recoils. It slams into my shoulder so unexpectedly that tears spring to my eyes. I feel blood building up beneath the skin, hot and painful, and scarcely have time to flip the safety on before dropping the gun to the ground and grabbing my shoulder in pain.

"You could have warned me," I say through gritted teeth, waiting until my tears have faded to raise my head.

"I said it would kick!" Samuel says, taking long, strong strides back toward me, a new sort of concern in his voice. He looks from the gun to me in surprise.

"Clearly we define 'a little' differently," I snap back, pressing my lips together. *Come on, Gretchen, get over it.* I can feel my shoulder starting to bruise but ignore it. The last thing I want is for Samuel to think I can't handle something.

"Sorry. I guess you aren't wearing much of a shirt for protection," he muses, the beginning of a laugh fading when I glare at him. "I can give you mine, if you want," he says, motioning toward his T-shirt.

"No," I say quickly, before I can reconsider. "No, let me try again."

"Okay, okay—hang on, though," he says, and tugs a navy handkerchief out of his back pocket. He folds it messily, then motions me to come close to him. He tucks his hand into the strap of my shirt and settles the handkerchief against the soft part of my shoulder; I try to ignore the trembling I feel when his fingers brush against my collarbone, the warmth that rushes to where his skin touches mine. Samuel clears his throat and steps away, nodding toward the gun.

"Okay. Pump it," he instructs me. I do so and take aim again. I already know my shot will be terrible—everything in my body is tense, waiting for the pain. I squeeze my eyes shut at the last moment and fire.

The second time hurts worse—it rips across the previous spot, blossoming down my arm until it burns. The tears spring back just as another roll of thunder echoes across the sky.

"Gretchen—" Samuel begins gently, but I ignore him and aim again. What if a wolf attacks me and then I have to shoot? The pain is just temporary. I have to deal with it. Thunder cracks again, and the dense feeling of rain in the air surrounds me.

I fire.

It starts to pour.

The raindrops hit me all at once, a river descending from the sky. Samuel is fast to my side, taking the gun from my hand and safely storing it away in his bag.

"Come on," he yells over the roar of the storm. "Let's go get under the trees till it stops." I rub my shoulder and nod. The pain is becoming a slow ache that's spread from my shoulder down my arm. I can already see it swelling. Samuel dashes toward the forest, and I start to go after him, but at the last moment I turn and run toward the target.

It's flapping in the rain, becoming soft and soaked; the marker lines from previous days are running like blue blood. I scan the target, looking for a single shot without a circle around it, a new shot. Instead, there's a peppering of tiny new bullet holes strewn across the page. Dozens of little hits. I grin.

"Gretchen!" Samuel shouts over the rain from the edge of the forest. I touch the rip in the paper gingerly, then turn and run toward him.

"What were you doing?" he asks when I reach him. Inside the trees is almost like being indoors during the storm; the thick canopy of leaves above lets only a few drops through. I'm soaked, and the water running off my hair carves a river down my back. I reach toward my shoulder; it radiates heat and is already darkening.

Samuel cringes and lets his fingers brush across the spot on my shoulder. "I'm sorry. Really. If I'd known it would hurt that bad, I wouldn't have made you shoot it."

I shake my head. "I hit the target. I mean, really hit it — right in the middle."

Samuel raises an eyebrow. "You what?"

"I hit it. I think the last shot, maybe," I say, grinning. The rain is already lessening, a brief summer thundershower on its way out.

Samuel's face, still hemmed in surprise, erupts into a smile that matches mine. He reaches forward and high-fives me, still shaking his head. He leans against a tree as we wait for the last drops of rain to fall.

I hit the target. Went through the pain. I can shoot, I can do this. I look over to Samuel, leaning against a pine, and step closer to return his handkerchief.

"I have to ask you something," I say as he plucks the handkerchief from my hand.

"What's that?"

"Remember when you said you'd help me keep girls from vanishing? Myself from vanishing?"

"Yes…"

"I don't want to wait for the wolves to come after me or anyone else in Live Oak," I say, casting my gaze to the ground nervously. The rainstorm stops, the sun shooting out from behind dark clouds. "And I don't want to just protect myself while other girls get chased and killed."

"What are you saying?" Samuel asks, folding his arms, eyes cutting into me.

"I want to go out after them. Like you do."

"You want to…go hunting?" Samuel asks, eyes widening.

"Yes."

"And you think charging into the Fenris-infested forest is a good idea?" Samuel says.

"I'm tired of waiting to be some monster's prey, Samuel. I want to be the one doing the hunting."

Samuel exhales hard and shakes his head. "I'll think about it. But for what it's worth, I think it's a stupid idea."

"I know," I say. "But I have to."

CHAPTER NINETEEN

S eriously, Gretchen. I don't need a haircut," Sophia says, nervously looking at the car.

"Come on. It'll be fun. Let's go." I yank on her arm. She pouts but finally gives in and follows me to the car.

By the time we reach Kool Kutz, it's almost four. The sun is scorching in the sky, driving most of Live Oak indoors or under the shelter of wide-brimmed hats. The parking lot for the "salon" is a mere three gravel spaces, all empty upon our arrival. It's a tiny cinder-block building with a shape that indicates it might have been a gas station or a drugstore before now. There are murals of fashionable women painted on the side — or at least, women who would have been fashionable in the mideighties. They sport headbands and short, poofy haircuts. I grab at the ends of my hair and begin to think Skittles hair is better than something more suited to a Jazzercise video.

"Don't worry," Sophia says, glistening in the afternoon sun. "As long as you only want something simple, she can't really mess it up."

"If you say so," I answer warily. Sophia grabs my hand and pulls me through the front door.

A blast of cool air strikes me, and chill bumps immediately appear under the layer of sweat on my arms. Kool Kutz smells like hair spray and perming solution, and the interior is almost entirely mauve. A woman in the back leaps to her feet.

"There's no way! It's not possible! Sophia Kelly! Back in my shop after almost two years."

"Hi, Ms. Minor," Sophia says with a warm smile. Ms. Minor is a stocky woman with a sharp nose and a tuft of bright red hair on her head, giving her the appearance of some sort of chubby bird.

"Don't you 'Hi, Ms. Minor' me. Haven't been here in ages—you haven't been driving to Lake City to get your hair done with those other hussy girls, have you?" Ms. Minor asks, putting her hands on her hips.

"No, no, of course not," Sophia replies. "I've just been cutting it myself, at home. There's so much to do there that getting out for haircuts is something of a luxury."

"And you're Gretchen. We met at the pharmacy that one time, remember?" Ms. Minor says brightly. I nod and hug her—she smells like floral soap—but honestly, so many people have introduced themselves to me that she's just one in a sea of faces.

"So what can I do for you ladies today?" Ms. Minor asks, eagerness spreading across her face.

"Haircuts," Sophia says. "I just want a trim, and Gretchen wants the rainbow cut out of her hair. And maybe some highlights or something for her too?" I raise my eyebrows at Sophia, who shrugs.

"About time," Ms. Minor says to me. She leans closer, as though she's letting me in on a great secret. "People talk here, Gretchen, and that hair has been the topic of much conversation. Ladies come in here like hens in a henhouse, bitchin' about how such a nice girl has gone and ruined her pretty head with colors like a two-dollar hooker. I'll trim that right out and they'll be beggin' you to come to church!"

"Oh," I say, because I can't figure out how to respond to all that.

Ms. Minor begins on Sophia's hair first, washing it, then trimming the ends and talking rapidly — Sophia hardly gets a word in edgewise, except to politely decline Ms. Minor's suggestion that they do something "really fun and innovative — something with bangs!"

Ms. Minor steps away from Sophia's hair and toward me. She hacks off the color quickly, leaving remnants of my former life curled on the floor like tiny rainbowed coins, then proceeds to process my hair with chemicals that make my eyes water. She's just gearing up to convince me to try layers when a bell rings as the door swings open. Our heads turn toward the front of the shop in unison; a dark-haired woman with streaks of gray walks in. Her face is saggy and tired looking, and there are dark crevices under her eyes. Something is familiar about her, but I'm not sure what; I'm certain we haven't met before.

"Merilee! Goodness gracious, hon, I was starting to think you'd forgotten about me!" Ms. Minor exclaims. She catches my eye in the mirror. "Merilee comes in on the first Thursday of every month to get her colorin'. Missed last week because of the busy holiday," she explains.

"And Deb gives away the secrets of my youth, tellin' everyone I get it colored," Merilee teases back. Merilee looks as though she's about to head to one of the waiting-room chairs but then sees Sophia, who must have been hidden behind me and Ms. Minor's wide hips. Merilee's face doesn't quite darken—it becomes wounded somehow, as though Sophia has just insulted her. I look toward Sophia, who is trying hard to avoid Merilee's eyes.

"I'll come back another day," Merilee says, voice flat. She turns to grab the door handle and I see Sophia wince.

"Merilee, come on, now," Ms. Minor says in a no-nonsense tone. "If you can't be civil at the hairdresser's, where can you be civil?"

"I won't—" Merilee begins.

"I'll go," Sophia offers at the same time, but Ms. Minor shakes her head.

"Sophia, we'll finish you and Gretchen up. Merilee, it won't be but a minute. Sit down. I've done your hair since the day I left beauty school and I'm not about to let you walk around town with your roots showing another day. People will think I've gotten too old to hold a pair of scissors," Ms. Minor says firmly. She's trying to keep it light and I'm grateful, but even her attitude can't lift the weight that's descended over the room.

"Merilee, why don't you go ahead and grab a smock while I finish Gretchen?" Ms. Minor says, tousling my hair with her hands. Merilee rises, jaw tight, and vanishes into a tiny bathroom. She shuts the door and I hear the water running.

"Poor thing," Ms. Minor says in a low voice, pursing her lips together and stepping away from me. "You don't mind her, Sophia. People always want someone to blame. You were just in the wrong place at the wrong time where Jillian is concerned—I know that."

Everything stops.

Layla. Emily. Whitney. Jillian. Danielle. Allie. Rachel. Taylor.

Jillian was the one who always wore the cross necklace. Last seen with Taylor and Allie, wearing a red sundress.

I feel cold. I knew I recognized that look on Merilee's face—I saw it for years. It was the look on my mother's face. The way she watched the forest, the way she convinced her heart that Abigail would come back, even though her head knew it wouldn't happen.

I realize that Sophia never wears that exact expression. She looks sad, she looks hurt, but she never looks like someone whose loved one has vanished.

Ms. Minor flicks on the deafening blow-dryer, sending my hair cascading around my face. I'm relieved—I'm sure

Sophia would be able to see the worry, the frustration, in my eyes.

When we're both through, Sophia pays for our cuts and we go to leave. Sophia lingers, however, and finally turns back toward Merilee, who is just taking her place in one of the salon chairs.

"Here, Merilee. Thought you might like these," Sophia says warmly, and pulls a bag of candies from her purse. Merilee looks at them but doesn't move to take them.

"Chocolate?" Merilee says in a heavy voice.

"With oranges," Sophia explains. I bite my tongue. There's so much hope in Sophia's voice and not even a glimmer of tolerance in Merilee's eyes. It'll take much more than candy to make Merilee give Sophia another chance.

Sophia's hand starts to quiver as Merilee's eyes slowly raise to hers. Merilee opens her mouth as if to say something, then slams her lips shut and shakes her head, disgust radiating from every line on her face.

Sophia's hand drops, and she swallows hard. She sets the bag of candy on the counter. "If you change your mind," she mutters hoarsely, and breaks for the door. I have to jog to keep up with her.

Sophia swings into the car and slams the door behind her—I duck into the driver's seat. The car interior is sticky and thick from sitting in the summer sun; I crank the engine for the AC but leave the car in park.

"Do you need a minute?" I ask her quietly.

"No. Just go," Sophia mumbles, folding her arms across

her chest. "I'm fine. She thinks it's just her, that...she's the only one who's lost someone..."

She's so close to telling me about Naida that I can feel it. *Please, Sophia. Just tell me. Tell me everything.* I realize for the first time that Sophia isn't all that different from the eight other Live Oak girls—she needs to be saved too. I'm just not sure from what, because she won't let me in.

But she doesn't speak again, so I back the car up and rumble down the main road, defeated. We pass Ms. Judy's house, and I peer around it to see Samuel's place in the trees; when I look back at Sophia, she seems calmer, as if she's forcing the emotion out of herself. I want to just ask about Naida and the other girls, throw my cards onto the table and let her do the same.

But I'm scared. I don't know how she'll react, and I don't want her to hate me, no matter what secrets she's keeping.

When we pull up to the chocolatier, my brother's Jeep is gone; Sophia and I reach the door to find it locked. She groans.

"I gave him my house keys. I figured he'd be back from Lake City by now."

"You have a spare hidden anywhere?" I ask.

"Nope. I'll have to climb in," Sophia says. Confused, I follow her around the side of the house to a spot just below her bedroom window. "I leave my bedroom window unlocked. Not like I have much of a choice, since the lock is broken."

I look up at the oak and bite my lip. "Okay. But I'm standing underneath because I'm pretty sure you're going to fall."

"I guarantee you, I won't," she says, and leaps up to grab

the lowest tree limb. She swings her legs around it like a gymnast and hikes herself up. She climbs, slowly but sure-footedly.

"You don't have to be all silent. I have uncanny powers to both talk and climb at once," she calls down.

But there's only one thing I want to ask her. I stare at her as she pulls herself into the sky. It seems easier now, without her sitting a foot away from me. I still don't want her to hate me, but I don't want to keep up this dance of secrets between us.

I take a deep breath.

"Why do you keep having the festival?" I ask casually, kicking at a fallen branch.

Sophia misses a step; branches swish and sway as she grabs on to a limb and regains her footing. Her eyes dart down to me for a single surprised, angry moment.

"What do you mean?" she says, trying and failing to hide an acidic tone in her voice.

"Just that, if girls keep running away afterward and people keep blaming you . . . wouldn't it be easier to just cancel? Wouldn't that make dealing with people like Merilee easier?"

"Well," she says, climbing a branch higher, "because . . . because I shouldn't have to."

"Well, yeah, but—"

"I shouldn't have to deal with them hating me. I shouldn't be the one people blame. It isn't my fault."

"Exactly, Sophia. What if we just canceled it this year? So no one blamed you?"

So no one vanishes?

Sophia stretches one leg out from the tree toward the roof, and I can see she's shaking a little. She pushes off the tree and lands her other foot firmly on the roof, then slides open her bedroom window. She hesitates, then turns to look at me.

"I just *have* to throw it," she says simply. "It's the only thing I *can* do. I don't really have a choice." She shrugs and smiles, but there's sadness to it, a secret hidden on her lips. She shakes it off. "Besides, Gretchen, it's only two weeks away. I can't cancel on such short notice!"

I nod, bite my tongue. She's lying. She's hiding something. She's keeping a secret, and it might be the reason girls die every year.

But I still want to save her.

Something wakes me in the middle of the night.

At first I think it was the dream I was having—a dream about Samuel with a beautiful, faceless girl who has Sophia's hair and a muffled voice.

No.

My eyes shoot open, stare at the vaulted ceiling above. I sit up quietly; Luxe raises his head sleepily, golden fur badly tousled. It was a noise—yes, I'm certain I *heard* something. I breathe almost silently, listening past the sound of the wind in the oaks outside and the ceiling fan clacking away above.

There it is. Footsteps.

I kick my legs over the side of the bed, careful to avoid the floorboard that creaks, and walk softly to the door as my heart picks up its pace. Luxe watches me for a moment, then flops his head back down on my blankets. I quietly open the door and slip outside.

It's not Ansel—that much I know immediately. My brother's quiet snores rise from the couch in the living room. I pass Sophia's bedroom. The door is closed—I assume she's asleep on the other side. *I should wake them up,* I think as I wipe the back of my neck, damp from fear and the nighttime humidity. What if it's time? Are they here, like they were for Jacob Kelly?

Shredded. I shudder and look at Ansel worriedly.

The footsteps move, rushed, hurried. I don't have a gun, just the one over the mantel downstairs. The steps are coming from the kitchen—maybe I can be quiet, slip down and count on the scent of candies to overpower my own. Or if I can't, at least I can scream—give Ansel fair warning instead of waiting for the monster to find its way upstairs.

When I said it on the rooftop at the Fourth of July party, I meant it: I can't be the scared little girl anymore.

I squeeze my eyes shut to find some semblance of confidence and open the door to the stairwell, jaw trembling. Were those claws? I listen closer, waiting for the yellow eyes to appear. I'd rather see them now than go another moment waiting.

A voice. A female voice, though one muffled by the walls. Not a wolf. Not a witch. I swallow the lump that had formed in my throat and force myself to take a few calming breaths. They haven't come for me, not yet. I tiptoe downstairs.

The chocolatier is darkened, though bits of moonlight

stream through the front windows and through the glass cases, as though the sky is intentionally illuminating truffles and candies. There's a dull glow from behind the saloon doors, a single light struggling to fill all the blackness. I edge around the display cases and peer into the kitchen.

Sophia paces. Her hair is down and frazzled, her nightgown wet with sweat. In front of her are a few truffle trays, mostly empty, and a bowl of candied orange peel that's been tipped over. There's also a bottle of dark rum, and I can tell even in the dim light that it's half empty. I remember it was intended for some sort of truffle, but judging from the glass beside the bottle and Sophia's face, I'd say it's largely been drunk.

Sophia winds her fingers through her hair and turns so I can see her face. It's hard to tell what's sweat and what are tears, but her eyes are watery and red. She slams her hand against the corkboard with the festival RSVPs and mumbles to herself, then stumbles back to the bottle of rum and pours herself another shot. There's a seashell beside the bottle—I think a new one. She glares at it, then releases another sob.

"Sophia?" I say gently, stepping through the saloon doors. Sophia clangs the glass back onto the counter and stares at me, confused, as if she's forgotten who I am. Her eyes suddenly flood with recognition and she crumples down to the counter, head in her arms.

"There aren't enough," she weeps as I hurry around the counter and put a hand on her back. "There aren't enough people coming."

"I'm sure some more people will RSVP. You have two weeks," I comfort her, quietly screwing the cap back onto the rum. She heaves and raises her head as I step away to put the rum back into a cabinet and toss what's remaining in her glass down the sink. She watches me mutely, as though I'm in a movie, then finds my eyes again.

"What if there aren't more?" she whispers, new tears spilling down her cheeks. She jumps off the bar stool and goes to the corkboard, where she begins rearranging the RSVPs frantically, dropping tacks onto the floor. I step around them and wrap an arm around Sophia's shoulders. I ignore the pounding in my chest, the knowledge that the party will result in some girls' deaths. That's Sophia's power: as much as I suspect her at times, I still care for her. I still want to comfort her.

"Then it'll still be a great party," I answer her soothingly, brushing away the strands of hair sticking to her face.

She looks at me and shakes her head, eyes wide with something like dread. "No, it won't," she says hoarsely. "I'm sorry, Gretchen. I don't know what to do. I don't know..." She reaches for the seashell on the counter, cradling it against her.

"Come on. Let's go upstairs and go to bed."

Sophia mumbles incoherently as I guide her around the fallen thumbtacks. Ansel is a heavy sleeper, but I'm still astounded that I manage to make it upstairs without his waking. I leave Sophia in her bed, then hurry to the bathroom to get a cold washcloth to wipe her face. By the time

214

I've made it back to her room, she's asleep, the shell resting on her bedside table beside the Nietzsche book. I run the washcloth over her red cheeks, cleaning the tearstains away, then rise to leave.

"Gretchen," she whispers, eyes closed.

"Yeah?" I ask, kneeling beside her bed. Sophia opens her eyes a little, lashes fluttering.

"I'm a good person, Gretchen," she mumbles drunkenly, pleadingly. "You have to believe me."

I want to believe her. I *mostly* believe her. But there are two versions of Sophia Kelly, two versions I've been trying to figure out since the day I got here. Now I understand that they were explained to me in the diner before I'd even met her. One is the patron saint of candy, and the other is the first sign of Live Oak's end days. And I'm not sure which version is stronger.

Sophia looks at me a long time, eyes desperate, helpless, then falls back to sleep.

CHAPTER TWENTY

I was thinking—wait, your hair..." Samuel says, squinting at me in the sunlight a few days later.

"I had the Skittle colors cut out of it," I say.

"Oh. Well...it looks...really..." It seems as if he's about to say something but can't find the word. He shakes his head and starts a new sentence. "I was thinking about what you said."

"What I said?"

"About hunting. About how you wanted to go hunting with me, I mean."

"And your thoughts are?" I ask eagerly.

"Well...if you're still interested...maybe that's not such a bad idea." Samuel shuffles his feet. I grin and walk forward, joining him in the shade of an oak.

"I'm still interested," I say, nodding.

"Okay, but...there are some rules. I don't want...I don't

want anything to happen," Samuel says, and I get the impression he prepared this speech. He continues. "You have to be able to hit a moving target. And you have to promise not to run."

"Not to run?"

"Like you did the night we met. You run into things. It's dark. Fenris chase things that run. It's harder to hit something chasing something I don't want to hit . . . if that makes sense. It's just a bad idea overall."

"So . . . when would we be doing this?" I ask.

"As soon as you can hit a moving target," he says with a shrug. "If you can hit this"—he holds up a tennis ball— "then you've got good enough aim to try hunting. With help from yours truly, anyhow."

"Okay," I say with a breath out. "Okay. I can do that."

Samuel shakes his head. "We'll see. Here," he says, handing me a rifle. "Your aim is best with this one."

The gray man is nowhere to be seen, and instead, Samuel throws the tennis ball hard. It ricochets off the ground as I try to aim for it. *Try* being the operative word—after several attempts, bullets have hit the dirt and a tree and skimmed through grass, all without ever making contact with the neon yellow ball. The afternoon fades into a mango-colored sunset, and Samuel checks his watch between throws. Still, he's yet to tell me we should call it a day.

"You don't have to hit it today," he reminds me as he brings the ball back for the millionth time. "I didn't plan for you to do it today. I just meant . . . that's the goal." He stoops to take a long drink of water from a bottle, which he then hands to me.

"But *if* I hit it once today, we get to go hunting, right?" I say before drinking. It's not that cold, but compared to the heat it's icy. I toss the bottle back to him.

"Do you really want to go hunting if you aren't truly ready?" Samuel says as he catches it.

I shake my head. "Yes. It sounds stupid, but yes. I feel like it'll change everything. It'll help me be . . . me. The me I want to become."

Samuel nods and looks at the ball in his hand, then rears back to throw it again. It flies from his hand and spins through the grass. I line up the sights on the rifle with it, then squeeze the trigger. Another miss. Samuel tries again.

The mosquitoes are coming out, nipping at my skin and distracting me even more than the fear of not hunting does. Samuel is right — it doesn't matter, it shouldn't matter. I have ages to hit the damn tennis ball.

Samuel picks up the ball and looks at it. He walks back to me slowly, with a look that reads "we're done for today." I sigh and empty the few remaining rounds from the gun, flip the safety on, and fall into the grass cross-legged. Samuel heaves himself onto the ground beside me. Lightning bugs emerge in the woods, where it's already dark.

"There's something I didn't answer, a while ago," he says, running the tennis ball between his palms. I raise my eyes to his.

"You asked me once," he begins, "if I still love Layla." He

gives me a long, intense look, and the remaining light from the sun reflects in his eyes.

"I..." I shake my head. "I was just wondering. You don't have to tell me."

"That's the thing, actually—I do have to tell you," he says. Even in the dim light, his eyes stand out in the piercing way that used to frighten me. Used to—it isn't until this moment that I realize they don't any longer. I still wouldn't say they comfort—they *challenge,* they dare, they shine.

"You told me your sister's name," he starts, "and if we're going to go into the woods together with, you know, loaded guns, I don't think I should have any secrets."

I inhale the scent of the trees and night. I'm not sure what to say, so I nod.

Samuel exhales. "I will always love Layla. That's what love is. It becomes a part of you. It holds you down sometimes; it becomes something you can't escape."

My stomach twists—I feel as though someone has hit me. I force a weak smile, nod, as if this is what I expected to hear. *Of course he still loves Layla.* I repeat it over and over in my head. That's the way it works. They always want the one who vanished. The one they can't have.

He gazes over my shoulder, into the dense trees, and when he meets my eyes again, there's an expression in them I've never seen—lurking behind the hardness, the bitterness, is an uncertainty that I can't believe I missed.

He opens his mouth and pauses before speaking. "But I want to make sure you know that that doesn't mean I'm still...

hers. She's gone. I know that. And just because I want to make things right in Live Oak doesn't mean I haven't moved on."

We watch each other, and then Samuel smiles and shakes his head.

"I just thought you should know," he says, then tosses the tennis ball to me; I catch it as it bounces off my thigh. He rises from the ground and makes his way to his motorcycle.

"Tomorrow night. We'll give it a shot. No promises—I *don't* find wolves more often than I *do* find them. But still."

"Wait, what?" I ask, scrambling to my feet. He doesn't answer, but I see a smile twitching at the corner of his mouth. I turn the tennis ball over in my hand and only then realize that there are fourteen holes in it, nearly hidden by the fuzz and swelling rubber.

I hit it.

Seven times.

I shout loudly, and before I can stop myself, I sprint toward Samuel. I drop the tennis ball and fling my arms around him, still yelling, sounds that were meant to be words if only I could translate my happiness into language. Samuel chuckles lightly and puts one arm around my head, then kisses me on the forehead, little more than a gentle brush of his lips. I step back, face wet with sweat and grinning.

Wait. He just kissed me.

Samuel seems to realize it at the same instant I do, and his face goes dark red. "Sorry," he says quickly. "I . . . um . . . forgot." Forgot what? That he doesn't kiss me?

"No, it's fine," I say, still breathless. The spot where his lips touched me tingles, memories of the way it felt replaying over and over on my skin.

"Come on," he says, voice still happy but now tinged with nervousness. He passes me the motorcycle helmet. "I'll take you home." I nod, spin in a circle to try to shake some of the enthusiasm from my veins, and climb onto the back of the motorcycle; for a moment, I try to keep space between Samuel and me, worried it'll make the strange kiss more awkward, but I can't help but draw closer to him as the bike rolls along.

Darkness seems to come quickly—from sunset to pitch-black is minutes, not hours. By the time we're a hundred or so yards from the chocolatier, the sides of the road are thick with lightning bugs and mosquitoes. Samuel gives me a hand to steady myself as I climb off.

"So really? Tomorrow?" I ask quietly, glancing toward the shining chocolatier in the distance.

"Might as well. Are you scared?"

"Yes," I answer without hesitation. "Terrified."

"I'll be with you," he reminds me. "I've shot them before."

"That's not really it," I say cautiously. "It's...I'm going after them. I've always been scared of the witch, afraid he'd find me, but...I'm going to look for him. It's scary in a different way. Scary because if this doesn't change me, if it isn't the last step away from being the scared little girl, I don't know what will be."

Samuel nods. "I'll meet you outside the Kelly place at... midnight? Sound good?"

"Yes," I say breathlessly. "That sounds great."

I turn and retreat toward the chocolatier; when I'm bathed in the porch light's glare, I hear the faint sound of Samuel's bike revving up and disappearing into the night. I turn back and try to see him in the darkness with no luck. My fingertips rise to the spot on my forehead. He kissed me, kissed me as if it was nothing, as though it was normal and right and I felt the same way for a moment.

He's Samuel, I tell myself, suddenly realizing that hunting wolves isn't the only thing suddenly scaring me. I turn to go into the house, but a voice interrupts the quiet.

"Who was that?"

CHAPTER TWENTY-ONE

I whirl around, hand to my chest. Before the scream of surprise can leave my throat, I exhale. Ansel.

"Who was who?" *Deny, deny, deny.*

"I'm not stupid, Gretchen," Ansel says. He walks around the side of the chocolatier and up the porch stairs, then collapses into one of the rocking chairs.

"Just a guy from town," I answer slowly as I take the rocking chair next to him.

We rock silently for a moment, the sound of Sophia sweeping the kitchen and the quiet radio interrupted occasionally by the noise of crickets. Some new emotion is threading between us, something rough and raw and new, but neither of us wants to point it out.

"Is it Samuel Reynolds?" he finally asks in a low voice. I turn my head toward him.

"What were you, spying on me?" I half tease, half worry. *What else has he seen?*

Guilt grows in the pit of my stomach. Ansel and I don't keep secrets from each other. We never have. We're the survivors, the ones who made it out of the forest, the ones who had each other when even our parents couldn't handle the world any longer. But now I'm keeping secrets—I *am* a secret, practically, this new version of me, this one that refuses to vanish.

"No," Ansel answers. "Seriously, no, I wasn't spying on you. That waitress from the diner ratted you out. Said she saw you on the back of his motorcycle."

I hold in a sigh of relief, though it does little to sway my guilt. Luxe head-butts his way through the screen door and trots outside, where he settles down at my feet. I rub his head with my toes, waiting for Ansel to go on, unsure what to say.

"So...are you? Dating him?" Ansel finally asks.

"What? No. We're just friends. I met him in town," I reply, my answer not entirely a lie.

"Okay...just wondering," Ansel says, holding up his hands defensively. "It's just that the waitress said...she said he was crazy. Like in a serious, clinical way."

I pause. "Do you believe her?"

Ansel sighs and looks down. "Do you?"

"No."

He pauses for a moment, then speaks. "It would be really easy for people to think you and I aren't exactly stable. I mean, our sister and...everything. And half of Live Oak thinks Sophia is crazy, and I know she's not. So I'm not going to take some waitress's word for it. If you trust him, I trust you."

I don't know how to answer — gratitude, surprise, relief, run through my head, but I can't think of a single all-encompassing word. Nor can I think of a word to express the feeling in my stomach, the tight, twisted frustration of knowing that my brother still trusts Sophia completely.

"Thanks," I finally say.

The radio in the kitchen turns off, and I hear the clicks and clatters of Sophia locking up. "I don't think you should tell Sophia, by the way. She'd probably be upset, hearing you're hanging out with the guy who hates her. *You* don't hate her now too, do you?" Ansel says suspiciously.

"Of course not." Why do I feel as if I'm lying to my brother? I don't hate her, I just... "But I agree — don't tell Sophia."

"Not yet, anyway," Ansel says. He drums his fingers on the edge of the rocking chair. I inhale and suddenly have to know something — an odd question, but one I feel as though I need to ask before I go trudging into the forest after witches.

"Do you miss Abigail?"

Ansel does a double take, then stares at me incredulously, as if I've struck him. "You said her name."

"Yes." I give my brother a long look, waiting for his judgment. I'm ready to say her name again, but is he? Can he understand just how much I've changed since we got to Live Oak?

"Right…wow…" He shakes off his surprise and inhales. "I…I didn't know Abigail." Her name is strange on his voice, as though it were a foreign word he doesn't quite know—but at least he said it. At least we're *both* ready to say it again. "I was seven. I know I'm supposed to miss her, but all I miss is the way things were before she was gone. When Mom and Dad were alive and things were normal."

"When we weren't the kids with the sister who disappeared."

"Exactly," he says. "When we weren't just the kids who survived some mystery attacker."

I consider once again telling him about the werewolves here, but…no. It wouldn't help. "Why do you think we survived, Ansel?"

He shrugs. "Luck? Our feet moved one step faster than hers?"

"But she and I were the exact same. She could have run faster. If I could, she could have."

"Maybe." Ansel frowns. "I don't know, then. Maybe it was fate. Maybe we were supposed to survive."

I raise my eyebrows at my brother—my practical, reasoning brother. It isn't like him to chalk something up to fate. But I realize that fate is actually the most reasonable answer. It's either that, or he has to think that her vanishing had no purpose whatsoever. Fate may sound unlikely, but it's a lot less painful than thinking your sister is gone for nothing.

"Why were we supposed to survive, then?" I muse in a whisper, as much to myself as to Ansel.

He exhales loudly, looks up at the night sky. "Maybe we're supposed to do something important. Something bigger than just survive."

"Like what? Save people?" I ask, thinking of the eight missing girls, of Naida, of the girls who have already RSVPed to this year's festival. If I save them, have I fulfilled whatever fate had in mind for me when it doomed my sister to vanish?

"Yeah, maybe so. Like Sophia."

I bite my lip. I nod. He's right, of course—it's just that I no longer think of Sophia first anymore when it comes to people I want to save.

Ansel looks relieved when we hear Sophia's feet on the stairs, climbing up to the bedrooms. He rises, knocks my hair into my face teasingly, trying to lighten the moment. "I'm going to bed. You staying out here for a while?"

Not without a gun is what I want to say, but instead I shake my head and follow him into the chocolatier. He flicks off the porch lights, and just as I'm about to turn around and shut the door, my eyes land on something by the foot of a rocking chair.

"What's this?" I ask, motioning Ansel back out. He frowns and flicks the lights on again.

"Goddamn," he says, shaking his head.

I reach down under the rocker and remove a shell, a blue and gray swirl that looks like a wave crashing into itself over and over. I turn to Ansel and hold it out.

"Oh, no," he says. "I'm not taking another one of these things inside." He takes the shell from my hand and, with the power of a former football star, hurls it into the forest. I hear it bounce into the leaves.

"'Another one'?"

"Counting the one you found, and the one she found in the middle of the night"—he probably means the night she was drunk—"this makes four since we've been here. I found one a week ago and showed it to her. She freaked out. I'll tell her about this one later, but I'm not bringing it inside again."

Seashells. They must be a piece to the puzzle of Sophia Kelly—I just don't know where they fit. "She's never explained them to you?"

"Not a word. She won't even answer when I ask about them," he says, looking at me grimly.

"There are more in the shed out back," I tell him. "Two boxes. They're all wrapped up in cloth. I wonder why won't she talk to us about them..."

"Yeah, well, if you want to try to get an answer out of her, be my guest," Ansel says, "but I've tried. Believe me. She shuts down. When the second one showed up and I tried to work it out, she wouldn't talk to me for the rest of the day."

"It doesn't make sense," I mumble, more to myself than Ansel.

"She'll tell us when she's ready," Ansel says, but he doesn't sound very convincing. I glance at the spot where the shell disappeared into the trees, another bread crumb in the mystery of Sophia.

CHAPTER TWENTY-TWO

❧

The day rockets by. No, that's a lie—the day drifts along lazily, dotted with helping Sophia fill bags and test out a chocolate fountain. Yet still, when it's dark outside and approaching midnight, I'm struck by how soon this moment has come. I peer out my window, worrying Samuel will be here early, that it'll start to rain, that he'll change his mind and I'll have to shoot another tennis ball seven times.

Strangely, I'm not worried about dying. I should be, I know I should be, but all I can think about is hunting. I feel powerful. Vengeful, almost. I won't vanish—I *can't* vanish.

At least, that's what I'm telling myself.

11:55. I rise from my bed and tie my hair back. I choose my clothes carefully—casual enough that if my brother or Sophia catches me, they'll pass for pajamas, but not so light that they'd impede my trudging through the forest.

Shoes in hand, I tiptoe out my door—earlier I complained about Luxe waking me up and got Sophia to lock him in her bedroom so he couldn't give my escape away. My heart bounces furiously in my chest as I creep past my snoring brother and down the stairs.

They don't wake. I turn the upstairs AC on so the fan drowns out any additional noise and slink under the Nietzsche quote above the front door frame.

Samuel is here. Somewhere. I can feel him, oddly enough, even though I don't see him.

"Gretchen," his voice calls out, louder than I'd have personally risked. I squint through the porch lights and finally make out his form by a tree. I hurry over to him. His eyes are sparkling in the starlight, and he looks younger than normal.

"You ready?" Samuel asks, looking into my eyes for a long time as he hands me a rifle.

"Yes," I answer immediately. I've never been so ready.

Samuel smiles and nods, then motions toward the forest. "After you, then." That's what I like about Samuel. He didn't have to ask if I'm sure. He touches my shoulder meaningfully—proudly, almost—and grins.

I step in first, and Samuel follows.

We crunch into the forest, our hushed whispers mirrored by the sounds of tree leaves sliding against one another. I have a moment of tense fear; it bubbles up in my chest and surprises me, an emotion illustrated by memories of the night Samuel saved my life.

I ignore it. We push forward.

"I'll cut back this way," Samuel whispers after we've been

walking almost a half hour. "I'll walk beside you a hundred or so yards out. I'll have a gun on you the whole time. Well, not on *you*, but on anything that comes near you. I promise."

"Right," I say.

Samuel gives me a sharp nod and long look before disappearing into the forest; I can't hear his footsteps after a few minutes. I move forward, slower now, breathing heavily to make up for the lack of Samuel's breath. The younger part of me, the scared girl, she wants to rear back up, to demand I run through the trees and out of the darkness. But she's overpowered—easily overpowered—by whomever this is that I've become. When a branch nearby cracks, I'm surprised to find I *want* it to be a witch. I want to see yellow eyes. I want to see them, then destroy them.

It's not a witch—just a raccoon, I think—something small that darts into the undergrowth. I turn around, waiting, watching.

Two hours later, I'm still waiting. I've readied my gun for a startled doe, a falling branch, even no noise at all, just my mind playing tricks on me. I flick the safety on and off, check the number of rounds, spin in circles around trees, even hum to myself. My legs are tired and I've walked through so many spiderwebs that I keep feeling invisible spiders on my arms. With a defeated sigh, I turn and walk toward where I think Samuel is.

I can see him standing, leaning against a tree. "Can we try again tomorrow?" Samuel shrugs.

I trudge closer, toward the patch of moonlight right in front of him.

"What, you're mad?" I ask when he lowers his head.

"Uh-uh," he mumbles, shaking his head. His eyes raise a little, meet mine tentatively.

His eyes are not green.

They are yellow.

I spin the rifle over my shoulder so fast that I almost miss catching it. My aim locks, everything lined up on his head. The man grins and takes a step closer. I should fire, I should kill him now, but he still looks...human, and that makes it impossible to squeeze the trigger. His hair is dark brown, but it's speckled with deadened silver and is rapidly growing into dirty fur. His teeth are grayed and pointed slightly, and his fingernails are yellow and black, diseased looking. He stretches his mouth open, and the jaw disconnects, cracks and pops, lengthening into a ragged mouth. My heart twists, stomach churns in disgust, as the world slows down.

The monster crouches, his pupils dilate wildly, and his back legs crunch and burst into fur. His teeth jut outward and erupt into long canines. My heart is stopping, the air in my chest stalling as the monster tilts his head to the side, studying me with wild, crazy eyes that are too wide for his face. I stare—I need to move, but all I can do is stare in wonder, in horror. He went from man to monster so easily, so—

The monster lunges.

The world speeds back up, flies into fast-forward. I fire.

It doesn't stop him.

The werewolf crashes into me, topples me backward. My head hits something; everything goes gray. I lose track of my senses — I can smell the rot in the wolf's fur but can't see him, can't feel his weight. I scramble, grasp at the ground with my fingers, squeeze my eyes shut and try to slow the whirring in my head. It won't be long before he bites down, before I feel his teeth. I have to —

Someone says my name, someone who sounds far away.

I gasp for breath; my vision gets clearer. Samuel is standing above me, eyes shining through the moonlight. He reaches down, hauls me to standing with rough hands.

"Talk to me, Gretchen," he says, shaking my shoulders. I'm confused — what happened? I look around, turn in circles.

"Where did he go?" I finally wheeze, coughing. I look around frantically, certain the monster will come raging from the darkness at any moment.

"What?" Samuel asks, putting a hand on my cheek to stop my frenzy.

"He jumped on me, he…" I shake my head, confused, as if my mind is moving faster than it should be.

"He's gone, Gretchen."

"You shot him?"

Samuel shakes his head, smiling. "No. You did. I was on my way; I saw you aim. You hit him just as he was lunging for you. He knocked you over, but he was shadows before you hit the ground. By the time I could have fired, he was gone."

I don't believe him. I relax my hand on my rifle, stunned. He's lying. He must have shot the wolf. I didn't even think I hit him. I search Samuel's eyes for the lie, for the truth, but all I see is sparkling, nodding.

"I killed him?" I whisper.

"*You* alone," Samuel finishes firmly.

And then it hits me. I grin, I laugh, I shout all at once, and a feeling of warm freedom sweeps through me. I don't need to be afraid, not anymore. My mind swirls. I'm *happy*. I'm happy.

I'm free.

I shake my head as my heart pounds in excitement. "I . . ." I don't even know what to say to Samuel, how to tell him what he's given me. "Thank you, Samuel. I mean, it sounds stupid and like it's not enough, but thank you."

Samuel's grin softens a little, becomes proud instead of ecstatic. "You're welcome, Gretchen," he says quietly, and I suddenly realize his hands are back on my shoulders, as though we're dancing.

And then it's silent—nearly so, anyhow. The woods fall still, with just the occasional swirling of fireflies and croak of a tree frog.

"I . . ." Samuel looks down. One of his hands slides off my shoulder, down my arm, then brushes along my fingertips just long enough that I could have ignored the touch if I'd wanted to. But something happens, as if my body made the decision before my mind could reconsider; I turn my hand over and entwine my fingers with Samuel's. Our eyes simultaneously move from our interlocked hands to each other's gaze. A cloud drifts in front of the moon, making everything darker, Samuel and I mere silhouettes in the night.

"No one likes me," Samuel says quickly, warningly.

"They all think I'm crazy. And I'm, well...I'm not easy to get along with."

I raise an eyebrow. "You're not that bad," I say, though it isn't until the words are leaving my mouth that I realize I'm whispering. "Once someone learns how to ignore half of what you say." Somehow his doubt gives me power, and I take a small step forward.

Samuel exhales and looks down—when he looks back up, I can just barely make out his bright green eyes in the blackness. He takes a tiny step toward me and then lets the hand still resting on my shoulder drift down to my lower back.

"Promise you won't ever hate me," he murmurs, so softly that I almost miss it. "I can't have you hate me too."

"I could never hate you," I say back, breath trembling in my lungs from a strange new longing, strange new desire for Samuel to pull me closer. "Believe me, I've tried."

My body kicks in, does what my heart wants, long before Samuel has the opportunity. I grab Samuel's arm and pull myself toward him.

Samuel releases my hand and brings his palm to cradle my cheek, and then the scent of bright leaves is all around me. When our lips meet, the scent swallows me, everything blurs, and I'm certain there's nothing to fear in this forest. There's nothing else here—no witches, no mysteries, nothing but Samuel and me.

CHAPTER TWENTY-THREE

illing a werewolf is no small task. You'd think I would remember every last moment—the scent, the feeling, the sight of a monster leaping toward me. But that's all blurred in my mind, overpowered by the sensation of kissing Samuel. I remember every moment of *that*—every sensation, every time he touched my skin, every time I took a breath and my lungs were filled with the scent of leaves and sandalwood.

We kissed in the forest—I can't remember if it was for hours or minutes. I locked my hand in his as we walked back to the street and didn't want to let go when he dropped me off at the chocolatier. Part of me thinks it's a mistake—that he's just confused. When I wake Wednesday morning, I spend a few moments trying to convince myself that I'd just invented the entire evening.

No. No, I don't have that good of an imagination.

Besides, if I try very hard, I swear I can still feel his arms around me. I couldn't have made that up. I rise and pull on shorts, then look for my brush to pull my hair into a ponytail. I desperately need a shower. But I'm hungry, way too hungry to wait on food. Wonder if it was the kiss or the hunting that left me famished?

"Morning, sleepyhead," Sophia says with a grin as I make it downstairs to the chocolatier storefront. She's fully dressed and holding a clipboard, doing inventory. I glance at the clock above the register—it's noon. My eyes race to the RSVP board by default. Six new ones. Seventeen altogether.

How many of those seventeen will vanish this year?

"Wow," I mumble, turning away from the cards. "Talk about oversleeping. Guess I was tired."

"No worries," she answers. She's particularly bouncy today, long waves of hair framing her heart-shaped face like a picture.

"You're in a good mood," I note with a grin.

"It's been a good morning," she says, nodding. Her cheeks flush pink and I groan.

"Ew—is this a story about my brother?"

"No!" Sophia objects, laughing loudly. "Well, not like that. I mean, I'm mostly happy because I got six more RSVPs to the festival. But Ansel...um..."

"Tell me," I say, letting my head fall backward. "Just leave out the squickable details."

"It's not that bad," Sophia assures me. She's bubbling over with the desire to tell me—I can see it from here, even through morning bleariness. "We just had a really nice night. There was some kissing. That's all. See? Not squickable at all."

I know I should recoil over what exactly "a nice night" might entail, but seeing as how I was kissing Samuel just last night, I find myself smiling. "Fine, fine, that's not so bad," I admit. I'm not sure if I'd be so cavalier, though, if my head wasn't swimming with the memory of how tightly Samuel had held me.

"You're still okay with it?" she asks, and I can tell that if I said no, she would break my brother's heart. The trouble is, I *want* to say no—but not because I don't want them to be happy. Because I don't trust her, and I know my brother does.

I nod, looking away. "Sure, it's fine."

Sophia grins and grabs a Coke from the refrigerator. "Are you going on another walk today, by chance?"

"No, why?"

"Well . . . I have to look for the festival tablecloths. They're somewhere in the attic. With the mice," Sophia says, wrinkling her nose.

"And you want help?" I ask knowingly. Sophia nods. "Okay, okay, but let's do it now, while I'm too tired to know what I'm getting myself into."

"Deal," she says. She motions for me to follow her upstairs, where she tugs down a ladder from the ceiling. Heat rushes out like a wave.

"I'm having second thoughts," I tease as we climb. Sophia

starts to laugh but instead coughs violently as a tornado of dust swoops around us.

"Okay, they're near the door somewhere, I'm sure. I wouldn't have hidden them—I use them every year..."

"Why not just keep it all in one spot?" I grasp either side of the hole in the ceiling and yank myself upward, into the attic.

"Things after the festival are hectic. I always end up throwing stuff around," she says thoughtfully, then takes a few steps away from me. I narrow my eyes and look around the dark attic, shrouded in golden light from a tiny arched window at one end. There are boxes everywhere, clothes racks covered in dry-cleaner bags with formal dresses and suits inside them. Piles of books, mostly candy related, trunks and old side tables and a laundry basket full of shoes. Sophia shuffles behind a stack of boxes taller than she is.

"Just look around. They aren't in anything, I'm sure... probably just on top of something," she calls out.

"Right," I murmur, and carefully step across the plywood floor toward the opposite corner of the attic. More trunks, old desk supplies, an ancient television... There's a stack of what looks like fabric on top of another laundry basket, this one filled with newspapers. I drop to my knees and grab the fabric. No good—baby blankets. The top one has Sophia's name embroidered on it; it's pale violet and well worn, with frayed hems. I glance over my shoulder cautiously before moving on to the second blanket in the stack. Not terribly surprisingly, it reads *Naida,* pink embroidery on a graying blanket that I think was originally yellow. I flip the top layer back, to the third blanket in the stack.

Lorelei.

I do a double take and pull the blanket out; it unfurls like a flag across my lap. It's brand-new, a sunny yellow with perfect creases, as though it hasn't been unfolded in ages. Lorelei Kelly...I fold the blanket up quickly and set it back underneath the other two.

"Any luck?" Sophia asks from the other side of the attic.

"No, not yet," I answer, scanning the room. There has to be something else here to tell me who the mystery sister is. I dash to a bookcase that's full of photo albums. On the top shelf are pale pink baby books with names on the spine—Naida, Sophia. No Lorelei—but I do see the tablecloths on a chair in the corner. I grab them, but as I do so, I unclasp the chain of my necklace and let it slide down my shirt to the floor.

"Got them!" I say triumphantly.

"Awesome!" Sophia answers. She emerges from the other side of the attic. "I've got to stop putting stuff up here." I hand her the pile of tablecloths and we head for the ladder, slipping out of the thick heat and into the cool upstairs.

"Can you get the stairs?" Sophia asks as she balances the fabric against her.

"Sure—wait," I say, and bring my hand to my chest. "My necklace...I was wearing it this morning..."

"Did it fall off?" Sophia asks, glancing around at the floor.

"I guess so — hang on, I'll go see if it fell off up there," I say with a shrug, and before Sophia can object, I head back up the steps.

"'Kay — I'll take these downstairs, then come help you look," Sophia says, and I hear her feet on the steps. I fly across the attic floor, snatch the necklace up, and halt in front of the bookshelf. Lorelei has a blanket — she must have a baby book up here somewhere... but no, everything other than Sophia's and Naida's books are outdated encyclopedias or ancient copies of *National Geographic*. I turn in circles, scanning the attic for any sign of her, listening carefully for Sophia's feet on the ladder. Frustrated, I yank Sophia's baby book off the shelf. Pictures, ultrasounds, hospital bracelets, stickers. No Lorelei.

Naida's book is crisper, used less. It's mostly the same, just with fewer smiles and laughs noted — being the second child means there's less thrill in a baby's first smile, I imagine. I flip to the front, to the ultrasound picture.

An ultrasound picture that doesn't look entirely unlike the one in Abigail's baby book back in Washington, before it was hidden away with everything else of hers.

Medical typography is fading across the top, but I can still make out the faint gray dot matrix letters. *14 weeks.*

Baby A. And beside her, *Baby B.* Naida was a twin.

I hear Sophia's feet on the landing. I turn the page quickly. Only one hospital bracelet, only one photocopied birth certificate. Only one baby in the photo of Mrs. Kelly holding her newborn. Naida's sister had vanished before she was even born.

I swallow hard. Another missing sister, another girl hidden away in Sophia's house. Girls who have vanished tucked under beds or hidden in attics. I feel shaky, as if I might collapse under the weight of the mystery, of the lies, of the secrets.

Why, Sophia?

"Did you find it?" Sophia's voice calls up. I inhale sharply and thrust the book back onto the shelf.

"Yeah," I answer. I swallow hard again. "Yeah, I've got it. I'm coming down."

I make my way to the landing and lower myself; Sophia closes the attic, sealing up her family's secrets once again. She turns to go back downstairs but finds my eyes.

"You okay, Gretchen? You look sick."

"Just the heat, I think," I say, shaking my head. "I'm gonna go lie down."

Sophia frowns. "I'm sorry, I shouldn't have made you go into the attic of hell. I'll get you something to drink and some crackers, okay?"

"Sure," I say, nodding, then turn and head to my room. No, Naida and Sophia's room. What was supposed to be Lorelei's room as well.

You and Naida are mirror images. The twin who survived, the one who didn't vanish — at least, didn't vanish for a little while.

You share the same destiny.

CHAPTER TWENTY-FOUR

It's cat-washing day, the only upside being that I'll have a chance to tell Samuel about Lorelei. And a chance to see Samuel for the first time since we kissed. It's been a week—a very long week—but with all the festival preparations, I haven't been able to get away inconspicuously.

Samuel zips up on his motorcycle and pauses for me to get on. I swing onto the back of his bike and am not afraid to hold on this time—but not only because I want to be near him; feeling the grind of the motorcycle and the rhythm of his breath is grounding. I hide my face against his shoulders till I feel like Gretchen, not like a reborn Naida.

When we get to Ms. Judy's, Samuel lets me off and steps away from me.

"Something's wrong," he says firmly.

"Yes," I answer.

"If you want..." He pauses and plays with the motorcycle's headlight for a moment. "We can pretend it never happened."

"What? No! No, not that," I say, and take his hand. It makes my heart jump nervously, excitedly, and when Samuel's fingers tighten around mine, I sigh and take a step closer to him. "Naida had a twin sister. Lorelei. She died before she was born."

"Before she was born? So you think she has something to do with Naida being the first?" he asks, eyebrow raised.

"I don't know, really, but it does mean Naida and I are even more alike than I thought. We both had twin sisters who vanished. That has to mean something, right?"

Samuel shakes his head. "Maybe. Look, have you thought about leaving the Kelly place? Maybe staying at a hotel or something? You can stay with me — hell, Ansel can even stay with me —"

"No," I say quickly, so quickly that I feel a little bad. "Ansel wouldn't leave her. And... I want to understand. I can't leave until I understand."

Samuel sighs just as Noodles springs out from behind the hydrangeas, looking particularly surly.

"Why am I more afraid of bathing that cat than hunting Fenris?" Samuel muses, shaking his head.

I smile and carefully — a little nervously — rest my head on his shoulder; he responds by turning toward me slightly, pulling me against his chest gently. He kisses the top of my head, as though we've been doing this far longer than we have. I've got nothing to base it on, but I get the feeling it isn't always this easy, this fast. My nerves slip away, are replaced with a glowing feeling.

"You catch the cat, I'll get some water," he says.

"How about the other way around?" I ask, looking at Noodles warily, but Samuel is already hurrying away from Noodles and me.

Samuel walks to the side of the house and fills a giant silver tub with water while I spend as much time as possible gathering the towel and bottle of No More Tears shampoo Ms. Judy left out for us. Samuel heaves the tub of water into the backyard and gives me a pitying look as I throw the towel on top of Noodles. I scoop the cat up before she realizes what's happening, but Noodles is still pretty quick on the draw—by the time I've heaved her over to where Samuel is standing, she's started yowling and I'm pretty sure were she not in a towel, my eyes would be clawed out.

"So, if you can hold her head down, I'll do the soap," Samuel offers.

"Deal," I say eagerly. "I'll drop her in. One...two...three."

Noodles barely hits the water before she takes off running. She finds shelter underneath Samuel's house—he crawls in after her and grabs her by the scruff of her neck, both of them emerging filthier than before, though only Samuel is bleeding. By the time we actually get her into the water, she's too exhausted to fight anymore. I still have to pin her down, but her new philosophy of "just wait to bite them when it's over" means her claws are no longer out and ready.

Fifteen minutes later, I grab for the towel that's already

covered in cat fur, but the cat has no interest in being dried. She leaps over my shoulder and bounds away, finally stopping at the porch to give us a hateful look and lick her paw.

"Done. I never want to be in Ms. Judy's debt again," Samuel says, tipping the basin of suds, water, and fur into the grass. He glances at the cut on my arm. "She got you good."

"No joke. I need to clean it," I say. "And," I continue, pointing to the cut on the side of his forehead, "you need to clean that."

Samuel leads me through the orchard to his house. The sky is a strange shade of gray now; sunlight still makes it to the ground, but the wind is picking up. Samuel leaves the door open so the cool air can come in before the inevitable downpour starts.

"Here," he says, handing me a bottle of peroxide and a pack of Band-Aids that look as if they were made in the early nineties. "I'm going to jump in the shower, okay?"

"Sure." I grab a paper towel from the kitchen, then sit down in the doorway, watching the wind whip leaves off the peach trees and cause the Confederate flag on Ms. Judy's porch to snap and pop. I tilt the peroxide onto the towel and grimace as I place it on my arm and the slow sting sets in. There's a howl in the distance that makes me jump—no, just a dog. But still, my eyes wander to the forest behind the orchard. That's where they are, watching, waiting for the festival…

"You okay?" Samuel asks, walking back into the room. Lightning cracks, a bright branch of light in the dark clouds. I rise and Samuel shuts the door, though the sound of rushing wind seeps in through the house's floors and walls.

"Yeah," I finally answer him. "I was just thinking about the festival. Sophia gave me one of Naida's old dresses to wear to it."

"You've got to be kidding. That's sick," Samuel says.

"I know. She won't tell me anything—I've asked her why she keeps throwing the festival, given her the chance to tell me about Naida...nothing. I don't know how to stop more girls from disappearing, short of hunting and killing all the werewolves we can in the next two days—the festival is *this Friday,* Samuel. How am I supposed to keep girls from vanishing if I can't even figure out why some girls at the festival disappear and others don't?"

"I don't know," Samuel says. "But you didn't know that when you killed the werewolf the other night either. Does it really matter?" The rain begins, ramming against the house's tin roof like a thousand tiny rocks; the house darkens from the storm, casting Samuel and me in blue-tinted light. We sit together on his bed.

I sigh. "Just to me. I just want to know why I'm still here."

"Because a crazy old woman made us wash her cat," Samuel says, crossing his arms.

I reach forward to playfully shove him, but instead my hand stays firmly on his chest. I can feel his heart beneath my palm, the beat quickening as my hand lingers. My fingertips slide up, to his neck, the side of his face, as though someone else is moving my body, some girl driven by desire and want and need. Samuel's eyes drift shut and he inhales.

The sound rushes me back into my own body—I pull my

hand away and try to hide the blush that's blossoming across my cheeks.

"Sorry," I mutter.

"Don't be," he answers, and I note that the tips of his ears are red.

"Um...I need to get back," I say quickly.

"Right, of course," Samuel agrees too fast. He rises. "Only...it's still raining. Give it another fifteen minutes— it'll be over."

"Oh. Right," I mumble stupidly. Samuel sits back down beside me, this time a few feet away. I want to kiss him, but clearly I have no self-control. *Come on, Gretchen, think of something else to say or do or anything—*

"Seashells!" I exclaim loudly. *Way to go,* I groan at myself. I don't even know if seashells are relevant to all this, but I had to say *something.*

"Seashells?" Samuel says, confused.

"I meant to tell you. Sophia gets these seashells. They show up on her porch and we don't know who brings them, and she's got boxes of them in the shed out back. You think it has something to do with the wolves?"

"Fenris don't deal in seashells."

"She freaks out when she gets them. It's like they're more than just seashells. I just don't understand how they fit."

"Live Oak is close to the beach. Could just be customers," he poses, clearly eager to have something to discuss. "Or it could just be Kelly finally cracking over guilt. People get crazy when they feel guilty."

"Always more questions," I say. "Maybe if I wait this one out, the answer will be in Sophia's attic again. It was almost easier when I was just scared of witches. The witch could have been anything, but with the wolves, there are...rules, and facts, and details and...I didn't know *anything* before."

"You want to go back to that?" Samuel asks with a grin.

"No," I answer with a small laugh. "Not for the world."

The rain stops, gradually fading from a downpour to a few scattered droplets. There's a rainbow outside, a faint streak of colors across the sky in front of the dark clouds. I climb onto the back of Samuel's motorcycle, biting my lips as I circle my arms around him tightly—the feelings rush back, the longing for there not to be three layers of fabric between us...

"Tomorrow night?" Samuel asks when we stop twenty yards down from the chocolatier—out of sight of the front porch.

"What?" I ask, startled—my mind was still on each thread, each seam, that divided us.

"Tomorrow night," he repeats as I get off the bike. "We can go hunting again. If your death wish continues. Besides, the festival is the day after tomorrow, right? We don't really have another chance."

"Okay," I say. Samuel gives me a quick smile, then drives away.

Two days to the festival. One night to hunt.

And then we're out of chances.

CHAPTER TWENTY-FIVE

When I come downstairs the next morning, there's a glaring, obvious absence. The RSVP cards are gone, leaving an empty corkboard and rows of thumbtacks. I hear laughter outside and run to the screen door to see Ansel and Sophia sitting in the bench swing. Sophia is crying and grinning at once, with the thick stack of RSVP cards in her lap and my brother's arm around her shoulders.

"What's wrong?" I ask, padding through the dew to where they sit. I lean on one of the fence posts, trying to figure out if Sophia is happy or miserable.

"Oh," Sophia sniffs, trying to pull herself together. "Sorry, Gretchen. I got the last of the RSVPs in. Just in time—twenty-three people are coming. I'm...happy," she lies. Even my brother knows it's a lie—he catches my gaze for a long time, shakes his head uncertainly. That said, there's something like relief hiding in Sophia's eyes. I take a step closer.

"Are you sure, Sophia? You're sure you're okay?" *Please, Sophia, just tell me about Naida. About why you throw the party. Tell me the truth. Let me help you.*

Sophia laughs, though it sounds a little more as if she's choking. "Really, I'm okay. I'll be okay." She lifts a glass of orange juice up. "I made mimosas to celebrate. I won't tell Ricky if you have one," she says with a watery wink.

"I'm good," I answer, though I notice Ansel is sipping on one.

"I'm going to go ahead and make the fudge and gingerbread today," Sophia says thoughtfully, wiping her eyes with her hand. "That means I'll just have the cakes to do tomorrow. Oh yeah, and I need to do the name tags. Will you help me, Ansel?"

Sophia rises, thumbing through her RSVPs, and slips inside; Luxe follows, happily trying to weave between her legs. My brother sighs and looks to the sky, slowly standing.

"Did she tell you what's really going on?" I ask him quietly.

Ansel frowns. "Kind of, but it didn't make sense."

"What do you mean?"

"She started crying because she says I'm going to leave after the festival. I told her I wouldn't—I promised I wouldn't—but she insists I won't want to stay. Said I wouldn't stay for her the way I'd stay for you."

"What about me?" I ask, remembering Naida's red dress, folded up in my dresser upstairs. "Did she think I'd leave too?"

Ansel nods. "She said she'd miss you. I don't get it. I just want this thing to be over. After this festival, Gretchen, we've got to get out of here. You know that, right?"

"Right," I say, though my voice isn't confident. "With Sophia?"

"Yes." Ansel shoves his hands into his pockets. "I don't know how, but we've got to convince her. And if Samuel Reynolds wants to come too, that's fine—we've just got to get out of this place. Sophia is..." But he doesn't seem to know what Sophia is.

I do: Sophia is lying.

"What if we can't save her, Ansel?" I ask quietly. "What if we can't save her either?"

His eyes flit to mine. They look wounded. "We've got to try, Gretchen. We can't just leave her out here."

Not like we did to Abigail is the phrase I know lingers in both of our minds.

"Of course not," I say, because I can't stand the look on my brother's face—the look of worry, of concern, for someone else that he wore so often in Washington, when the concern was for me. I had thought that look was gone for good. I hate to see it again. "We'll help her, Ansel. I promise."

I am not sure if I'm lying or not.

CHAPTER TWENTY-SIX

I slump down onto one of the asphalt hills, the conversation with my brother from earlier in the day still roaming my mind. *Saving Sophia. The way we couldn't save Abigail from the witch.* I turn to look at Samuel, who's staring up at the sky beside me. The old drive-in is already almost engulfed in darkness; I wonder if this is around the time movies started, back when this place was open. I wish I'd been here. I wish I'd known Live Oak before it was full of For Sale signs and monsters.

"It's still not the werewolves I'm most scared of," I say quietly. "It's not knowing what will happen. Not understanding what Sophia will do tomorrow night at the festival. I thought everything would be fine once I knew what the witch was, but there are so many other mysteries now."

"You can't save everyone." Samuel's words are so blunt that they surprise me, so opposite of my brother's mentality that they feel foreign. He sighs and shakes his head. "I've been trying to save the girls in Live Oak for two years. Sooner or later, you have to realize—you can't save them all."

"Then how do you choose?" I ask, afraid of the answer.

"Where the wolves are concerned," Samuel says, inhaling, "you don't really get a choice. It's whomever you get to first."

Maybe *that's* what really happened in the forest twelve years ago. Maybe the witch just got to Abigail first. Maybe it's just that easy, just that stupid, how people live or die. I nod at Samuel but look away, embarrassed at the tears that are building in my eyes. He takes interest in a bunch of clover bursting through the loose pavement while I gather myself together.

"You ready?" he says as the sun fully disappears behind the trees and the dilapidated movie screens.

"Yeah," I say through a deep breath out. "One night to kill as many monsters as possible."

"Don't think about that," Samuel says sternly. "The minute you start thinking of it that way, you'll lose your focus. I don't want to go hunting with you if you aren't focused. I swear to god, I'll never forgive you if you shoot me in the leg."

"What about the arm, then?" I tease as he helps me to my feet.

"As long as I get a free shot at yours," he answers. He points to one of the old screens. "So here's what I'm thinking—what if you stay here, and I climb up on that for a better vantage point."

"Are werewolves going to come out here? Without the trees nearby?"

"I think so," Samuel says, walking away backward. "And I'll have a clear shot, just in case you need help. Between the two of us we can't lose. You just stay still and ..."

"Look tempting?" I finish his sentence.

"Something like that," he says, tripping a little over one of the hills. He slings his rifle over his shoulder and grabs hold of a thin, rusted ladder that leads up behind the screen — for a moment I'm pretty certain I'll have to haul him out of the debris when the whole thing buckles beneath him. But it seems stable enough once he's reached the top, standing on a platform that runs the length of the screen. He knocks a piece of the screen out so he can aim and sticks his rifle through it.

"Move backward," he calls down quietly. I obey, backing up till I'm at the top of one of the hills.

"You're going to be able to hit one from there?" I say doubtfully, looking at the space between us.

"You don't trust me?" he asks, grinning — I can just make out the sparkle in his eyes and the white of his teeth in the dark.

"I'll never forgive you if you shoot *me* in the leg," I tell him firmly.

"Yeah, yeah. Now be quiet." I'm about to remind him that he's the one who started talking but instead just scowl at him and bend to run my hands over the moss poking through the broken asphalt. A few moments go by; Samuel vanishes entirely in the darkness. Fireflies arrive, glowing bright green. I catch them, watch them blink in my hands, then let them fly away.

"You need to make more noise," he calls quietly from above.

I stomp around, brush my feet across the pavement, kick a few rocks.

"More noise that makes it's obvious you're a girl, not a wild boar," he says.

"Are you calling me a wild boar?" I hiss.

"Sing or something."

"I don't sing."

"Then you don't kill wolves. Sing," he whispers, but he can't hide the hints of humor in his voice. I catch the cocky grin on his face in the moonlight and glare.

I meant it when I said I don't sing, but I bitterly hum, quietly at first until Samuel waves his arms, indicating I should get louder. I show him my middle finger but oblige, and finally my lips form words.

"In the Big Rock Candy Mountain, there's a land that's fair and bright." I sing in a half whisper. Something moves in the forest that surrounds us—something small, a bird, maybe, or a raccoon.

"I haven't heard this song in years—I don't suppose you can play guitar too?" Samuel asks.

"Shut up—I'm attracting werewolves," I snap back. *"Oh the birds and the bees and the lollipop trees..."*

I make it through the song twice, then peer into the trees. This may be the stupidest thing I've ever done. I hum another verse, letting a few words slip through my lips. I'm about to tell Samuel his idea was moronic when there's a sharp crack. I hear Samuel shift and know his gun is aimed, waiting for something to spring from the woods. I don't raise my own, not yet.

"*Where the rain don't fall and the wind don't blow...*" I whisper, urging my voice to get louder. The fireflies are scattering—soon they're far from me, leaving me on a lake of black pavement alone.

Don't give up now. Don't be afraid.

"*I'm going to stay where you sleep all day*—" A stick pops in the trees, something moving fast. I whirl around, gun raised.

Just in time.

The wolf glares at me from the edge of the tree line, the opposite end of the drive-in from Samuel, hatred and hunger radiating from his golden eyes. He's dishwater gray, with greenish teeth. He hunches down, prepared to leap—but I'm prepared to shoot. I breathe slowly, carefully. One shot. *Don't shake, Gretchen.*

Think of what's at stake.

My mind flashes through the eight girls, Naida, and Sophia, and I tighten my finger on the trigger. The monster growls, a hisslike noise. He springs forward. Fast. I fire.

He crashes into my knees, which buckle beneath me. I careen onto pavement, skinning my elbows and shins. A gun sounds out, not mine, but it doesn't stop the monster. The werewolf pins my arms by my side and lowers his head toward mine. Blood from a bullet wound on his shoulder spouts like a grotesque fountain. It splatters onto my neck and rinses over the werewolf's canines. Another shot, one that ricochets off the ground beside me, and suddenly it feels as though my upper arm is on fire. My gun is pinned beneath me, its corners cutting into my back as the monster presses against me, heaving. A third shot. I squeeze my eyes shut, fighting to inhale.

Then the wolf is gone.

I cough and gasp when he becomes shadows, lungs burning, staring at the sky. The scent of the monster is thick in the air and sticks to the sides of my throat. There are footsteps running toward me, but I'm too busy trying not to faint to focus on them. I reach up and gingerly wipe at the wolf's blood on my neck, then stare at my fingers. It was so close to me, so close to killing me.

Hands are on my back, on my arms; Samuel is on his knees beside me. He hauls me to sitting, leaning my body against his for support. The fireflies move in, sparkling around us as I catch my breath and the world stops spinning.

"Are you hurt? Let me see your arm," he says, pulling my arm to his face to see in the darkness. It's bleeding and burns when he touches the skin around the line-shaped cut. I shake my head, cringe as the sting from the scrapes on my elbows sets in.

"Sorry," I say as I strain to breathe normally. He brushes my hair from my face roughly. "I couldn't shoot him in time."

"It's fine. Come on," he says. "You can walk, right? I can't believe I hit you."

"Yeah, what—did you *shoot* me?" I ask in surprise, looking at my arm. The line-shaped cut makes sense now, the fire I felt on my arm.

"It just grazed you. I couldn't get a decent aim on the second shot. I thought I'd be able to kill the wolf long before he got to you, but the next thing I knew, he was on you..."

"So you shot me?" I ask, alarmed.

"I have excellent aim."

"What if this had been my head!" I say, pointing to the mark. It oozes blood slowly in response.

"Then you wouldn't be yelling at me," Samuel says. "Come on. Movie screen wolf hunting doesn't work, apparently."

"No kidding." I rub the bruise that's forming on my chest from the monster's weight.

"Be ready to shoot, in case there are more," Samuel says. I tug the rifle over my shoulder, check the safety, and take a step.

To my surprise, instead of broken concrete, my foot rolls over something smooth and hard. I raise an eyebrow and lean down to pull whatever it is off the dark ground.

My hand comes up with a perfect peach-colored seashell.

CHAPTER TWENTY-SEVEN

shell?" Samuel asks quietly.

"They...the werewolves are the ones bringing them," I say in shock. "No, it doesn't make any sense. Witches don't deal in seashells."

"Clearly they do," Samuel says, but seems as amazed as I am. "You said there are more—how many?"

"I think this is twelve," I say after I count in my head. "But in the shed, there are more." I inhale as I realize what this means, as everything slides into place in my head. When I speak again, my voice shakes. "She knows about them, Samuel. She knows about the wolves, and she's never said anything." I can't breathe, as though the wolf is on top of me, pressing down on my lungs all over again.

"Maybe it's a warning. Maybe she's marked," Samuel says, eyes wandering through the circle of trees around us. "Come on. Let's get out of here." We begin to walk quickly, whispering to each other as we hurry down the drive toward his bike.

"Why mark her? Why not just kill her? Did Layla and everyone else get shells?" If she really is marked, how much danger is she in? I speed up, worried.

"Layla never got shells," Samuel says quickly. "I've never heard of this until now."

"So . . . Sophia is special too, somehow, that they'd mark her?" I mutter as we emerge on the street. My mind is racing, too full of ideas to think clearly.

"How many shells are in the shed?" Samuel asks.

"Um . . . eight. Three in one box and five in another."

Samuel freezes. I slowly turn to look at him, confused.

But his eyes say everything, explain far more than words could.

"Three, five. Three girls the first year, five the second year," I say breathlessly. Samuel's jaw tightens, but he nods.

"Twelve this year," I murmur. "Including this one. That's why she panics when she gets them."

"We've got to stop the festival," Samuel says firmly.

Samuel yanks the bike off the ground and I jump on, grab his waist tightly. I rehearse what I'll say to her, what I'll tell her. I can do this, I tell myself. I can make things right. I can save us. I can stop the first sign of Live Oak's end days.

We roar into the night, past the point where he normally drops me off. The chocolatier appears ahead, glowing like the stars above. He slows as we near it, then stops by the mailbox. I swing my legs off and turn to face Samuel.

"Let me talk to her. She won't listen to you."

Samuel nods curtly. "Want me to wait?"

I pause for a heartbeat. "No. No, it'll be fine. I'll tell her, and then...she'll listen. I—"

"You know where to find me if you need me," Samuel cuts me off.

I kiss him, and he wraps an arm around my waist and pulls me against him, letting his other hand wander through my hair. I grab his shoulders and hold them tightly, kiss him back as though I'm drowning and he is air. He releases me but watches as I run down the chocolatier's drive and up the steps.

I fling open the door and hit the stairs just as I hear Samuel's motorcycle rev up. Luxe bounds out of my room to meet me at the upstairs door, panting as though he thinks I've woken up merely to play with him. I brush past him and dive onto the couch where my brother is sleeping.

My arms hit pillows that squish beneath my weight. I toss the pillows aside from where they're carefully tucked under the blankets. He isn't here. He has to be here—he has to get out. I leap back to my feet and run to Sophia's room, flinging open the door.

"Sophia!" I shout. She shoots up in her bed, hair frazzled, eyes wide.

"What, Gretchen? What is it?" she asks frantically. I'm about to answer when I see movement beside her in the bed. Sheets move, swirl, and finally, my brother's head emerges.

"What are you doing?" he asks, cheeks flushing. "I thought you went to bed early."

There are a lot of things I want to say about finding my brother sleeping in Sophia's bed—I want to admonish him for hiding it from me via pillows on the couch, I want to demand to know why they were keeping this level of a relationship from me—the level where being in bed together no longer means they're simply having sex, but that they want to just *sleep* side by side.

No time. Besides, you didn't tell them about Samuel.

"Sophia," I repeat, still breathing heavily.

"Gretchen? Are you okay?" she asks, eyes flitting from Ansel back to me. Sophia kicks her blankets aside and hurries toward me in a camisole. I reach forward and grasp her hands.

"Sophia, listen," I plead, searching her eyes for something, though I'm not sure what. "The shells. I know about them. Three girls the first year, then five, and this year. Sophia—you can't go through with the festival."

Sophia's face changes so quickly that it's almost like magic—from careful understanding to wide-eyed, sweating fear. She shakes her head, and her fingertips tremble in my hands. She yanks her palms from mine and turns sharply to go back to her bed, where my brother sits, looking bleary and confused.

"What? What are you talking about?" she demands. Sophia struggles to find the edge of the sheets, struggles to avoid my eyes, struggles for every breath.

"Sophia, you know it's true. That's why you're scared of the shells — you know what they mean. The witches — I mean, the werewolves — they're leaving them to scare you —"

"What?" Ansel interrupts, voice icy.

I turn to my brother in desperation. "Ansel, the witch, the witch that chased us and took Abigail, it was real — it was a werewolf, a Fenris. And now there are more of them here. I'm sorry I didn't tell you. I didn't want to ruin it for you — I wanted us both to be free. But they're here, and they're trying to scare Sophia by leaving the shells. I shot one in the forest —"

"The witch... what?" Ansel asks, shaking his head. He thinks I'm crazy, thinks I'm cracking somehow, drunk, maybe. I take a deep breath, try to slow my racing thoughts.

"There are three shells in the shed from the first year. Five from the second. Eleven this year." In my mind I wonder what would have happened if we hadn't shot that wolf tonight. Would twelve girls be marked? I continue aloud. "Sophia, you have to cancel."

"No, don't be silly," Sophia says, voice shrill. "They're just shells."

"They're more than that and you know it!"

"Gretchen, why don't we go downstairs? You can get something to drink and some candy —"

"I know you're scared, Sophia," I cut her off. "But we can leave, if that's what you want. We'll pack up Ansel's Jeep right now and we can leave, pick up Samuel — the four of us can go anywhere you want. We won't let any more girls disappear. But you have to stop the festival. You have to cancel it."

Sophia is shaking now, so hard that she looks as though she's freezing in the midsummer heat. She shakes her head and tears erupt in her eyes, spilling down her cheeks. "No, no, I can't..."

I don't know what to say. I look desperately to Ansel, who looks as if he's certain this is a dream—that after all this time, there's no way I'm pulling the witch into our lives again. Sophia shakes, mumbles. I can't understand what she's saying, only that it means no.

No, she won't cancel the festival even if it costs eleven more girls.

"You really are the first sign of Live Oak's end days," I whisper aloud. "Why, Sophia? Why?"

She has no answer, only more tears. Ansel wraps her in his arms, strokes her hair, tries to comfort her.

"I'm not staying here," I tell him. "I'm not helping her do this, knowing—"

"No! Gretchen, please!" Sophia's words explode from her mouth. "You have to stay. Please, just through the festival." There is so much desperation in her voice that Ansel releases her and leans back. Her eyes are wide, crazed; her lips tremble, and she chokes on each breath. "I'll do anything, Gretchen, please!"

"Why?" I ask breathlessly. Sophia gets out of bed, falling to the ground at my feet and grabbing my hands, sobbing with every breath. My chest tightens. I feel tears building that don't make it to my eyes.

Her words are watery and forced. "We'll do what you said after that—we'll leave. You and me and Ansel, we'll all leave. Just wait, please wait, till after the festival—"

"Why?" I ask again, more forcefully this time. She stares at me through fountains of tears but doesn't answer. "Why, Sophia?" My voice grows angrier, frustration breaking through. "Why do you keep doing this if Naida disappeared too? And if you know girls will vanish? You said you'd do anything—just *tell me why!*"

Sophia crumples forward, heaving, like a drowning girl. She curls into a ball on the floor, and I can't understand her words, can't understand what she's trying to tell me, can't understand anything except that she isn't telling me why. I want to love her, I want her to be the patron saint of candy, but I just...

Can't.

"Gretchen," Ansel says softly, gently, words barely heard over Sophia's moans. "Go stay with Samuel till after the festival."

"Come with me."

"I can't...I can't leave her like this," he answers, and drops down beside Sophia. She collapses against his body, mumbling, murmuring pleas for me to stay. He holds her tightly, and I think he might be the only thing keeping her from falling apart entirely. Her rock. She has never looked so breakable.

Of course he can't leave her. He loves her.

"I'll watch out for the girls at the festival and make sure nothing...happens. And when it's over, we'll..." He looks from Sophia to me, swallows hard. "We'll sort all this out. You and I will. Just us."

"Ansel—"

"Gretchen, please. She can't handle this." He reaches into the pocket of his pair of jeans on the floor, grabs his keys; he tosses them to me so swiftly that I barely catch them. "Take my car and go."

I exhale. Nod. Turn sharply, unsure what else I can do. I feel as though this is a dream—someone else is running my body; this isn't really happening.

"Gretchen?" Ansel calls after me. I don't mean to, but I see Sophia's eyes. She still wants me to stay, so badly that she doesn't even seem able to form the words to beg me again. Ansel continues, and his voice sounds the way it used to, back when he was my only rock. Serious, protective, soft. "Gretchen, listen to me. Just in case this is all... Just stay inside the night of the festival. Promise me."

"I promise," I say immediately.

I force myself to turn around, to walk to my bedroom, Naida's bedroom, Sophia's bedroom, what would have been Lorelei's bedroom. I throw clothes and books into my suitcase hastily, driven by tears and hopelessness. Luxe barks and drops a tennis ball at my feet. I kiss him on the head just before yanking my suitcase out the door. I let it fall down the stairs—I don't think I'm strong enough to carry it.

I throw my things into the back of the Jeep and urge it out of the driveway, swerving a little. *Keep moving forward, keep driving, keep going.* If I look back, if I think about what just happened, I won't be able to stop crying.

I park the Jeep next to Samuel's motorcycle and leap from the driver's seat, then sprint through Ms. Judy's dew-laden grass. Samuel opens the door when I reach the halfway mark, a confused but happy expression on his face—but when he sees my tears, his expression falls. He takes a single step toward me, but in that amount of time I've closed the space between us—I collapse into him, and he wraps his arms around me, lifting me up off the ground.

And then, finally, I really cry.

CHAPTER TWENTY-EIGHT

Waking up in Samuel's arms is comforting; I ignore the realization that the chocolate festival is this evening and instead push myself closer to him, kiss his chest before snaking out from under his arm while he's still sleeping. I pull on fresh clothes, open the front door, and inhale the fresh morning scent, dew and grass and hay smells. The sun is barely up, and a light mist is settled over everything. It makes the world look beautiful, innocent. It makes everything look safe, as though maybe last night were a bad dream.

But it wasn't. A helpless feeling, rooted somewhere near my stomach, grows and pushes into my heart. I've failed. I couldn't save Sophia, I've been thrown out, and I have no plan for saving the other Live Oak girls tonight—if it can even be done. I wrap my arms around my legs and watch the sky for a few moments. I don't know what to do. I'm finally *not* the scared little girl, and I'm just as helpless as if I were.

I have to move. I can't just sit here and dwell—I need something to occupy my mind. I rise and cross the lawn, get into Ansel's Jeep, and drive toward Judy's diner. Live Oak is already busy by its own standards, with all the old townspeople out watering flowers or going for walks. I cut through the center of town and see Judy's on the horizon.

Wait. As I slow down by the Confederate soldier statue, I see an old man with a cane hobbling up the steps to a crumbling brick storefront with arched windows and two flags—one Confederate, one American—hanging out front. A hand-painted sign in the window reads SEE GEN. ROBERT E. LEE'S RIDING BOOTS HERE! I wanted something to occupy my mind, didn't I?

I slow the car and pull it to the side of the street just as the old man gets the door open. He looks over his shoulder at me and gives me a crooked smile—I recognize him from the Fourth of July block party, the man with the moonshine. Sara's grandfather.

"Here to learn about the general?" he asks.

I hesitate. "I guess I am," I say, then smile back and hurry up the steps behind him.

The old man enters the museum first, turning to get the keys out of the lock as I walk toward the center of the room. The museum has high ceilings that allow sunlight to pour in but is only one floor. Straight ahead is a monstrous portrait of Robert E. Lee in his uniform—the painting is so large that it takes up most of the wall space, and Lee's bluish eyes give me a hard stare. The other walls are decorated in similar

270

memorabilia — portraits, some that look torn out of magazines or calendars, and one large, somewhat poor painting of Lee mounted on a sorrel horse.

"Come on, over here," the old man says, hustling past me. He smells like medicine and aftershave, so powerful that it almost makes my eyes water. I follow him toward the back corner of the museum, where there's a glass countertop display not unlike Sophia's. The old man walks around it, opens his mouth to speak, but then cuts himself off with a sharp breath. He ducks behind the counter, grabs some cleaner and polishes the glass, and finally meets my eyes with his faded blue ones.

"These," he says, pointing into the case, "are the riding boots of one of the greatest Americans to ever live, General Robert Edward Lee. Commander of the Confederate Army of Northern Virginia during the War of Northern Aggression. Lincoln himself wanted the general to lead the Union Army, you know, but Lee wouldn't abandon Virginia. He wouldn't fight against his homeland. That's courage, young lady — that's real courage right there."

I kneel down to peer inside the case. They just look like boots — worn over-the-knee black boots with scuffed toes and heels. There's a tiny picture on top of the case of Lee wearing them. When I look back up at the old man, he's beaming, and I can't help but grin. All Live Oak's signs, all the banners, all the pride — all over a pair of boots.

"Over here," he says, motioning to another case, "we've got the horseshoes of one of his second most famous horses, Lucy Long."

I'm just looking down into a case below the painting of the sorrel horse—Lucy Long, apparently—when a shadow appears in the open door. It's a teenage boy, pimply faced and with headphones jammed into his ears. His parents are behind him, and they file into the museum one by one.

"Excuse me," the mother—a plump woman wearing too much makeup—says to the old man. "We're trying to find the interstate? We've been lost in the country for an hour now."

"You're practically there—when you see Judy's, you'll see the on-ramp. But how about you take a moment, since you're here, and learn a piece about the great General Lee?" the old man says. He's moved closer to them and ushers them forward even though the family clearly wants to sprint for the door. The husband and wife exchange wary glances while the boy rolls his eyes and turns his music up loud enough that I can hear it from across the room.

I put my hands into my pockets and turn, looking at all the paintings again. It's not so much that they're Robert E. Lee—I barely know a thing about him—but rather that they, in some way, are Live Oak. All this history, all this past that they're clinging to, even while the town falls apart around them. Even while the first sign of Live Oak's end days prepares for another nail in the coffin of this town.

"Take the damn things outta your ears, boy, and come learn about history," the old man tells the teenager, who sighs but yanks the headphones out. He slouches over to the glass case and looks in, pressing his hands against the glass and leaving fingerprints on the surface. The old man begins his spiel about Lee, and I turn to go—I've got to get to Judy's and back, preferably before Samuel wakes up.

"How do you know these were his?" I hear the boy ask.

"Well, there's a photo right there," the old man answers.

"Of him in some riding boots. He was a freakin' general. He probably had a million pairs. How do you know these aren't just fakes?"

I wait in the doorway for the answer, but the old man just makes a few defeated sounds, starts a few sentences, and then falls silent. I turn around to see the boy shaking his head and jamming his headphones back into his ears. The family files past me, gets into a minivan full of laundry baskets and suitcases parked behind Ansel's Jeep, and wheels away toward the interstate.

I look back inside the museum to see the old man hauling out the cleaner again, polishing away the prints the boy left on the glass. He shakes his head at me and puts the cleaner down, then proceeds to begin setting out a pencil holder full of tiny Confederate flags and a few T-shirts on the counter.

"You can't trust outsiders, you know," he says, and my stomach twists at the thought that the old man thinks I'm like that boy. "They're always looking to turn you about. Mess with your head. Make you stop believing the things you know to be true." The old man looks lovingly up at the massive painting of Lee, then back to me, tipping his head in my direction. "Us Live Oakers gotta stick together. Gotta stand up for one another. People are the only thing holding this place together, so every person is precious."

"Us Live Oakers." I am not like that boy.

And he's right. People are the only thing holding this place—holding any place—together. It doesn't matter if those are really Lee's riding boots or if Sophia is the first sign of Live Oak's end days. They're both a part of me now, a part of the place where I became a new version of myself, where I faced the witch, where I wasn't afraid. Live Oak's broken and troubled but still holding on, still fighting. I can't abandon it—or anyone in it—no matter what kind of promises I've made, no matter what kind of risks I'll have to take. I'm not a scared little girl anymore—and I haven't been for a while.

I smile at the old man and wave good-bye; he responds by starting up an old tape player that fills the room with a quiet narrative about Lee's life.

By the time I make it to Judy's and back to the house, it's been at least an hour. Samuel must have been reaching for the front door right when I open it—I nearly run into him.

"Are you okay?" he asks immediately, glancing at the bag in my hand.

"I'm fine," I answer, pulling him back into the house and tapping the door shut with my foot. "I was getting us breakfast." I set the bag of food down on the floor and turn to him.

"Oh. Right," Samuel says, shaking his head as if he's trying to toss darker thoughts away. "I thought maybe...maybe you left."

"No," I say, and put my arms around the back of his neck. "But I went and saw Robert E. Lee's riding boots."

"Impressive?"

I pause, then nod.

"Learn anything about him?"

I smile a little. "I learned that I have to break a promise to my brother, which I feel bad about." Poor Ansel. He's only trying to keep me safe. He's always tried to keep me safe. But it's time I repay him.

"What promise?" Samuel asks.

"I told him I'd stay inside tonight. But I have to go to the festival."

Samuel steps back and meets my eyes. "Why? You don't have to go to save the eleven. We can set up on the roads going out of Live Oak, pick off the wolves there."

"That'll save the eleven, maybe," I admit. "But it won't save Sophia. And it won't get me any answers. I still won't know why some of them are special. You won't know why Layla and Naida are gone but other girls are still here. We have to help them, and I have to know the truth."

Samuel and I look at each other a long time. I want to say so much, but I'm not sure any of it would make sense. Naida, Sophia, me—there's an answer I still don't have, and while I don't entirely know what the question is, I know it has nothing to do with the roads out of Live Oak. I might be able to break free of the wolves, of my destiny, of Naida's destiny, but I won't do it if it means abandoning someone else to the monsters. Abigail and Sophia both deserve better from me.

"I know," Samuel says in a low voice, answering my unspoken words. "Okay, we'll go. Just tell me what you need me to do, Gretchen. You lead, I'll follow."

CHAPTER TWENTY-NINE

At sunset, I put on Naida's dress, wrinkled from being shoved into the bottom of my suitcase. It seems as if I should wear it, though—and besides, the red flowery fabric will probably help me blend in at the festival. I rip the sleeves so I can hold a gun easier, practice aiming, skip matching sandals in favor of tennis shoes I can run in.

I am still nervous. Still scared. I just don't care anymore— I can't allow myself to care anymore.

We are mirror images, but we are not the same. A reflection is you but reversed, after all. We are not the same. I chant this to myself over and over, trying to build up my courage. It works—it becomes something of a battle cry as I check my rifle, load my pockets with spare rounds, affix Naida's face in my mind.

We are not the same.

The festival starts at seven, but Samuel and I don't leave

till later—after eight o'clock. There's no way we'd be able to slip in unnoticed if we arrived on time. I wrap my arms around Samuel's chest and bury my face against his neck as we zip through town. Most of the remaining stores are long closed, though we get a few strange looks from old people sitting on their porches, gabbing away as they sip sweet tea or beer.

Samuel stops his bike just a hundred or so yards from Sophia's house. He climbs off, then helps me. We both have rifles on us, and we pause to pack our pockets with extra handfuls of shells.

"Where to, fearless leader?" Samuel says, squeezing my shoulder gently as I slide the rifle strap over my chest.

I inhale. No turning back now. I have to warn them. I can't let them vanish like Abigail. "This way," I say, and take the first step toward the chocolatier.

The noise grows as we close in on Sophia's place. A dull hum of conversation quickly morphs into a roar. There's music, acoustic guitar of some sort, and laughter that's bright and cheery, along with a few lower, male voices. When the house finally comes into view, it appears to glow from the strings of paper lanterns that illuminate the backyard. Every downstairs light is on, and cars are parked throughout the front yard and even down the street.

Strangely, though, no one is in sight—everyone is in the field out back, leaving the front deserted. We slink through the yard, using trees and cars for cover. The front door and storefront are darkened, but the kitchen is brightly lit.

Together we tiptoe up the porch steps, ducked down low.

I crack open the front door to the chocolatier and peer around it. No one, of course. We cut across the storefront, toward the display cases. I pause, leaning against them. It doesn't sound as though anyone is in the kitchen. Samuel hunches down beside me, looking uncertain.

The kitchen's screen door opens, then slams shut. Footsteps—Sophia's, I presume—pad across the kitchen hurriedly. I try to analyze where she is—the refrigerator, I think, now over by the oven. I rise, ready to confront her, to beg her, to plead with her again. To call her my sister and hope it reaches past her fear to her heart.

The screen door opens again, slams again. *Ansel,* I think as I hear heavy booted footsteps on the hardwood. I'm about to signal Samuel to move, to step in and surprise them, when the second person speaks.

"I'm disappointed, Miss Kelly," a sly, low voice says, barely a hiss over the sound of the party outside.

That isn't Ansel.

My eyes widen in confusion, and I dare to look up and through the glass. The saloon doors keep me from seeing faces, but I can see torsos and legs through the rows of candies in the case. The man is close to Sophia, very close, and she wrings her hands behind her back and steps away from him. She's trembling.

Who is it? Samuel mouths at me. I shake my head—I've never heard this voice before in my life.

"I'm sorry. I know...I..." Sophia begins. Her voice sounds as though she's on the verge of tears.

"You don't have eleven," the man says, taking an intrusive step toward Sophia. She backs up into the counter and grasps the skirt of the pink party dress she's wearing.

"I know," Sophia pleads. "But there just *aren't* eleven this year—one of the girls didn't show up. Look out there—there are plenty of seventeen-year-olds! I can make up for it next year!"

"Be quiet," the man says. I can see his hand—his fingers ripple and transform to claws, then turn back.

"He's a Fenris," Samuel whispers almost silently. I meet his eyes—they're livid, burning.

"B-but…S-Sophia…" I stammer, trying to make sense of whatever it is that's going on. Nothing is adding up.

Or worse yet, everything is adding up, however slowly. Sophia doesn't only know about the wolves, know about the shells, know about what's happening to the Live Oak girls. Sophia knows the wolves. She's talking to them. She's…My mind fumbles, trying to find a word, trying to work out what she could be to the monsters. Worse—what they could be to her. *Not Sophia,* I think Not the girl who is like a sister, the girl my brother loves, the girl whom I wanted to be just like.

No. My jaw tightens, teeth grinding, fists clenched as my mind swirls, watching her talk to a killer.

"Please," Sophia says, voice cracking. "Please—"

"You'd better work this out," the man—no, not a man, a wolf—says, and then storms out the screen door. It slams shut, and Sophia crumples to the floor. I see her face for only a moment, but it's racked with grief, guilt, sorrow. Her mouth is twisted in a silent wail, and her eyes are squeezed shut. I hear her choke down a few sobs, and then she rises. She breathes deeply, brushes down her skirt, and clears her throat.

"Sophia?" Ansel's voice sounds through the other side of the screen door.

"Yeah?" Sophia answers, voice brighter than I know she feels. She sniffs away the last of her tears, an old pro at some deception I still don't understand.

"There aren't any more hazelnut truffles. Did you have any extras? People are asking for them."

Sophia laughs cheerily, and I'm amazed that she's able to do so given the emotions I just saw her go through. "I've got some more in the storefront. Not a lot, though! Tell them to slow down!" she teases. Ansel laughs, the sound fading away as he rejoins the party.

The saloon doors swing open.

There's no point in hiding. No point in pretending she won't see us. No point in pretending I didn't just overhear a strange conversation. As the saloon doors swing shut, I stand and face Sophia.

She jumps, clasping her hand to her chest to suppress a scream. Her eyes flicker: first anger; then fury; then, more powerful than either of those, sorrow. Sophia shakes her head, and her eyes fill with tears.

"Gretchen, I . . . you're here," she whispers hoarsely as tears slip down her cheeks. Tears of . . . relief? I'm not sure.

The gun feels dead in my hand; I can't lift it toward Sophia, no matter whom she was talking to.

"That was a werewolf. Sophia, you know that was a werewolf," I whisper. Sophia jumps as Samuel stands up beside me, eyes dark. He isn't afraid to raise his own gun and aims it squarely at her chest. I continue. "You know they're real. You know..."

"It was...it isn't what you think," Sophia stammers, shaking her head. She breathes hard and begins yanking hazelnut truffles from the display case, as if the act of doing so will keep her sane.

"You're with *them*," Samuel says, his voice low and threatening. His hands are tight on the rifle, knuckles white.

"Sophia, tell me what's going on," I demand in a low voice. "Just tell me the truth."

"I can't," she says, words barely audible. "Gretchen, I'm so sorry. Never forget—never forget that I'm sorry." Sophia kneels to the floor, a silent cry escaping her lips.

"Samuel, get my brother," I say quickly. He nods and takes a step but Sophia cries out, half scream, half words.

She shakes her head pleadingly. "Please don't tell him. Please, Gretchen."

"Then start talking," I whisper.

She nods meekly, swallows, begins to speak. "They wanted eleven girls. You had that part right. But the shells weren't just them trying to scare me. It was...they were..."

"Instructions," Samuel says in disbelief.

"Yes." Sophia nods pitifully.

"It isn't the wolves cutting girls off as they leave town," he says, voice filled with fury. "It's you. You're marking them, sending them out after your party to die."

"I don't want to!" Sophia cries, her voice suddenly loud, pleading, begging for mercy, though I don't think she seeks it from us. "I don't want to, Gretchen. I just have to!"

The back screen door slams. I don't think twice; Samuel and I immediately take aim together, guns pointed and ready.

But it's just Ansel. He sweeps through the saloon doors, confusion on his face—especially when he sees his sister holding a gun. Ansel and Samuel stare at each other for a moment before my brother speaks.

"Gretchen, what's going on? What are you doing?" Ansel says, and I'm relieved that he doesn't sound as though he thinks I'm crazy—he sounds as if he's worried. As though he wants me to fill him in so we can be allies again, the two of us running side by side.

"Saving eleven girls," I answer, lowering the gun. Samuel does the same but takes a step closer to me.

"She was talking to a wolf. She's with them," Samuel growls at Ansel.

"What?" Ansel asks, and his eyes narrow. "A wolf?"

"The witch. The werewolf," I remind Ansel, but he doesn't seem sure how to react.

"Listen to your sister," Samuel snaps.

Ansel glares at Samuel, then reaches for Sophia. But she

doesn't fall into him, doesn't let him hold her—she stares at me, as if she and I are the only people in the room.

"You have to understand, Gretchen. I have to do it. For my sister."

"They killed Naida," I whisper through gritted teeth. "Why would you work with them—kill other girls—"

"No!" Sophia cuts me off, shaking her head frantically. "They took my sister. But they didn't kill her. They did something worse."

"Explain," Samuel snarls, and I see no compassion for Sophia on his face. I can't blame him—she marks the Fenris's victims. Which means Sophia marked Layla.

"They killed my dad," Sophia says, lips trembling. "And then they came back and took Naida."

"What do you mean, they 'took' her?" Ansel asks, reaching for Sophia's hand.

"They took her with them. But they didn't kill her. They promised to give her back one day if I cooperate. They have her somewhere, somewhere by the ocean. My sister loved the ocean," Sophia says, mournful nostalgia in her voice.

There. My answer, right there. I am not special for surviving. The eight others aren't special for dying. My sister isn't special for dying.

Naida is the special one.

For whatever reason, Naida was *taken*. Not killed, not devoured. She's special to the wolves. All this time, all this wondering, and it turns out Naida really did start it all.

And now I realize: I am not a mirror image of Naida—the

wolf didn't take me. I am a mirror image of Sophia. The surviving sister. The one who knew about the monsters in the forest, the one with the guilty eyes and broken heart. Abigail is dead—the wolves didn't come to Ansel or me with any deadly bargains—but Sophia and I still play the same role. I once went into the woods to see if the witch wanted me; Sophia is doling out new victims too.

My heart sinks, lungs catch, trying to bear the weight of it all. Trying to balance pity and fury. I understand—what wouldn't I have done to bring Abigail back?—and yet I don't want to. I don't want to understand this kind of darkness.

"What about the shells…" I whisper. Now that I have one answer, I want them all.

"Proof of life," Sophia chokes. "Every year they bring me new ones from her, new ones that she picks just for me. They bring me one for each girl I need to have at the party for them. This year it was eleven."

"This doesn't make sense," Ansel says to me, looking for some sign of agreement in my eyes, as if he wants to prove that Sophia is simply crazy, that I'm simply wrong. "Why would *werewolves*"—he has trouble with the word—"wait around? If that's what really chased us through the forest, Gretchen, it didn't wait us out. It just attacked."

"You're not from the South," Samuel says, shaking his head. "Not from farmland. It's the first key to successful farming." Sophia looks up at him, and I know that whatever Samuel is about to say is the truth. "Wait until your crop is mature to harvest."

Sophia nods tearfully. "They want girls at eighteen. The closer they are to eighteen, the better. It's their favorite age—they say it's when a girl's blood is sweetest. They leave the younger ones—wait till the next festival. They take the ones in the red dresses."

Horror bubbles into my throat. I can't breathe. I want to speak but the words are... I look to my brother. His eyes are wide. We both look down at the red floral dress I'm wearing. The one Sophia picked out. Ansel looks as though he might be sick.

"I'm eighteen, Sophia," I finally whisper, groan, almost, because my throat won't form the words well.

Sophia inhales, trembles, looks as if the words that are about to leave her mouth are knives on her tongue. "You're number eleven, Gretchen."

CHAPTER THIRTY

I cry out; Samuel breathes hard, angrily; but it's Ansel's actions that seem to hurt Sophia the most. He steps away from her, horrified, as though he can't bear to touch her, can't bear to even look at her. Sophia takes a step toward him, extends a shaky hand.

Ansel slaps it away.

"I'm sorry, I'm so sorry," Sophia pleads with him. "You have to understand. She's my sister. She's my little sister. I have to protect her."

"Protect her?" I ask, voice becoming shrill. "Sophia, these are monsters. They're *never* going to give Naida back. They never give anyone back!"

"Don't say that!" Sophia screams, her face sheet white. "Don't say that...I..." She rocks back and forth; I think she might faint. "They promised. And if there's a chance, a tiny chance they'll let her go...she's my sister. I love my sister, and she's all I have left."

"She's *my* sister. You...you *are* the witch," Ansel hisses. There's so much hatred in his voice, so much rage, that he sounds like a different person.

I shake my head and suddenly understand why Sophia loves the Nietzsche quote over the shop door. *There is always some madness in love. But there is also always some reason in madness.*

Love this powerful? Powerful enough for her to...I thought she loved me. I thought she was my friend, despite her secrets. No wonder she was so desperate for me to come tonight, so kind to me, so eager for me to stay here at any cost. No wonder she knew Ansel would leave her after tonight.

"I didn't want to, Gretchen. I'm a good person. I'm a good person," Sophia repeats, choking on sobs.

"Why was Naida special? Why didn't they kill her, if they killed everyone else?" I ask.

"They—" But she doesn't get the opportunity to explain. The screen door in the kitchen slams shut.

Samuel and I lift our guns. Ansel balls his hands into fists and steps up beside us, meeting my eye for a glimmer of a second.

"No, please, no, you can't shoot him," Sophia whispers haggardly behind us.

He's slick, handsome. Wearing a polo shirt and torn

jeans. He has bright yellow-brown eyes and high cheekbones, and his hair is a gentle wren color that looks tremendously touchable.

The girls outside don't have a chance with a monster like him around.

"What's going on here?" he asks, stepping through the saloon doors. My aim is perfect; I know Samuel's is as well. *It's okay, no need to panic. Everything is under control,* I tell myself.

"It's her," Sophia chokes, then hides her face. "She's the last one."

The werewolf laughs, an emotion that doesn't make it past his voice. His teeth sharpen, his fingertips quiver, and claws ease their way through his fingertips in tiny bursts of blood and skin. The touchable hair slicks, mats, breaks down into mangy fur.

So Samuel shoots him.

Sophia screams. Blood splatters onto the saloon doors. The party outside silences. But the Fenris doesn't die; he rears back, charges out the door of the chocolatier, trailing thick blood behind him.

And then it begins.

Outside, the screams of twenty-three teenage girls rush over us like a wave of terror. Samuel and I charge forward, knocking the saloon doors aside. We burst through the screen door into the pink-and-orange-tinted party, a world of tables lined with candles and paper and beautiful, elaborate sweets.

Everything is still beautiful, still perfect, except for the handsome guys. They're transforming, melting from men into monsters. The girls scream in horror, choke on air, try to run but find their feet don't move.

Samuel tilts his head; he's going right, I'm going left. Ansel, ever wanting to save people, runs straight ahead. *He doesn't know what he's facing, I have to watch out for him.* I aim, fire, miss. God, the girls are so close—what if I shoot one of them? Is it better to be shot than devoured? I aim again, exhaling for balance. Fire. The nearest monster vanishes with a sharp howl, explodes into shadows that make the girl standing closest to him faint. Another monster, an enormous gray one, steps out of the remains of his clothing. He charges at me, zigzagging. I follow him with the gun, hit him with a bullet that doesn't even slow him down.

Ansel slams into his side, football skills put to use, and sends him flying into the grass. I want to make sure my brother is okay, but there's no time. A girl runs into me, grabbing my arm. I can't hear what she's saying over the sound of gunfire and screaming, but it's clear from her wide blue eyes. *Save me, please; please save me.*

"Gretchen! Watch your left!" Samuel's voice roars over the fray. I look over, try to aim for the tawny werewolf that's galloping toward me, mouth open and tongue lolling around bloodstained teeth. The girl by my side is on her knees, gagging on cries, pulling on my arm—I can't aim with her there. The werewolf dives at me; I duck down and ram the stock of the rifle up as hard as I can. I feel it crack bones and ribs, and the werewolf roars in pain as he rolls away. I kick the pleading girl away, aim, fire as the wolf turns around. Shadows.

I turn back to the festival, gun ready. Someone's knocked over a table lined with pillar candles; the flames have caught a string of downed paper lanterns, a dozen little bonfires right beside the chocolatier's kitchen. Ansel is strangling a werewolf, tugging him to the ground, but right beside him is a huge black beast with his head buried in something bloody, something that was once wearing a cherry red party dress. It eats ravenously, hungrily.

When the wolf's teeth crunch down on the girl's delicate, perfectly manicured hand, I lose it.

I run at the monster, gun aimed, firing desperately. He rears back as the bullets hit him, strings of blood and tendon swinging out of his mouth. He staggers and growls, snaps at me, then collapses over the body of his victim. He glares at me with one yellowed, furious eye and tries to find his feet again. I place the tip of my gun between his eyes and fire.

When he becomes shadows, I'm left staring at a dead girl's open body. I gag, almost vomit, and turn away just in time to see Samuel shoot two werewolves, one right after the other. How many are there? The monsters have caught on to the guns—they're moving, running, darting behind girls who are desperately trying to run for their cars or who are curled up on the ground, screaming. Ansel swings at another monster. There are blood streaks on his back, claw marks that sliced through his shirt and into his skin. Another wolf is coming up behind him—

"Get down!" I scream at my brother. Ansel looks up to see me aiming; he yanks the wolf to the ground. I hit the one coming up behind him. The beast's body slams into Ansel's before it becomes shadows.

I hear Sophia's voice.

I look up to see her walking across the lawn as if there's nothing going on at all, as if tables aren't overturning and the lanterns aren't flickering and dying. As if the wolves aren't here. The wolves treat her much the same—as though she doesn't even exist. *Of course they don't hurt her—she's their meal ticket,* I think, stomach swirling in disgust. Sophia steps over a body as if it's nothing, but when she reaches me, I see how hard she's trembling.

"Gretchen, go," she says. She looks back at the chocolatier—flames from the lanterns have started licking at the kitchen walls. "Just go. It's too late for . . . I can't . . ."

I aim over her shoulder at a wolf; he stops, steps back. He explodes to shadow when a bullet that isn't mine hits him; Samuel nods at me, then continues, taking down wolves so quickly that I can't understand how there are so many left. I reach into my pocket, fumble for more bullets—I've got only one left in the rifle.

"Tell me why Naida is special," I snap at her as I reload. I didn't come this far to go away without every single answer.

"They're using her," Sophia whispers. "They say she has

two souls. One died when they bit her; the other becomes dark, like them."

"I don't understand," I shout, furious, scared, hurt.

"She had a twin sister who died before they were born— when one twin dies like that, the other absorbs her. I guess Lorelei's body *and* soul went into Naida." She swallows, as though what she's saying hurts her throat. "The wolves take one soul by biting into her heart, and then the other will die slowly, in the ocean, until she's all darkness." Sophia opens her mouth, but it takes her a long time to say the final phrase. "Until she's a monster," she finishes hoarsely.

I remember the ultrasound, Lorelei and Naida tucked against each other. Two little souls, resulting in one little girl—a girl whom the wolves would essentially be able to kill twice.

"Why do they want her dark?" I ask, trying to ignore a raspy growl from the other side of the lawn.

There's a look of horror in Sophia's eyes when she answers. "They can't have mortal lovers; they kill them. But the ocean girls—they're dark, they're kindred evils—"

Sophia kneels to the side and vomits, choking. I try to help her up but then somehow, through the noise, I hear a clicking sound. A hollow, light noise that signifies a gun is empty. I whirl around toward it.

Samuel is out of bullets; he struggles to reload as the wolves take notice and press in on him. I fire at one; the bullet slices through the monster's shoulder and then skims through the air right beside Samuel's head. He looks at me but doesn't say anything, desperately pushing bullets into his rifle.

A wolf charges him. Samuel stumbles. Golden bullets light up in the moonlight before raining to the ground, and the gun goes over his head. I hear myself screaming, not words but sounds, as fury, frustration, and bullets fly out of my gun. Two wolves go down, but there are more. One dives on top of Samuel. He punches the monster, and I hear his jaw break, but Samuel can't stop the second one. The beast's teeth sink into his side. Samuel roars in pain.

There's a hissing sound in the air, and my brother emerges behind the wolf that's attacking Samuel, slamming the monster in the head with a thick wrench. His skull cracks and his head opens up, blooming blood into his matted fur. I aim and kill him. Ansel heaves Samuel to his feet just as I reach them to cover Samuel while he reloads.

The three of us stand back-to-back-to-back as girls rush past us, sprinting for their cars. Car wheels squeal, but it's hard to tell the sound from the cries. There are still monsters, still so many monsters, and the chocolatier is genuinely on fire now. Smoke is beginning to billow across the lawn. The kitchen door falls off the hinges; the fire grows.

Violet dashes across the yard toward Sophia, who is on her knees in the grass, gazing at the sky. Violet takes her hand, tugs, pulls, screams at her. Sophia's head bounces like a rag doll's against Violet's efforts. Violet shakes her head and finally releases Sophia's hand to save herself when a wolf charges at them.

The wolf snares Sophia by the arm, slicing into her skin. I recognize him—it's the wolf Sophia was speaking to inside, the one with the yellow-brown eyes. He's only partially transformed—his nose is split in two, an animal snout between two human nostrils. Fur bursts out along his spine, and his hands have long, yellow, and thick nails that are dripping blood. A shadow of the attractive man who spoke to Sophia not even a half hour ago. Sophia doesn't make a sound as the remaining wolves group around her, growling, huffing, glaring at us.

Samuel and I take aim; the leader's eyes find mine for a scattered instant. I see him squeeze tighter around Sophia's arm till her skin turns purple. A threat as clear as if he'd spoken aloud: *Shoot, and I'll kill her.*

I swallow hard but take my finger off the trigger.

CHAPTER THIRTY-ONE

The wolves back up near the chocolatier, unable to get too close—fire is now gnawing the pale wood into dark, brittle ash. Their glassy eyes flicker, daring us to make the first move, to give them an excuse to rip our skin from our bones.

Sophia's pale pink dress is covered in grime and blood. Her eyes are swollen and her lips part. "Please. I can do it again. Another town, anywhere else. P-please," she stammers. I barely hear her over the crackle of flame, the pounding of betrayal rocketing through my mind. She'd do it again. All this, and she'd do it again.

The witch considers this as strings of bloody saliva drip from his mouth—a human jaw dislocated by enormous, jagged teeth. One shot—I can do this; I can hit him before he takes one of us out. If I can hit the first wolf, Samuel will have time to take out another, I can hit a third, then Ansel . . . Sophia. Sophia could die.

She deserves to, I think darkly.

But no, I have to try to save her. We're mirror images. I have to wait till the wolves make the first move, wait till I have the advantage. The leader looks at Sophia a long time, till something sinister crosses his lips. I aim.

"Kill the others," the leader hisses. He nods toward me. "Save her."

I fire.

The leader moves slightly at the last moment, but the shot flies true and a monster behind him falls backward, then erupts into darkness. I don't care; I don't have time to look — I aim again, fire, aim, fire, until I feel like a machine.

Samuel fires at a wolf charging toward him. Five left, including the leader, who is coming for me. Sophia is yelling, running at Ansel, desperate to save him. Her screams slice through the meadow, a shrill cry about the growls.

"Run, Gretchen! Please, run!" she shouts at me.

Her voice is drowned out by the sound of gunfire. The leader gets closer, rage in his eyes. I aim, fire, miss, aim, fire — I choke on smoke just as the leader lunges at me.

My brother's arms appear behind the wolf, wrapping around his neck. Ansel twists around, elbows the monster in the throat, slams against his ribs, and yanks his claws backward as the beast roars in fury. The wolf bites Ansel — the leg, then the arm — but Ansel is determined. He flips him over and punches his gut.

296

A dishwater-gray monster sees the leader struggling against Ansel and starts for them. I freeze, aim, fire. The wolf flails backward with an angry hiss. For a moment I think it'll take a third shot, but he staggers, then explodes to shadows. Four left; Samuel is surrounded by three. Sophia is pleading with them, begging them to stop.

Samuel kills another; I realize I'm out of rounds just as I reach him. I shove my hand into his back pocket and grab another handful of bullets to reload. *We can do this. We can fix this.* I wheel around toward my brother to see if the leader is among the dead yet.

I feel a wolf's teeth gnashing into my legs at the same moment I see his glittering eyes. The monster closes his jaws around my shin, teeth slipping between bones. I scream and my vision goes watery. *Fight, fight*—I slam the stock of the rifle down on his jaw. Something cracks, forces him to release me, but he's about to go in for a second strike.

A shot flies through the air, splattering the wolf's blood on me. He becomes shadows that skitter over my body. Samuel helps me to my feet.

"Help your brother," he yells. I turn and see Ansel still fighting the leader. His arms are slick with blood from the monster's claws. The wolf tosses, turns, twists to the ground to get Ansel off his back. I can't shoot; I'd hit my brother. Ansel cries out in pain as the wolf's back claws find his thighs and dig in. Ansel thrashes; he and the wolf spin backward, through the doors of the shed. They crash into darkness.

I run to the shed, try to aim, but it's black. The smoke

from the fire makes my eyes water; I can barely breathe. *Come on, Ansel, all I need is one shot. One shot—I can help.* Behind me I hear the remaining wolf. I hear Samuel fire twice more. Did he kill it? I don't know. I have to shoot. I take a step closer, aim—

There's a roar of noise, a slide, a fall, things moving strangely. The shed pitches to one side, and I hear wood shatter. The entire upper half of the shed collapses in scarcely a moment, transforming a broad doorway into a cage of wood planks and old boxes. The resulting breeze sweeps out over me, along with a dull, low creak.

Ansel is trapped.

I scream his name and run toward the pile of wood, boxes, bent metal, broken glass. I throw rubble over my shoulder carelessly, scratching my hands, tearing apart my legs as I thrash for some semblance of my brother. I hear Samuel shooting. I don't turn to see if he's hit anything; I just need to find—

"Gretchen!" my brother's voice breaks through. I hear shifting, moving, and then there's an explosion from behind the debris. The lead monster tears through the fallen wood and lands firmly on the ground outside.

The wolf turns to me.

He licks his lips hungrily.

The witch charges.

I fire, fire, fire, over and over again, aiming carefully but unable to keep up with him. He knows how to dodge the gun, swoops his head down, gets closer and closer. *Die, please die.* Blood trickles from bullet wounds but he won't *die.*

My gun clicks. I lost count of the rounds. I'm out.

I grit my teeth, raise the gun, ready to strike him. Ready to fight, somehow.

Samuel's roar is so animal-like, I think he's another wolf. He slams into me, knocking me to the ground so hard that my rifle bounces away. I scramble backward in the dirt toward the gun, desperately searching my pockets for more bullets. I don't see the other wolf anywhere—Samuel must have gotten him.

The monster is livid. Anger radiates from his eyes, yellow disks that pierce the night. His jaws open, teeth snapping for Samuel's skin. Samuel shoots, but the beast slashes at his arm. Blood flows, but Samuel doesn't let go of the rifle. He spins away from the monster, fires again. The bullet tears through the wolf's ear, sending bits of fur and flesh scattering. But it isn't enough.

The wolf wraps his jaws around Samuel's chest, slick teeth cutting into flesh. He tosses his head back and forth violently. Samuel's limbs flop like a rag doll's. His eyes roll back in their sockets. Blood streams down his chest, but the wolf doesn't stop. I have one bullet left, lodged in the corner of my pocket. My hands shake as I load it. *Come on, hurry—*

By the time I've aimed, the monster has released him. Samuel's body skids across the ground, tumbling to a stop where Sophia is standing, horrified. Samuel doesn't move. I don't think he's breathing.

The noise that escapes my throat is hard to recognize. I run toward them, sliding to my knees, grasping Samuel's hands. In the same instant, Sophia lets out a long, low scream. She charges toward the wolf, yelling words, noises, shouting, face dark purple, eyes wide.

"We had a deal! I would have done it for you; I would have done all of it for you again! Naida and Ansel and Gretchen...I...love...reason..." Her words don't make any sense, broken apart by sobs and cries. Tears are splashing down my face—he's breathing, thank god he's breathing, but his eyes are closed...

"Enough," I whisper, trying to steady the tremble in my voice. *One way or another, enough.* I let a hand caress Samuel's shoulder lightly, look back to the shed where my brother is still trapped, then stand. I lift my gun and aim at the witch.

One shot.

I won't run.

The wolf half transforms, snout sucking into his face. Fur flies off, mottled skin giving way to human flesh dotted in puncture wounds. The claws remain, with the glistening eyes and the jaw so enormous that it looks cracked. Sophia is still screaming in front of him; he reaches out and grabs her. She falls against his body, where he squeezes her close, so close. He leans in and takes a long, awful whiff of the skin on her neck. The monster licks his lips and gives a dark laugh, using her body as a shield, and backs up close to the chocolatier. He turns to me. I think my heart is stopping.

"Come with us, girl," the monster says haggardly. His

300

eyes are so locked on me that they feel heavy, as if they're going to bore into me and force me into the ground. "Leave with me, and she and her lover can go." The monster's gaze flickers to the shed. I can hear Ansel shouting, yelling my name, Sophia's name, but his voice feels far away, background to the wolf's raspy breaths.

I am frozen. I don't understand. Why would they want me to come with them? Why would they *take* me, instead of kill me? The question must be clear on my face, because the wolf speaks again, voice almost sweet, almost familiar; he's trying hard to make me think he's making this offer out of pity, not hunger. Trying to make me think he doesn't want to rip into my skin, tear apart my bones.

"I can smell it on you. A twin. When one dies, the other always gets her soul. You're connected." He inhales the air again, as though he's tasting me from a distance. "And your twin is long gone, by the smell of you."

Abigail. They've already killed Abigail.

"Which means you"—his voice is low, a hiss, but somewhat almost horribly seductive—"are ready to join us." He looks down at Sophia, smiles at her, the skin around his mouth cracking as he does so. "She's ready to join your sister."

I can't think. Everything has stopped working; everything is still.

They think I am ready to become darkness. I am ready to become a witch. That I am ready to be Naida's mirror, instead of Sophia's.

Ready to vanish.

"You have the chance to save them," the wolf says, voice growling as he tightens his grip on Sophia. He sees my eyes graze across Samuel's bleeding body. "We'll leave all of them here."

I look at Sophia, hear my brother pounding on the shed, feel Samuel nearby, still bleeding, still hurting. I am special, and I have the chance to save them. Just like I wanted to. I can save them all, just by walking away with the witch. And unbelievably, I find myself thinking something else, something selfish, something I haven't thought since I went into the woods years ago to see if the witch wanted me:

It would be so much easier just to vanish.

Sophia's eyes widen in fear. She didn't know any of this, the details about twins, I can tell—didn't know that I'd be special just like Naida. She looks at me desperately, pleadingly. There's one word, however, that filters through the air to me even in the silence: *Don't.*

"Deal?" the wolf hisses. His grip tightens on Sophia's shoulder, cutting into her skin. She's so weak, she doesn't notice the blood that dribbles down her dress. Samuel groans beside me; his eyes flicker open—but he can't help. No one can help now.

Sophia whispers something under her breath. I shake my head—I can't understand. She whispers louder, louder, until it becomes a chant.

"Do it. Do it, please, do it." The words fly off her tongue like a prayer. I furrow my brow. She wants me to do it? To make the trade, my life for hers and Ansel's? Even though I'm considering it, I'm still hurt, betrayed — and then I see her eyes.

And I understand what she's really asking me to do.

Even though I hate her, I don't want to do it.

I aim. The wolf ducks down behind Sophia. I adjust the rifle to match. *Forgive me, forgive me, please,* I beg her silently, but her face is peaceful, her eyes are shut. The smoke-heavy wind sweeps her chocolate-colored hair around her face. She looks magical. She looks beautiful.

I fire.

The bullet cuts through Sophia's chest into the wolf's head. He becomes shadows instantly, blackness that blooms around Sophia as she falls backward, falls through the papery wood that used to be her kitchen wall. I abandon the gun and run forward, ignoring the flames licking at my arms, scorching my clothes. My hands hit the edge of the oven, the iron sizzling against my skin, but there's no time to draw away. I choke as I grab Sophia's body, yank her from the hungry fire and into the grass. Blood is soaking through her dress; her skin is black in places from soot; she coughs violently — more blood spatters her lips.

Ansel shouts her name — no, Ansel pleads her name, shouting from his prison. There's a scuffle behind me; I dare to glance back to see Samuel struggling to stay upright, hauling boards aside, flinging debris away with a sort of desperation, the power that must come only from knowing what it's like to lose the girl you love. Blood is soaking the side of his shirt, but it doesn't slow him down — he reaches into the darkness and emerges with Ansel's wrist, then tugs my brother out of the wreck. Ansel is beaten, an eye is bloody, his leg looks broken, but he runs across the lawn and falls down beside me. Beside Sophia.

She's still alive, alive for now. Ansel takes her hand. Tears drip from his face to hers.

I don't want to look at her. Not like this. Her blue eyes are wide and cloudy, and how can there be so much blood? It looks like a rose blossom on her chest. She grasps for my hand, then turns her eyes to me. I can't tell if she actually sees me or not.

"I'm so sorry, Gretchen."

"I know," I answer, words forced past the thickness in my throat. "Sophia . . ."

What do I say?

"I didn't mean it. I swear, I didn't mean for it to go so far. I just . . . I didn't know what else to do," she whispers. A wet sound emerges from her throat, and she chokes for a moment before continuing. "Forgive me?"

"Yes." I'm not sure I really forgive her, I'm not sure I can ever forgive her, but I won't let her die knowing that. I *can't* let her die knowing that. Her eyes lose focus for a moment, then wander to Ansel. His hand is tight on hers.

He opens his mouth several times before the words come out. "I love you," he says. The words emerge on a sob.

Sophia squeezes Ansel's hand as he brings it to his lips to kiss her fingers. Sophia smiles, and her lips part slightly to speak, to return the sentiment.

But instead, she dies.

CHAPTER THIRTY-TWO

*E*veryone in the South has a family burial plot.

The Kelly family members are all buried in a section of the Live Oak cemetery that's surrounded by wisteria vines. The scent of the flowers pours over us as an old and frail pastor talks about the kingdom of heaven, about Sophia's beauty, about her kindness. All of Live Oak stands around Ansel and me; we sit up front, in chairs usually reserved for family, because we're not sure where else to sit. Samuel's hand rests firmly on my shoulder, squeezing tightly.

They blamed it on wild animals. Stray bullets. Some of the survivors tried to tell the truth, but who would believe them? They're all here too, eyes wide and shaky, looking for wolves to dart out from behind headstones.

Her coffin is white. I picked out her dress—deep periwinkle, because I thought it would match her eyes. I gave the undertaker a Nietzsche book to put in her hands, and the photo of her and Naida at the beach as children. I wanted to give him more—pieces of candy, hair ribbons, blankets, seashells. I wanted to give him everything, so she would have everything she needs in the ground with her, everything the patron saint of candy needs and nothing to remind me of the first sign of Live Oak's end days. Nothing to remind me of the witch.

I should be mad. I should hate her. I should judge her. But there is some madness in love.

They put out the fire before the entire chocolatier was consumed. The kitchen is gone, and part of the storefront, making it almost entirely unstable—Ms. Judy lets Ansel and me stay in a spare room in her house, even gives me a few of her own books to add to my collection. People drop by constantly to see us; they bring seventeen different kinds of casserole, pies, Jell-O, plastic milk jugs full of sweet tea. Luxe won't stay at Judy's though—he often disappears, and without fail, we find him sitting on the chocolatier's singed front porch. Loyal to the end.

We're trying to clear out her house. We don't know what to do with the things she thought were precious. We don't know what to do with the things we've never seen, the things stashed in the attic, the things only the Kellys really know about.

Samuel and I sit on the porch, hands clasped, Luxe at our feet. Ansel is on the swing out back, where he spends most of the days staring at the sun rise and set. There's not really anything left for him to fix.

"What now?" I ask—I didn't entirely mean for the words to be aloud. Samuel looks at me, then shakes his head.

"I don't know," he says through a sigh. "I don't know."

I pause. "Do you think there's really any helping Naida?"

"Probably not. Who knows? I've never heard about the wolves wanting girls like that before." He lifts my hand and kisses it gently; I rise and move toward him, then sink into his lap. I pull my knees up and lean against his chest.

"I don't want to stay here." I didn't want to say it—I hate myself for saying it, honestly.

"Me neither," Samuel confesses somberly.

We pause, rocking slightly in the evening breeze. The lightning bugs are just emerging, illuminating the yard like Christmas lights. Whip-poor-wills call out, and flying squirrels dart from the attic into the oak trees. It's beautiful; everything about this place is beautiful.

"Where do you want to go?" Samuel asks.

I turn to face him before resting my head on his shoulder. "The ocean," I answer.

"There are wolves there, too."

"I know."

Samuel nods. "Then that's where we'll go."

EPILOGUE

The air-conditioning in Sophia's car—well, *our* car, I suppose—is broken. It doesn't matter much, now that it's the beginning of autumn, but we still have to wipe beads of sweat off our foreheads by the time we reach downtown Live Oak. We breeze past the square, the Confederate soldier statue, Judy's diner. Luxe barks at ducks waddling beside the road as we turn onto the interstate, and we shush him.

Samuel, Ansel, and me.

Ansel doesn't want to let go of the chocolatier, of Sophia. He aches for her, sees her in his dreams and nightmares. I understand. I understand completely. My brother lies down across the backseat of the car with Luxe and closes his eyes, swallows hard, as though it'll be easier to pull away from Live Oak if he doesn't have to watch it happen.

"You want to drive?" Samuel asks as wind rushes through the windows, almost deafeningly.

I shake my head, squinting as my hair flies around my face. "Not yet. I want to be able to look at everything when we get there. I can't do that if I'm trying not to wreck."

Samuel smiles. "You'll like it. I went there a few times with Layla. It's beautiful."

"I know," I say. "I know it will be."

We cut through forest, through farmland, and finally, palm trees start to spring up on the sides of the road. The oaks still loom, draped in Spanish moss, but the ground is sandy and the scent of salt swoops into the car around us. I inhale deeply, letting it filter through me.

Samuel turns down a tiny road lined with cottages, which ends in a parking lot by a set of wooden stairs. He cuts the car off and turns to me, watching, waiting for my reaction.

I slowly open the door, step out of the car. The sound of waves crashing soothes me, gulls calling, flat blue water that stretches out until it touches the setting sun. I whistle for Luxe, who wakes Ansel when he hops out. My brother emerges from the car, squinting in the sunlight, and gives me a weak smile.

Together, we walk toward the ocean.

Acknowledgments

Sweetly seemed like it would be an easy book to write. I loved the characters. I loved the story. I sat down, raring to go, excited to see it take shape...and it turned out to be what seemed, at times, an impossible book to write.

I can say with absolute certainty that I would still be huddled in my bedroom crying were it not for the heroic, practical, and kind acts of the following people. I owe you endless thanks and bottomless boxes of chocolate.

Julie Scheina, Jill Dembowski, and Jennifer Hunt, for their sage advice and brilliant ideas that talked me off the cliff and back to my chair.

Carrie Ryan, Maggie Stiefvater, Tessa Gratton, and Brenna Yovanoff, for hours upon hours of e-mail, instant messages, and late-night conversations about how to be a better reader, writer, and author.

Tessa Gratton, the only person I'd trust to read my or Gretchen's tarot cards.

Saundra Mitchell, for reading and rereading *Sweetly*,

shining it up, lifting my spirits, and for being the only person who will watch *Deadliest Catch* with me.

The 2009 Debutantes for continued advice and support during everything from middle-of-the-night meltdowns to jubilant "It's done!" parties.

Jim McCarthy for adopting *Sweetly* and loving it as his own.

Granddaddy Pearce and my father, Brad Pearce, for teaching me how to shoot a rifle and a shotgun—and for not picking on me when I cried over the recoil.

Ames O'Neill for being as excited as I am to share my books with the world.

StrawberryLuna for giving *Sisters Red* a cover that gave me chills.

Sarah Basiliere for helping me find my way up the Big Rock Candy Mountain.

Most of the 2010 PRHS color guard senior class, for contributing their names to the list of the Live Oak missing—thanks for volunteering to be eaten by wolves, ladies.

My parents and sister, for their continued tolerance of my high levels of crazy, for clipping every newspaper article, and for being at every event to cheer me on. Also my grandparents, for shamelessly telling everyone who crosses their paths to read my books.

CHARACTER INTERVIEW: GRETCHEN AND ROSIE

Get a glimpse into a conversation between Gretchen from *Sweetly* and Rosie from *Sisters Red*, a companion novel to *Sweetly* by Jackson Pearce.

I've always thought that Gretchen and Rosie, in some ways, are two sides of the same coin. Although they've never met in the novels, each has experienced both the Fenris and the weight of making a seemingly impossible decision about someone she loves. Each carries the responsibility that comes with those experiences differently, yet they still have common ground. I started thinking about what they might talk about if they got together and how their different stories would impact their answers to questions. The result is the following interview, which starts in what I envision as the middle of their conversation, perhaps several months after the events of their individual stories.

Rosie: There's an understanding, isn't there, between everyone who knows about the Fenris? It's like we all know one another, even when we don't really.

Gretchen: I think so. Sometimes I feel like I got exclusive tickets into some sort of club. A club with monsters. That can't be normal, being happy about being involved in a monster club....

Rosie: I know what you mean, though. Besides, what is normal, anyway?

Gretchen: I don't know. Sometimes, before we got to Live Oak and I knew the truth about the monsters, it was like I had a normal life. Every now and then, when I'd get caught up in the moment and for a little while forget that I had a missing twin, I'd feel like I fit in, like I was the same as everyone else. But with your sister, you always had to be a hunter. Did you ever get to feel normal?

Rosie: Normal compared to what? It was normal, as far as I was concerned, to wake up and stretch and go get in a fistfight with my sister to practice attacking monsters. For some people it's normal to get up and go to school. I think you create your own normal, for better or for worse. Did I know I was different from other girls? Yes, of course. I mean, forget the Fenris. Other girls went to school and had mothers and fathers and dogs and didn't know anything about knives. But I still felt normal. Do you think you're more or less normal now than you were back in Washington?

Gretchen: I feel…more normal, actually. Which is weird, because it's not more normal to know about monsters and go looking for them to shoot them and see the sort of horrible things I've seen. But knowing the truth about what's really in the woods makes me feel more normal because it's kind of like…knowing what *they* are helps me know who and what I am. Weren't you scared, though, growing up knowing what the wolves were?

Rosie: No. I mean, yes, of course—they're scary. But my sister was never afraid, not really, so I wasn't either. Because she knew we could take them, I knew we could take them. If I'd been alone, though…I would have been scared if I was alone. Sometimes I'm still scared, being apart from her. Are you and your brother like that?

Gretchen: I…I'm not sure *what* my brother and I are like. I think he's still getting used to the idea that I'm not the same person I was back in Washington. That I'm not fragile anymore. I don't think he dislikes it, but sometimes he talks to me like we've just met. I guess we have, in a way. Things like what happened in Live Oak change you from your core; all tragedies and victories do. When my sister vanished, it changed my parents. When Naida was taken, it changed Sophia….I think when you're healing, sometimes things grow back different from what they were before. The chocolate festival definitely made me and Ansel grow back different.

Rosie: Sometimes I'm worried that Scarlett and I will be like that when we're back together again—whenever that is. I'm different now, and she is too. I'm worried everything won't click into place like before.

Gretchen: Would you go back and change things, though, if you could? Stay with her?

Rosie: No. That would have been easier, maybe, but I know going our own ways for a while was for the best. But knowing you've made the right decision doesn't mean that it was an easy decision. I was happy before, hunting with her, but I'm happy in new ways now. I'm happy in ways that feel permanent. What about you? Would you change anything?

Gretchen: I'd change almost everything. Or at the very least, I'd find a way to save Sophia. I know she was doing something horrible, unforgivable, but...I don't think she meant to. I think she made a choice a long time ago, a terrible choice, and then turned around and realized she'd gotten in over her head, too far in to back out. I think she would have been more like you, maybe, if she'd had the chance.

Rosie: She did have the chance, though — she didn't have to help them. I sound like Scarlett when I say that, but...Sophia made a choice. Just as you did. It's not your fault her choice led to her death.

Gretchen: No, but...I don't think she had much of a choice. Wouldn't you do anything to save your sister?

Rosie: Yes. That's true.

Gretchen: I think she made the only choice she could. And then I feel bad for thinking that, since so many girls died at her festivals...but I can't bring myself to hate her. All I can do is feel sorry for her and feel guilty that I couldn't help her.

Rosie: Now *you* sound like Scarlett. You're going more her path than mine at the moment, really — going out to help Naida, to fight more Fenris....

Gretchen: Are you and Silas done for good? No more hunting?

Rosie: No. Being a hunter...it never really stops for good. We'll start again, eventually. When the time is right. And you and Samuel will stop when the time is right. But for now...I'm happy. Are you?

Gretchen: I am. Despite everything, I really am.

BENEATH THE WAVES . . .
MEMORIES ARE FORGOTTEN.
SECRETS ARE KEPT.

LIVES ARE STOLEN.

Turn the page for a sneak peek at Jackson Pearce's
dark reimagining of Hans Christian Andersen's
"The Little Mermaid."

Coming September 2012

PROLOGUE

There are lights at the surface.

Lights so unlike the sun, that can't reach down into the depths of the ocean. Lights we can see only when we look outside the water. She turned the thought over and over in her mind, imagining the lights as best she could until she had to ask her sisters for help again.

"What about the carnival? Are the lights *on* the rides? What are the rides?" she asked one of the oldest, who just turned away—that sister rarely spoke anymore. Lo sighed, turning back to one of the younger ones, whose first trip to the surface was more recent. "Tell me, Ry?"

"Lights. Lights everywhere, I think on the rides. I don't know what the rides are called anymore," Ry said, sounding irritated at the notion of lights. "And noise. Really, Lo, it's nothing to be excited about. It's not the way you remember it."

That was what they kept telling her—it wouldn't be the way she remembered it. Because the last time she saw the human world, she was human.

She walked on land and sat in the sun and sometimes went so far inland, she couldn't even see the ocean. These were things she barely remembered, things that felt like dreams and grew fainter and fainter each day she spent underwater with her new sisters.

The girls here weren't her real sisters, but sometimes she convinced herself they were. When they streaked through the water, laughing, minds linked by some sort of electric current that skipped through the ocean, when they'd been under so long that they forgot a human world existed...then they were her real sisters, her real family, and this was her real home.

But even as she forgot her old life—first the strongest memories, then the moments between, and then the smallest details of who she was—there was one thought, one memory that never left the recesses of her mind: She'd been happy as a human, happier than she was now underwater. And that tiny thought refused to let Lo fully embrace a lifetime under the waves. She had to at least *look* back to the human world.

Once every deep tide—every fifteen months—the sisters surfaced together. Some to remember, most to remember why they forgot. Why the ocean took the memories of their old lives one grain at a time, the same way the tide pulled the shore out to sea. Why the ocean took their souls. Turned them from humans into...this.

There are lights at the surface. I just need to see them, and I'll never forget what they look like again, Lo told herself. She still felt it was better to remember, to know what she was missing. Most of her sisters had long decided that it was easier to forget.

"Ready?" one of the oldest sisters asked. Her voice was bell-like, musical. All the old ones were beautiful, from their voices to the palms of their hands. They would grow more so every day, until the day they'd float away with the low tide, or maybe in a storm, and never be seen again. They became angels, according to the stories. Most of her sisters believed the angel tale, that old ones went to the surface and were greeted by beautiful men, beautiful women who welcomed them into the sky. Lo had her doubts—most of the girls her age still did, but as they grew old, their doubts faded until they believed steadfastly. She wondered how many days, months, tides this sister had left.

"Is it time?" Lo asked.

"As soon as you feel the tide coming in. Any moment now..."

The old sister paused, waited for the tiniest shift in the ocean, in herself. Changes Lo hadn't noticed when she first arrived, changes she suspected only creatures of the water could appreciate. Lo found the water more marvelous every day, found living in it to be more perfect, more wonderful....

But she still wanted to remember.

The ocean shifted; her sisters rose and slipped upward like a single creature. She followed, the old sister just behind her, waiting for them to call her back, to hold her down to the sea floor like they'd done when she first arrived and fought to break the water's surface for weeks and weeks. But no, it was time. She was several months into her new life; she could be trusted to glimpse the old one. The weight of the water above them grew less and less until...

Lo gasped, dry air filling her lungs. It hurt, but she grinned and forced her eyes open despite the wind. Wind — she remembered wind. Standing in a field near a tiny house, people behind her, her family. When she first arrived at the ocean, she would pick out the most beautiful shells from the ocean floor, send them away in the waves, and hope her family would find them. She would imagine they'd see them, know they were from her, know she was alive... and now, she couldn't remember their faces. She couldn't even remember how many family members she had.

The lights. I need to see the lights, she thought firmly — maybe they'd remind her of her family. She looked up at the stars, the moon, and finally the shore. Two bright lights shone from a spot in the sand, moving along slowly, waving back and forth —

Hands — they were handheld lights, grasped in the palms of humans walking side by side. Walking. *I used to walk*, she thought, but she couldn't stop herself from thinking how ungainly it looked compared with being in the water. She swam forward a little, silent, to get a better look.

A boy and a girl, laughing, talking, the sounds barely audible over the crashing waves. Brilliant-colored lights in pinks, reds, greens, yellows, from the carnival beyond the pier, bounced off their faces—all that light, and yet the two of them somehow looked brighter in comparison. They looked warm. They shone. They looked happy.

"Are you going to try?" one of the sisters asked.

"Him?" Lo answered. "How would I get to him?" The two crossed in front of several houses, then a white building with glowing porch lights, making the couple appear in perfect silhouette.

"You can sing. It works sometimes. And they think we're beautiful. That helps."

"But he has her. He's already in love."

"Maybe you can break it," another sister suggested.

"Don't *you* want to?" Lo answered, looking back at them. This boy's soul, why weren't they fighting over it? They were all older than her, more beautiful, more practiced. Make him love you, kiss him, drown him. Earn his soul, and you get your humanity back—the escape from the ocean that the older girls told her about on her very first day. Yet they were letting her have him, if she wanted.

"Go ahead, Lo," Ry said.

Lo swallowed. She loved her sisters, but she knew—they all knew—they weren't originally meant for the sea. And she wanted to remember her former life completely, return to it, before she became old and beautiful and had forgotten her humanity entirely. *It won't be fair, what will happen to the boy, but it wasn't fair what happened to me, either. That makes it all right, doesn't it?*

She couldn't remember what happened to her, what turned her into an ocean girl. It was the strongest memory, the first to go. All Lo remembered was standing at the shore of the ocean with a man whose face she couldn't remember. Her body ached, and there was a jagged wound over her heart. The man sent her into the ocean, told her the other girls would find her. He was one of the angels, Ry told her when she arrived.

Lo doubted that as well.

She touched the scar on her chest, almost faded entirely. There was a voice in her head telling her to stop, to turn back, but she ignored it and swam closer, closer to where the waves crashed against the shore.

Sing, a different voice said. A voice that longed to be human again, the voice of the girl she used to be.

The sisters sang all the time, songs that melded together to form one voice that made the ocean thick with music. Lo opened her lips, let the notes emerge.

The boy stopped first, then the girl. They looked at the ocean. Did they see her? The thought was exhilarating, dangerous. She sang louder; behind her, she heard her sisters join in, voices quiet, guiding her along in the song.

The boy stooped to set his light down in the sand, pointing at the ocean, talking with the girl. He waved at Lo, big arms over his head. He saw her. *He sees me; he's coming for me*—yes, he took tentative steps into the water. *Come, where it's deeper, please....*

The girl yelled, shouted, tried to pull him back, but he

took another step, another, another. The song grew louder. Lo extended her hand in the moonlight. He had a handsome face, sharp features like a statue. His clothing, now soaked, clung to his body as he reached toward her.

She took his hand. *Don't be scared.* When he touched her, more memories of her old life slammed into her mind. Being held by her father, the scent of his cologne. The smell of things baking, the way fire leaped up from kindling. She swallowed hard, held on to each memory as long as possible before looking back to the boy's eyes.

"Hello," the boy said. He sounded dazed and blinked furiously. Lo stopped singing, and her sisters' song grew louder in response.

"Do you love me?" Lo whispered.

The boy looked surprised for a moment. Her sisters sang louder—he was having trouble fighting them. "I..." He looked back to the girl on the shore. "I love her. The girl by the church, I love her."

Lo's jaw stiffened; her fingers on the boy's hand tightened. "No, no, you love me."

The ocean shifted again, and some of her sisters stopped singing, started whispering. They were tired of the air touching their skin; they wanted to go back under—they wanted to leave. Lo bit her lip, ran her fingers along the boy's shirt-sleeves. Fabric hanging on a clothesline, laundry being folded, the way towels felt drying off her skin, more memories that proved even harder to hold on to. They skirted out of her mind like little fish, then darted back to the recesses they came from. Forgotten.

By the next deep tide, I'll have forgotten everything, just like them, she thought, glancing back at her sisters. *That's why they didn't want the boy for themselves. They don't care about their souls anymore. I won't care in another fifteen months.*

Now. It has to be now. Be brave. It has to happen.

She pulled the boy closer to her, so that his breath warmed her skin. "Love me."

"I…"

There was no time. Maybe he loved her already, maybe that was good enough, maybe — the ocean changed again, and the oldest sisters ducked back underwater. Lo inhaled, grasped both edges of the boy's shirt, pulled him against her lips, and kissed him, pleadingly, sorrowfully, desperately.

Then she pulled the boy under.

He hardly fought at first, still entranced with their song, confused, and she was so much more powerful than him in the water. It was easy to pull him into the deep, down to the ocean floor, so easy that for a minute, Lo was able to forget what she was doing to him. His eyes were growing wider; he began to fight for air, struggle against her. *This is it. It's happening. My soul, I'll go back —*

His eyes rolled back in his head. Lo realized her sisters were everywhere, watching, waiting. She leaned over the boy and kissed him again as the last precious bit of oxygen left his lips and floated to the surface.

And then he was dead.

And nothing else had changed.

Lo stared at her hands, at her feet, waiting for the pale blue color to turn back to shades of peach and pink. Waiting for the urge to surface, to gulp air happily, to swim to the shore and run on the sand.

It didn't come.

"Everyone has to try it for herself," Ry said gently, swimming closer. The boy's body listed on the ocean floor like seaweed. Lo felt sick; she doubled over and hid her head. "We all did. But it never works. You can't make them love you that fast."

"I don't think it's even real, that you can get your soul back," an older girl added. "It's a fairy story. Oh, Lo, don't cry. You have us. You don't need their world now. You don't have to worry about remembering anymore. You can just be happy here. And one day, the angels will come back for you, and it'll be beautiful, Lo. It'll be perfect."

Lo turned and cried into her sisters' arms, for her soul, for the boy, for the memories. Her sisters brushed out her hair and held her close. They pushed the boy's body away so she couldn't see it. They sang songs and began games to take her mind off what had happened.

But when the night ended and her sisters went to sleep, Lo stared at the sun from deep beneath the waves, at the tiny threads of blue light that made their way through the water, down to where she was.

Her soul was gone for good. The boy was dead, the girl left alone on the shore. And for nothing, nothing at all, other than a fairy tale and a few scattered memories of life on land. *Let it go. Let it all go.*

And she allowed herself to forget.

A novel about love, loss, and sex—
but not necessarily in that order.

purity

JACKSON PEARCE

"A hilarious and heartfelt story about what happens when
a teenage girl actually tries to honor all the promises that adults
demand from her while staying true to herself. I loved this book."
—Jennifer Echols, award-winning author of
Endless Summer and *Love Story*

Available wherever books are sold.